# Finally Fitz

ALSO BY MARISA KANTER

*What I Like About You*

*As If on Cue*

# Finally Fitz

## marisa kanter

SIMON & SCHUSTER BFYR

NEW YORK   LONDON   TORONTO   SYDNEY   NEW DELHI

An imprint of Simon & Schuster Children's Publishing Division

1230 Avenue of the Americas, New York, New York 10020

Text © 2024 by Marisa Kanter

Jacket illustration © 2024 by Louisa Cannell

Jacket design by Krista Vossen

SIMON & SCHUSTER BOOKS FOR YOUNG READERS

and related marks are trademarks of Simon & Schuster, LLC.

Simon & Schuster: Celebrating 100 Years of Publishing in 2024

For information about special discounts for bulk purchases, please contact Simon & Schuster Special Sales at 1-866-506-1949 or business@simonandschuster.com.

The Simon & Schuster Speakers Bureau can bring authors to your live event. For more information or to book an event, contact the Simon & Schuster Speakers Bureau at 1-866-248-3049 or visit our website at www.simonspeakers.com.

Interior design by Hilary Zarycky

The text for this book was set in Calisto MT Pro.

Manufactured in the United States of America

First Edition

2  4  6  8  10  9  7  5  3  1

Library of Congress Cataloging-in-Publication Data

Names: Kanter, Marisa, author. Title: Finally Fitz / Marisa Kanter.

Description: First edition. | New York : Simon & Schuster, 2024.

Identifiers: LCCN 2023031674 (print) | LCCN 2023031675 (ebook) |

ISBN 9781665926072 (hardcover) | ISBN 9781665926096 (ebook)

Subjects: CYAC: Online dating—Fiction. | Social media—Fiction. |Interpersonal relations—Fiction. | Bisexual people—Fiction. | BISAC: YOUNG ADULT FICTION / Romance / Contemporary | YOUNG ADULT FICTION / LGBTQ+ | LCGFT: Novels. Classification: LCC PZ7.1.K285 Fi 2024 (print) | LCC PZ7.1.K285 (ebook) | DDC [Fic]—dc23

LC record available at https://lccn.loc.gov/2023031674

LC ebook record available at https://lccn.loc.gov/2023031675

*For Vanessa—*

*We don't choose our family, but I'd still choose you*

# Finally Fitz

*I* pose in the Washington Square Park fountain, a turquoise kiss on my cheek.

"Chin to the left," Dani says from the bottom step of the basin.

Hooking my thumbs in the belt loops of my shorts, I tilt my turquoise kiss ever so slightly toward the camera while my girlfriend sets up the perfect shot. Dani slips out of white flatform sandals and takes a step down, submerging her hot-pink toes in fountain water that's warm from concrete baked in summertime heat.

She squats. Raises my phone. Lowers it.

"Fitz. A smidge more stage left."

Danica Martinez, an actress first and foremost, speaks in stage directions.

It's adorable, but I can't smidge.

Instead, my head snaps forward, my eyes meeting Dani's mirrored sunglasses. "You know any farther left is borderline profile."

Dani kicks a splash in my direction, the gold hoop in her

left nostril sparkling in the sun. "*Smidge* left. Trust your photographer."

Look. I don't hate my face. I unpacked the trauma of internalized beauty standards in middle school. I'm my Grandma Dee, strong nose and all. I embrace it. My nose. The character it adds. That I can transform myself into the spitting image of Miranda Priestly from *The Devil Wears Prada*. Which I did. Halloween. Freshman year. My first post to get over 1K likes.

I just also embrace flattering angles to minimize the bridge bump.

So I turn my cheek as far left as I'm comfortable with. "This is max smidge."

She rolls her eyes and her turquoise lips blow a raspberry, but she raises my phone again. "I suppose I can work with this."

Dani might be able to work with this.

But *I* can't.

I'm way too in my head about the bridge bump to focus on the rest of the shot. It's only when she directs me to switch it up and look at the camera straight-on that I can relax back into the shoot.

Some artists express themselves with words on a page, with the composition of perfect harmony, with the *swoosh* of acrylic on canvas. Clothes are my medium. Photos are my channel. Today's work of art is a patch-sewn crop top paired with high-waisted shorts, styled with oversize gold hoops by Lola Chung and loose pigtail braids that are long and blonde and pink at the ends. (Dani convinced me to let her oVertone them last weekend. Mom hates it—the pink—but I love the change.) A neutral no-makeup look emphasizes my turquoise kiss coordinated to match the crop top, which is the star of the photo. It's a triumph in color blocking with cap sleeves that I lovingly hand-stitched from shades of blue scrap fabric. Behind me is water shooting toward the sky, the iconic arch, and the blurs of strangers all showcasing that I'm finally here.

In New York City.

And for the first time, my followers will see my designs out in the world, not staged in a suburban bedroom.

If the Shoe Fitz started as an Instagram account to show my three older sisters—Maya, Clara, and Tessa—that I'm a visionary with the clothes they abandoned when they left our childhood home. Clothes I refused to leave behind when *I* left that home. At thirteen, when my parents and I moved from Texas to Massachusetts, I schlepped their closets halfway across the country. In them, I discovered endless possibilities, mixing and matching patterns and contradictory color palettes to transform their hand-me-downs into something reminiscent of them, to keep us connected despite the physical distance between us.

It worked at first.

But lately, my sisters are too busy being adults to engage with my posts.

At least other people do.

Over the last four years, I've gained thousands of followers, all invested in the creative and innovative ways I reuse textiles and style outfits. It's why I care so much about the angle of my face in a photo and agonize over every decision, from business opportunities like accepting my first brand partnership with a sustainable jewelry designer to editorial direction like choosing the fountain I'm standing in as the location for this shot.

With so many eyes on me, I won't post anything less than my best.

Right now, my best is a top I made months ago, born from fabric left over from costumes I designed for the school musical. It's the last thing I made that I'm truly proud of—and this city, this fountain, is the perfect place to show it off and announce my fashion-focused summer.

Some minutes later, I sit next to Dani on the stone steps and swipe through the shots, searching for the one that screams, *I am thriving*.

"Hot," Dani whispers in my ear.

But I see the bridge bump. Ugh. I smidged too much.

*Next.*

"Hot," Dani repeats at this one, and it is. I am.

If I wasn't being photobombed by a shrieking toddler.

It's a talent, my ability to find and fixate on the minute detail that renders an entire photo unusable. If it's not my profile, it's the wind wrinkling the top I'm trying to showcase, a weird reflection in the water, the arch of the background getting cut off at the top, my awkward hands.

I never know what to do with my hands.

"Can we take a few more?" I ask.

Dani sighs. "You really don't have enough pictures?"

I shake my head. "None of these are *The One*."

Am I being even more hypercritical than usual? Maybe. But it's a huge deal, my passion taking me from my suburban home to one of the fashion capitals of the world. A step up meant to signal to brands, to designers, to college programs, to *my parents* that fashion is more than just a hobby. It's my life.

"What about this one?"

She stops on a candid photo of me laughing, mouth open, full bridge bump on display. It's cute, but in a behind-the-scenes-blooper-for-Stories way . . . not in a post-on-main way.

"It's not perfect."

"It's *real*," Dani says, nudging my shoulder. "But fine. Go ahead. I'll stay in character until we lose the light."

I raise my eyebrows. "In character?"

"As Hot Photographer."

I almost blurt out *I love you* on the spot.

Instead, I let Dani wrap her hand around mine and pull me back into the fountain. Our toes submerged once more, she raises my phone and *tap, tap, tap*s until we lose the light.

In the final moments of golden city glow, she lowers my phone and says, "You know, we can spend every day in this fountain now if we want."

I grin. "I guess we do kind of live here now."

Her turquoise smile is so wide it nearly knocks me over—

as does the fact that I got so caught up in the moment that I forgot the qualifiers.

*Dani* lives here now.

I'm just visiting.

When her internship at the Public Theater ends, her freshman year at NYU begins.

When my summer at FIT ends . . . I go back to Massachusetts and my senior year of high school.

*I already miss her so much.*

But I shake off the feeling as soon as it snakes its way into my heart, replacing it with memories of laughter and musical theater references and the taste of bubblegum lip gloss that all started six months ago with rehearsing lines in her bedroom. I rewind back to our beginning, sitting on her bed and losing my mind over the furrowed brow that accompanied her request for notes, becoming obsessed with her talent and how seriously she took a student-run musical. Reading the lines of her love interest over and over.

Pausing at the kiss. Skipping it.

Until we didn't.

*You like girls*, I said when we pulled apart.

*I'm still figuring out my labels*, she answered, biting her bottom lip. *I like you.*

We never skipped the kiss again.

And now we're here, sitting in the Washington Square Park fountain, on the precipice of an entire summer together, pursuing our dreams and solidifying our happily-ever-after.

Dani, interning at the theater that previewed *Hamilton* and taking improv classes. Me, learning new upcycling techniques and meeting people who love clothes as much as I do. Us, pretending we're locals or playing tourists, depending on the day.

And before our programs begin, we have an entire week to start exploring the city hand in hand, her fingers pressed against mine, freezing despite the humidity that lingers even when the sun goes down. I've planned a whole week of adventures culminating in our six-month anniversary with the terrifying and exhilarating declaration:

*I love you.*

Dani hands my phone back to me. "What're we thinking for Monday?"

"I made a reservation. It's a surprise."

She raises her eyebrows, golden-brown eyes meeting mine. "For six months? Fancy."

*Because I love you.*

Damn my Irish lineage and the fierce blush I inherited from my dad. "I just thought . . ."

Dani sends another small splash my way. "Hey. I'm teasing."

She reaches into her purse for her wireless earbuds and hands one to me. A second later, "Welcome to New York" blasts in our ears because we are Swifties to our core—but also because damn it, New York *has* been waiting for us. Dani sings along as she pulls her hair out of its messy bun, sending dark brown waves cascading over her shoulders in the shadows, her lamplight profile and perfect pitch killing me slowly.

"Don't move."

I pull out my phone and in one take snap a perfect photo of Danica Martinez at dusk.

Then I take her hand and pull her closer, closer, closer until her turquoise lips meet mine.

## TWO

*A*  week later, I snap shots of plated dishes in portrait mode—a bread basket; burrata; a bowl of house-made cavatelli.

"Never has cheese been so photogenic," I declare.

At Serra by Birreria, everything is. A trendy Manhattan rooftop has been transformed into an Italian countryside, lush and overrun by a vibrant swirl of flowers and greenery covering the ceiling and twisting down columns. Our corner table has a view of the entire garden in the clouds and all the staged vignettes I've seen in countless #SerraByBirreria posts. All beautiful. Trendy. Romantic.

And I want every memory captured.

Plants in bloom.

Flowers in our hair.

Fresh burrata before it's on our tongues.

*Us.*

I've been doing this all week—snapping memories to make into a scrapbook of us, designed to leave Dani with a piece of me and to promise that the end of the summer won't be a goodbye, just a "see you later." So far, my camera roll includes us window-shopping in SoHo, taking the ferry to Ellis Island, and scoring cheap student rush tickets to see *The Lion King* on Broadway.

Also mixed in are some shots Dani took for If the Shoe Fitz. Content creation is never done, so I've had to devote a little bit of our week together to accessorizing my clothes with Lola Chung's jewelry. It's a huge deal that brands have started reaching out to me . . . and pretty much the only reason I can afford to be here. Mom and Dad couldn't bankroll my summer. Even if they *could*, I know they wouldn't. Fashion, to them, is a *frivolous hobby*. Direct quote. And my part-time hostess gig definitely wasn't bringing in summer in New York money.

So I monetized my platform and made it happen.

Thankfully, Dani gets it. She's as serious about acting as I am about fashion. It's one of the things I love most about her, that she loses time mastering her lines the same way I obsess over crafting the perfect outfit for a photo.

"We're inside an Instagram filter," Dani says, processing the aesthetic.

I tilt my camera up in an attempt to get a stylized photo of Dani with the burrata. "I'm obsessed."

It's not just the burrata that I'm obsessed with. It's Dani in a navy midi dress with tortoiseshell buttons, lips burgundy this time, her hair in two loose braids over her shoulders. She wears them better than me, the braids.

Click.

*I love her.*

Click.

*I love her.*

Click.

*Say it, Fitzgerald.*

Dani stabs the burrata with her fork, ruining my shot.

"Sorry," she says, her tone implying that she's very much not.

Shit.

I'm ruining this.

I upload a shot of just the burrata to my Story, then drop my phone in my purse and pull on a loose thread from a flower I hand-embroidered on the bohemian sleeves of my cream maxi dress. It's not that I *needed* to share the most beautiful cheese I've ever seen with my followers. It's just bonus content. I sprinkle impersonal slice-of-life anecdotes like makeup-free selfies, food porn, and the occasional book recommendation between my design tutorials and sponsored content as a reminder that there's a real person—a real *teenager*—behind my account.

But right now?

These photos are a distraction.

It's just, I've never said it—*I love you*—in a not-platonic way before. I've *thought* it. Hand-lettered it in sketch pads tucked under my bed. Wrote unsent love letters in the Notes app on my phone. I've *wanted* to say it. To Becca, the first person I came out to at theater camp in middle school after a tragic ankle sprain from attempting basic choreography. To

Drew, the boy who helped me make sense of Shakespeare in exchange for help with his math homework on the bus freshman year. To Luna, a BookToker who also understood the pressures that come with a platform. Every time, I felt it. Love.

Feelings happen fast.

Words? Not so much.

Because when I let myself feel out loud . . . I'm too much. Always.

So honestly? It was a relief when Dani asked if we could keep things casual after our first kiss. *I like you*, she'd confessed. *But I'm moving to New York after graduation, so, like, I'm not looking for anything serious. Is that chill?* I let my mouth against hers be the answer and have played it chill, cool, *casual* ever since. Let myself feel those three words without any pressure to say them.

Until Dani came to me with the application for this life-changing summer program at FIT.

*You can see if New York fits*, she said. *Maybe this doesn't have to end.*

That was the moment I knew she loved me, too.

"Sorry. I've never done this."

Dani's lips curl up in a smirk that makes the tension in my shoulders disappear. "Eaten burrata on a Manhattan rooftop?"

"Well. Yes. But I mean—"

"Fitz. This might be better than Olive Garden."

I exhale and smile at the Holy Grail of praise. Dani believes that Olive Garden breadsticks are their own food group. "Not bad for an Instagram filter?"

She takes another bite and moans. "So good."

"Maybe it's too good."

Dani laughs, a loud cackle that results in a snort, which only makes her laugh harder.

It's so sexy.

*I love you* slams against my rib cage with such incredible force.

*I love the way you commit to every performance as if it's on a Broadway stage. I love how your sister is your best friend in the whole world. I love that Pixar shorts make you cry. I love your rants about corporate social responsibility. I love that your socks never match. I love literally everything about you.*

I want to reach for my phone, to text my best friend, Natalie. *Is this how it's supposed to feel?* Because it feels like a medical emergency. But I'm done being chill. So over *casual*. We're in New York City. Together.

There's never going to be a more perfect moment.

"Dani, I—"

"Wait. *No way.* Fitz?"

*—love you.*

The words die in my throat as an unfamiliar voice has the audacity to cut me off mid-declaration. I turn my head and make eye contact with a short teen standing over our table sporting a blunt bob and bright blue eye shadow. Should I know this person? I must. They obviously know me.

"Hi—?"

"Wow. Okay. I thought I saw you from my table—" Blonde Bob points across the patio. "I *love* your posts, like, so much. I'm Gina."

Wait.

Blonde Bob, *Gina*, follows me?

"I think she's short-circuiting," Dani teases.

"I'm just . . ." I gape. "Gina, you just made my entire *life*."

I know my metrics. 12.4K followers. Enough for small brands like Lola Chung to start to reach out to me and for biphobic trolls to enter my DMs. But like. I'm a baby influencer. 12.4K is not a *meet a follower in the wild* number.

And yet.

"Can we take a photo?" Gina asks.

"Oh my God. Definitely!"

Gina hands her phone to Dani, who takes it, her lips pressed in a thin smile.

"I'm making my own homecoming dress," Gina says. "Well. I'm trying to. Your prom look inspired me."

"Incredible," I say. "What are you working with?"

I can't process the fact that Gina wants a photo with me, but I can talk design.

"I'm a dancer, so an abundance of tulle."

"Bold, I love it. Pro tip: if your machine doesn't have a Teflon foot, clear tape is a lifesaver."

Gina and I are incapable of keeping our eyes open at the same time, and when Gina asks for one more after assessing the photos, Dani doesn't even try to hide her eye roll.

"Sure! My camera is great in low light," I say to cover, handing over my phone instead.

Am I annoyed that Gina interrupted our moment? A little. But I'm not going to be rude. Plus I'm still processing being recognized. I find and follow Gina on Instagram, note the she/her pronouns in her bio, and DM her the photo. But confirming receipt turns into her showing me her dress progress, extending this impromptu meet-and-greet. Eventually, Gina leaves us for her food with a wave goodbye and I'm floating. I interact with my followers' comments and DMs daily. I know there are people behind the screens. But meeting someone who knows my work—and not only cares about it but also is *inspired* by it?

It's so validating.

"Is this fame?" I joke.

Dani stabs her ziti. "I don't think so."

I laugh. "Definitely not. Still. How does it feel to be dating an influencer?"

"Honestly? Not great."

I float right into a concrete wall. "What?"

Dani drops her fork. Her lower lip wobbles.

*I did something wrong.*

"You didn't introduce me to Gina."

I frown. "The interaction happened so fast, and it caught me off guard. I didn't mean to—"

Dani cuts me off. "You didn't even remember I was here. Until you needed a photo."

I'm so confused.

"You're mad about taking a photo?"

"Not *a* photo. Every photo. Is it too much to ask that we go one day without taking a fucking picture?"

I blink away tears. "That's . . . really harsh."

"I spent my first week in New York City—the place I've been dreaming of moving to only my entire life—taking photos of you."

"Photos of *us*."

"Seriously?"

"What? It's an important distinction!"

I reach for my phone to open my camera roll and scroll through the hundreds of photos of us—setting up our suite in Union Square, holding up the Mamoun's falafel we stood in line for, being basic tourists roller-skating in Rockefeller Center.

"It might start with us, but then it becomes about you. It *always* becomes about you and your content."

"It's not—"

"Even tonight is just about photos. You brought me to an overpriced Instagram filter and spent so much time taking a picture of cheese that I sat here in silence. For ten minutes."

I—

Did I really fixate on burrata for that long?

She continues, "Sometimes it feels like I'm just your photographer."

No. No. *No*.

Dani is reading this all wrong.

I shake my head. "Dani. Listen. I'm sorry for all the photos . . . but it's my work. And those photos are how I can afford to be here this summer with you. So really, even those photos are for *us*. You know that! You seriously cannot think you're just my photographer. That's bullshit."

"Is it?" Dani whispers, looking down at her plate.

Does she really not know?

I reach for her hand and press her fingers against my pulse. "You are not my photographer. You're my favorite person. All week I've been trying to find the words to tell you that I'm over pretending we're casual because the way I feel about you is anything but casual. I—"

"Don't."

"—love you."

*Finally.* The phrase tumbles out in a rush, so quick I don't register the word that's meant to intercept it—not until I'm met with silence and a lift in the pressure of her icy fingers on my wrist. I look up and see tears streaming down Dani's cheeks this time.

*Don't.*

"I didn't want you to say it," she whispers to her plate, unable to even look at me.

"What?"

Dani reaches for her purse and stands. "I need space."

Space? Since when? This summer was *her* idea. *You can see if New York fits. Maybe this doesn't have to end.* New York was my dream too, before I even knew Dani, so I applied without hesitation.

Now . . . she needs *space*?

Never has a word made less sense.

"Dani. We live together."

We each have our own roommate in a shared suite, but still. When I got in, Dani was the one who suggested rooming together. I asked if she was sure and her kiss was definitive.

*Yes.*

But now she says, "A mistake."

Nope. I take that back. *Mistake* makes even less sense.

"Because of some pictures?"

"Yes. And no." Her burgundy lips stretch into a sad smile. "You beam when you talk about clothes. I never understood that description in a script—how to convey it—until you. I don't think you even know it. I'm so addicted to your glow. And I guess I thought this summer could be about that, us connecting over our art . . . but it's just been me following you around as you search for the perfect backdrop to promote fucking ugly bracelets."

"Lola Chung's bracelets are not ugly."

"Fitz."

"I'm sorry! Not the point. I'll—"

She cuts me off. "These last few days made me realize I haven't even seen that glow in a while. Your Instagram-life balance was nonexistent even before the brand deals. Now you're always looking for a photo op for your followers. Isn't it exhausting? *I'm* exhausted. And if that's what you want to focus on, if you'd rather have a follower or a photographer than a girlfriend . . . maybe we should've left our relationship in high school."

I blink.

Oh my God.

Danica Martinez is breaking up with me.

"But I love you," I repeat. I don't know what else to say. "I love you."

Her eyes meet mine, shimmering tears streaming down her cheeks, before she pivots and walks away.

Just leaves me.

Then, my phone pings . . . with a Venmo notification.

*Danica M. paid you—*

My phone slips out of my hand before I finish reading.

I hear the crack of glass on concrete.

And I shatter too.

# THREE

*I* sob mascara tears on an uptown 1 train, comforted only by meaningful eye contact with a corgi and sad-girl music. Yes, Phoebe Bridgers. I *do* have emotional motion sickness, and it was triggered by the worst one-syllable word in the entire dictionary.

*Space.*

As the train screeches to a stop at each station, I count the number of blocks between us.

34th Street. *Eighteen.*

42nd Street. *Twenty-six.*

50th Street. *Thirty-four.*

I count all the way up to 110th Street. *Ninety-four.*

Morningside Heights. Tessa's stop.

I exit the station and follow my cracked phone two blocks north to my sister. *Ninety-six.*

Tessa lives in a tiny apartment in a brownstone steps away from Columbia's campus. She studies brain stuff there as a first-year PhD candidate in a program with a long, pretentious title that I don't remember. I can't remember. My brain is mush from counting city blocks and *space*.

Is ninety-six blocks enough space for Dani to realize what a huge mistake this is?

My finger hovers over the buzzer of unit 4D.

*Phoebe, give me strength.*

I press it.

Once. Twice. Three times.

Nothing.

I reach for my phone to call, but the music cuts off mid-song and the screen goes black. Dead. And Tessa isn't expecting me—our reunion is meant to be after our classes tomorrow, at her favorite Thai restaurant on the Upper West Side. It's not meant to be now. I'm not meant to be a sobbing mascara-stained mess at her door, but I don't know where else to go.

Sleeping in my room—*our* room—is the opposite of space.

Absolutely not an option.

So I press the button again and again and—

"Wrong—"

*"Tess."*

Silence. Then, "Fitz?"

Her voice is intercom static.

"Yeah," I say. "I'm—"

The door buzzes. I swallow my emotion and haul ass up four flights of stairs. I take the steps two at a time at first, a bold and overly aggressive move that leaves me out of breath by floor two. My heart might actually explode before this day is over, taken out by the word "space" and a four-story walk-up.

Tessa's door opens before I knock.

She's in an oversize Lumineers concert tee and olive sleep shorts, with tired, almost annoyed eyes behind her round rose-gold glasses. "Fitz. You can't just—"

Then she sees my face.

"Dani?"

"I messed up."

Her expression instantly softens as she opens the door wider and gestures me in. As soon as the door closes she wraps her arms around me, and I let her because I'm broken and too tired to push her away, to not let her take care of me.

It's what my sisters do.

Growing up, I hated it. I wanted sisters . . . not *babysitters*. But I'm the baby in my family, by a lot. Tessa is twenty-five and she's my youngest big sister.

I pull away from the embrace and floorboards creak under my feet as Tessa leads me through the small entryway to give me a tour. Her apartment is "charming"—Tessa-speak for *what it lacks in square footage, it makes up for in natural light*. I bend down to take my shoes off and when I stand back up I whack my head on a hanging plant.

"She didn't mean to hurt you, Henrietta," Tessa says, steadying the planter.

Okay. Tessa talks to plants now. Names them, too.

Noted.

Before I can ask about this, she tosses me a Paramore shirt and bike shorts so I can change out of my tearstained dress.

After I do, I sink into Gertie, the puke-green couch that has been passed back and forth between my sisters ever since Clara and I picked it up at an estate sale in Dallas when I was, like, eleven. I inherited Clara's penchant for thrifting, but I have much better taste. Evidence: this couch. It's early-twentieth-century ornate and the *worst* shade of green, but I don't tell that to Clara to spare myself a defense of its character.

I miss thrifting with Clara.

I don't tell her that, either.

Clara and Maya, my oldest sister, never left the Dallas suburb that was home until my parents uprooted me mid–awkward stage in the name of Mom's dream job. That job? Director of Parks and Recreation in Boston. My mom is pretty much Leslie Knope. Dad is a neonatal nurse and Boston isn't lacking in excellent hospitals, so for my parents the move made sense. But my sisters were all adulting by then. Maya had just moved in with Sarah, her then-fiancée, now wife. Clara was in her first year as an art teacher at the high school I thought I was going to attend. Tessa was a junior at UT Dallas. Their lives were firmly, solidly in Texas . . . but I was thirteen.

I didn't have a choice.

My bat mitzvah doubled as a goodbye party.

No one asked how I felt about moving 1,700 miles away from my sisters. Or how it felt to see them together, constantly, after I was gone. Or how it still feels to primarily stay connected with them via social media posts and monthly FaceTime check-ins.

Not that I hate Massachusetts.

I have snow. I have real friends. I have Dani.

Had Dani.

Tessa puts a kettle on the stovetop. "What happened?"

I squeeze my eyes shut and see Dani's pinched eyebrows, her mouth forming *Don't*. "Someone recognized me tonight from Instagram."

Tessa places two ceramic mugs on the counter. "What? That's incredible."

My eyes well up. "Dani, um, didn't think so."

"Oh."

"She said she feels like my *photographer*. Now she needs space"—I hiccup—"but I love her. I finally told her . . . but I'd already messed up so bad. Fucking Gina."

Tessa's forehead crinkles. "Gina?"

"The person who recognized me and ruined my life! I should've thought to introduce Dani. I'm so stupid."

"Ava."

It's cold water dumped over my head. "Ava" is only invoked by my sisters when I'm being my most dramatic self. I am Ava Fitzgerald, but I've just never felt like an Ava. It always felt itchy in my throat. Not quite right. I started going by Fitz in first grade and it feels so much more me. Ava is acceptable in only very specific circumstances and this is absolutely not one of them, because I'm not being dramatic.

"Unnecessary!"

"Sorry," Tessa says, pouring boiling water over mint tea

bags. "I'm sorry, but you are not stupid. Dani sounds like she's being an unsupportive, insecure asshole."

"And Bennett is so fucking perfect," I snap, then instantly regret setting up another long-winded defense of her douche-bag boyf—ahem—*fiancé*.

I don't expect Tessa to drop the sugar spoon and burst into tears.

Oh no.

"*Tess*," I whisper. "I'm sorry. Bennett is . . . fine."

It's not a compliment, but it's the closest I can get. Bennett Covington III is MFA candidate with prep-school origins insufferable. Literary douchebro who has spent the entirety of their (seven-year!) relationship writing but never finishing the next Great American Novel insufferable. Introduces himself as *I'm the next Kerouac* insufferable.

*Fine* is a generous descriptor.

"I'm sorry," I repeat as Tessa picks the spoon back up and stirs our tea in silence. "I think I'm in shock."

Tessa walks over and hands me a mug, then sits criss-cross on the other end of the couch while I brace myself to be chewed out for daring to comment on her relationship, for being *too young* to understand. She doesn't. Instead, she inhales the scent of mint tea for an extended beat, then says, "Bennett is an asshole, actually."

My jaw is on the floor.

"Note all the new plant children on the shelves," Tessa says.

I didn't notice before. My sensory input is pretty shot at the moment. But I see it now—a plant-filled, Kerouac-free apartment. Bennett believes it goes against the natural order of the universe for plants to exist indoors. Like I said. Asshole.

"What did he do?"

Tessa shrugs. "Someone from his workshop."

"I'm going to kill him."

"I didn't even notice or catch him. He *confessed*. Then turned it around on me, like, I haven't been emotionally available. We were planning a *wedding*."

"He's dead."

Tessa snorts. "This isn't funny."

"I'm not laughing."

"You hated Bennett."

I shrug. "You loved him."

"I really did."

There's a beat of silence, then a question comes to me.

"Wait. When did this happen?"

"He moved out last week."

"Oh."

It's not shocking that Bennett fully vacated the premises before I knew about it, but it still hurts. We've texted every day this week. More than usual, but only about all things New York—a crash course on the subway, the best local spots downtown, how to avoid tourists, et cetera. Not once did Tessa even hint at the pain that's so evidently displayed on her face.

"Maya and Clara know?" I ask.

Tessa shakes her head. "No."

Wow. I am never the first sister to know anything.

"It's just so embarrassing."

"For *Bennett*."

Tessa wipes her cheek. "Fuck Bennett. Dani, too."

I blink, but no tears come this time. "It's not over. Dani just needs space."

"Sure."

Tessa's eyebrows rise, like *that's cute,* and it's kind of incredible, how a single expression can make me feel like I'm ten years old again and render me the baby sister once more. It doesn't matter that I know about Bennett before my other sisters do. Tessa didn't *want* to confide in me. I mascara-sob stumbled my way into this information.

It's so annoying.

"What?" I ask, defensive again.

Tessa stands. "Nothing. I have an eight a.m. lab tomorrow. So . . ."

"Wait. Did I wake you up?"

She yawns, effectively ending the conversation. "The fridge is fully stocked and we—*I*—have every streaming platform. And I have a whole empty side of a king bed now, so no need to crash on Gertie. It's always a mistake."

I nod. "Can I borrow a charger?"

Tessa retrieves one from her bedroom and hands it to me. Her eyes linger on Gertie's free cushion as I rummage through my purse in search of nothing in particular. But if I look at

Tessa, my expression will scream *stay* and I don't want to have to ask.

I want Tessa to want to stay up late for me.

"Night, Fitz."

As expected, Tessa retreats to her room and I'm left alone again with my phone and my thoughts. Pretty much the worst combination. As soon as my phone glows back to life, the notifications begin. *Natalie. Henry. Natalie. Henry. Natalie. Henry. Natalie.*

Of course my friends know by now.

Henry, Natalie, and I are a trio but Henry and Dani are also close, like, *we drunk kissed once and got over it* close.

I don't read their messages. Instead, I open If the Shoe Fitz's Instagram feed and doom-scroll through all the beautiful people who populate my timeline. People I compare myself to. People I think about when I pose for a photo and obsess over flattering angles. People I want to be, with the kind of platform I can only dream of growing—

Oh my God.

Maybe Dani has a point.

I do fixate on perfect photos, on writing an effortless caption, on the thousands of hearts of validation every time I post a new look. Online I'm fashionable, filtered, *fine*. A curated version of myself that Gina was so excited to meet.

A version of myself . . . who hurt the person I love.

I open my camera roll and scroll past twenty, fifty, *one hundred* versions of me posing in the Washington Square Park fountain. *Shit*. A tear slides down my cheek and falls onto my cracked screen.

I pause on the candid that Dani liked. *It's real*, she said. Maybe that's it. I need to focus on what's real, and why I am here. I'm here to learn and grow and become a better designer, not just a better influencer. I'm here because I am so in love with Danica Martinez. I—

I know what I have to do.

# FOUR

*D*id you know?"

Henry Chao is a mosaic on my screen, sleepy, wide-eyed concern distorted by broken glass. It's a dick move, calling him so early, but I don't care. I stayed up until three a.m. editing the best photos featuring Lola Chung's jewelry, drafting captions, and scheduling enough posts to satisfy my contract. After I finished, I saw Dani's face every time I closed my eyes in an attempt to fall back to sleep. So I've been staring at the ceiling, obsessing over this question, wondering if I'm the only one who didn't see it coming.

Then realized I can just ask.

"Did you know?" I repeat.

He pushes his clear plastic frames up the bridge of his nose. "Shit, Fitzgerald. I think I deserve more credit than that. Dani is—"

I disconnect because it's not the *no* I need to hear, but when my phone immediately vibrates in my hand, I answer.

"Sorry!" Henry says. "I love you and I'm *so* sorry. No, I didn't know."

"Okay," I say.

"What do you need?"

This is why I love Henry. He always knows the right question to ask.

"Is that Fitz?"

It's Natalie's voice, far off in the background. Natalie Jacobson and I are soulmates, bonded by super-specific Jewish feelings and a mutual understanding to not be woken up before the sun. But she's here. Awake.

There's only one explanation.

"We're going to the Vineyard," Henry says, confirming it.

"Oh."

Martha's Vineyard without me. It's not like I expect my friends to sit home and miss me all summer, but New York is eight weeks. Optimal Vineyard weather will very much still be a thing when I'm back. They don't have to go jump off the *Jaws* bridge or wait in line at Back Door Donuts without me.

And yet.

"Reid leaves for Albany next week," Natalie says.

"We'll go again when you're home. Obviously," Henry adds.

I press my lips into a thin line, refusing to emote. It's just— Vineyard days are a *process*. It's a one-hour drive to a forty-five-minute ferry. It's hauling beach chairs on our backs and tote bags overflowing with Hot Cheetos and Starbursts and no less than five varieties of sunscreen because my pasty-white skin has two settings: ghost or lobster. It's a once-a-summer endeavor.

And it's always been *our* thing—Henry, Natalie, and me.

Not Henry, Natalie, and her boyfriend, Reid.

I like Reid. He's passionate without being pretentious and will do literally anything for Natalie. But if I'm that replaceable on a trip that's always been our thing . . . have I misread our friendship as much as I misread my relationship with Dani? Has my platform been getting in the way of that, too?

"It's whatever," I say, letting my Dani feelings swallow these friendship ones. "Dani . . . is she okay?"

Henry's head-shake is emphatic.

"Did she tell you why?" I ask.

The second *no* is extra emphatic.

"If the Shoe Fitz."

Natalie steals Henry's phone. Her dark curls are pulled back in a messy beach bun. "What?"

"It's my fault," I say. "I—"

I share the highlight reel of our entire disastrous anniversary dinner and every mistake I made in the week leading up to it. It hits different this time, admitting to my people how fixated on my platform I am, that I didn't realize how self-absorbed I was being, how bad I am at turning my social-media brain off, how massively I messed up.

"—but I have a plan to fix it," I finish, with a pause for the drama. "A hiatus."

Henry swallows. "I mean. I think it's more of a breakup—"

I cut him off. "From If the Shoe Fitz."

In the silence that follows, Natalie and Henry look at each

other and I see it, a wordless conversation in real time. I hate that. My sisters have it too, an entire nonverbal language, and the weird twinge in my chest right now is too familiar.

"I just need you to change my passwords to lock me out of my accounts."

Henry frowns. "Me?"

"Yeah. Natalie will crack the moment I ask for them back."

Henry snorts and Natalie's face scrunches in offense, but then she shrugs. "Valid. But is this really the move?"

I nod. "Dani's right. New York is so alive. I want to take a break and live in the moment, you know? And it's the only way to prove to her that I heard her and that I can change. I can focus on the clothes and *us*."

"And yourself," Natalie prompts.

Okay. Natalie and Reid's chaotic will-they-won't-they codirector dynamic that defined junior year does not really put her in a position to make therapist-esque declarations.

"Obviously," I say. "Instant validation is my serotonin, so being offline is going to be huge for me. And Dani will see the change and know it's because I love her and she makes me better."

I can't read Henry's expression—if he understands my vision or sides with Natalie's skepticism.

Natalie starts again. "What if—?"

Henry cuts her off. "I'll do it. Of course I will."

I exhale. "Oh my God. This is an act of heroism, Chao. Truly."

Henry shrugs. "I got you."

I recite every password of every account associated with If the Shoe Fitz and he methodically locks me out of each one of them. We even change my phone number in the accounts to Henry's, so I can't hack my way in during a moment of weakness. And there will be many moments of weakness.

"All my sponsored content is scheduled, but my hiatus announcement is in drafts. Can you post it?"

One cannot go from daily updates to just weekly sponcon on main without an announcement. I don't want anyone to think I'm, like, dead. I chose the candid photo of me in the fountain at sunset, mid-laugh. Dani's favorite, imperfect photo.

Geotag: *on hiatus*

Caption: *time for a summer adventure & refocusing on what's real.*

Simple. Direct. Lowercase.

Just don't ask me how long it took to craft that single sentence.

"Now?" Henry asks, because after this there's no going back.

I nod.

"Done."

I'm still processing the reality of this moment when Natalie says, "Fitz, we—"

"Have a ferry to catch," I realize, noting the time.

"I am so, so sorry," Natalie says.

I wave her off. "Stop. Go! Thank you. I love you. Miss me a lot!"

"We love you too," Henry says. "Let us know—"

"—everything," Natalie finishes.

The twinge is back when we disconnect and I think about them on their way to catch a ferry without me, but I shake it off and sit with the weight of what I've just done. I expect to feel hopeful, free, *something*. But I just feel . . . hollow.

*No.* Social media withdrawals cannot possibly happen this fast.

I stand, leaving Gertie's clutches in pursuit of a shower and find a note left on the table, scrawled in messy script. A silver key sits on top.

> There's peach yogurt in the fridge and extra towels in the bathroom. If you need a place to crash on the weekends, this is home. Or whenever, really! But fair warning, the commute downtown WILL be a sweaty nightmare. —T

For the first time in four years, Tessa and I are in the same place, and the potential of us is almost too much to process. I assumed we'd get the occasional dinner. I didn't expect a key and an open invite to her apartment. But I also didn't expect Bennett to not be here. Without Bennett and his books taking up so much space, quality sister time feels possible. Maybe heartbreak will bond us. Even if mine is temporary.

It *is* temporary.

A hiatus is the grandest gesture. I know this because my

fingers are already twitching at the inability to scroll through Instagram.

It's going to be worth it.

She'll see I meant what I said and say it back.

*I love you.*

And we'll get our perfect summer back on track.

## FIVE

*I* am melting.

Tessa's note? Extremely accurate.

I'm on a downtown 1 train in an air-conditioner-less car and bodies are everywhere. My various joints—shoulders, knees, elbows—are pressed against strangers' sweaty skin. Personal space is nonexistent as we screech to an abrupt halt between stations. I inhale a sharp breath that's a mix of lilac deodorant and general body odor. It's miserable. Is this how I die? A slow, sweaty, asphyxiated death stuck underground?

Fortunately not.

Motion resumes at last and the train crawls into the Times Square–42nd Street station, where half the train exits as soon as the doors open. Bless. I squeeze peach vanilla hand sanitizer onto my palm and rub it onto my shoulders where stranger sweat touched my skin. Then I wipe my own sweat from my upper lip. *It's a two-shower day*, I do declare, as the train jerks to yet another impromptu halt. At this rate, I'll have to book it to my dorm to change before sprinting to make it to my first class on time. How this transit system is even operational is mystifying.

My phone buzzes twice in my lap.

**Dani Martinez**
em says you didn't come home last night, what the
fuck?
8:31AM

they think you're dead
8:32AM

Oh my God.

Em, my roommate, seems chill. As in, cool and indifferent to my existence. Dani is clearly the one checking in on me. I have to bite my lip to suppress a smile. She must have seen my post and understood what it meant. I can't wait to see her, to initiate a romantic reconciliation and erase the last twenty-four hours from our memory. To be us again.

i'm fine!
8:33AM

I press send without overthinking it.
"Fitz?"
Shit. Again?
Why does this keep happening? How am I even *recognizable* right now? I look like a swamp monster in the bike shorts and tee I slept in last night because no way was I subjecting my

high fashion date dress to this rush hour subway experience. My damp hair is bunched in a mop on the top of my head. I have a massive zit on my chin. My *eye bags* have bags.

And okay, yes, I'm on hiatus.

But I still have an image to protect.

"Please. No photos."

"Excuse me?" the voice, a soft tenor, asks.

I look up and make eye contact with a ficus first. Its leaves are sad and droopy, like it's suffering from heatstroke along with the rest of us. I blink. A full *tree* is being transported via the 1 train, the pot secured between white Adidas on feet belonging to someone with a soft tenor voice who knows my name. I can't see much of their face, but they're dressed in cargo shorts and a green polo. Light brown hair peeking over the leaves is styled in a longer-on-the-top crew cut. I don't typecast my audience, but I can't say I'm not the tiniest bit surprised that Ficus Follower knows who I am. *You follow fashion influencers, yet you wear cargo shorts? It does not compute.* Regardless, I see it now. Ficus Follower telling the world what a vain, superficial bitch I am . . . while I'm on hiatus with no way to defend myself.

Shit.

"I'm so sorry," I say to the face, whose features become more discernable after they gently nudge ficus leaves to the side. "I swear, I never just assume someone wants a picture with me. Being recognized is still a very new, extremely weird thing for me and I've had a *day*."

Ficus Follower's mouth quirks up. "It's not even nine."

"A *day*," I repeat.

Deep brown eyes behind square plastic frames meet mine and hold my gaze, wordless.

Oh no. I overcorrected. Ficus Follower is looking at me like I'm positively unhinged.

"As have you," I add. His thick eyebrows shoot above the spectacles, so I wave at the ficus. "You are transporting a person-size plant."

We pull into Penn Station and the seat to my left is vacated with a tote bag *thwack* to my shoulder. Cool. I feel a bruise forming as we speak.

"It was a rescue mission," Ficus Follower says, taking the free seat and repositioning the pot with a gentle tenderness. It's, like, Ted Lasso–level endearing. Somehow it's enough for me to just know that Ficus Follower is Good People.

I pinch one of the drooping leaves between my thumb and index finger. "It does seem sad."

"Eloise just needs some love. Someone left her on the sidewalk in direct sunlight in the middle of a heat wave. Asshole."

I blink again. Who is this plant rescuer?

"I'm sorry," Ficus Follower, Caretaker of Eloise, says. "I have, um, a lot of feelings about the commodification of plants. People want them for aesthetics but forget that they're alive. They need—*deserve*—to be treated that way."

"Absolutely."

Ficus Follower laughs. "You don't have to humor me."

"I'm not. You're a hero."

"Eloise is worth it."

I laugh, embracing that New York can be a sweaty, claustrophobic mess one second and meaningless banter with a stranger on the subway the next. Ficus Follower's mouth quirk goes full smile in response, complete with two bottom teeth that overlap in a perfectly imperfect way. It's not a bad smile. Objectively.

"Next stop, 14th Street," the static voice of the conductor says over the loudspeaker.

My stop.

I stand and turn toward the ficus. "It was really nice to meet you, Eloise. You too—"

"Levi."

I smile. "Levi."

Of course Plant Hero is a Levi. Levi is a good name. The best name.

Memories wrapped in that name resurface as the subway slows to a stop, triggering a visceral, nostalgic reaction. Wow. It's been a minute since I thought about those days spent with my first favorite person before he left me. Since I wondered, *Where in world is Levi Berkowitz?* I used to stare at the ceiling at two a.m. and let my imagination take me to any answer. I gravitated toward the absurd—the Galapagos Islands, the Australian Outback, Antarctica.

Anything to justify why he never called.

Or emailed.

Or responded to my bat mitzvah invitation.

When the likely truth of it all is that childhood friendships are based on forced proximity—and when you're ten, Dallas and Austin feel like opposite ends of the world.

The doors open and I step onto the platform and out of the nostalgia haze, attempting to discern the best exit using Google Maps and ignoring the reality that this means I have service again and there are exactly zero new Dani texts. Okay, so maybe immediately initiating a romantic reconciliation is not the move. Maybe Dani still needs a beat of space to see I'm taking this hiatus seriously before she comes to her senses.

I can give her that.

Route determined, I take two steps forward, but I hear my name from that same tenor.

Not "Fitz."

*"Ava."*

I'm not Ava online. I've *never* been Ava online.

Holy shit.

I turn toward the subway and see Ficus Follower, Plant Hero, *Levi* attempting a last-minute exit. I can't explain how I didn't know before this moment, because watching this lanky plant boy attempting to quickly haul a ficus that is almost as tall as him off the train, it's so damn obvious.

Plant Hero isn't *a* Levi. He's *the* Levi.

In a past life, *my* Levi.

"Berkowitz?" I ask, but despite his efforts, the doors close between us.

I see Levi mouth *Shit* as the train rolls away from the platform.

He's gone.

And I really, truly, can't believe it. I cannot believe how wild and magical the subway is. How all these years, I wondered, *Where in the world is Levi Berkowitz?* only to not recognize him when he was right in front of my face, giving a dissertation on plants' rights.

Once the shock wears off, my stomach drops to the floor, the mortification setting in.

Because after *seven years*, Levi Berkowitz recognized me.

And I thought he wanted a picture.

## SIX

*I* am the worst first impression.

Creaky hinges and a door slam accompany my entrance, cutting off my hero, Mallory Burton, mid-sentence ten minutes into the three-hour course that is "Closing the Loop: From Curating a Feed to Building a Brand." My eyes scan the room for a single free seat and find one . . . in the front row. Eleven sets of eyes shoot judgment in my direction. I get it. Fashionably late doesn't apply here.

"This seat has your name on it, Ava," Mallory Burton says, her tone kinder than I deserve. She looks runway ready in a navy jumpsuit that cinches at the waist and complements her pale, freckled skin.

"Fitz." I walk over and pull out the middle chair at the three-person table, scraping metal against linoleum. To my left, a dark-skinned Black kid with a silver bar through their eyebrow above incredible smoky purple eye shadow winces. "Sorry, I mean. I'd like to go by Fitz, Ms. Burton."

"Got it, Fitz," she repeats with a smile, her deep green eyes meeting mine. "Ms. Burton is my mother. I'm Mal."

She then hands me a name tag and tells me to write down my name and pronouns and it takes every ounce of control to not swoon because *Mallory Burton, CEO of Revived by Mal, just said my name.*

Tucking a strand of Ariel-red hair behind her ear, Mal continues her spiel from where she left off. "The twelve of you have been selected out of hundreds of applications because I saw potential in your portfolios. I built a successful YouTube channel over a decade ago," she says, then winces like she's dating herself. "When I decided to transition Revived by Mal from a fashion vlog to an actual business, I had no clue what I was doing. No one to guide me through the process of how to write a business proposal, how to find investors, how to build strategic partnerships for sourcing and distribution, how to *scale*. I made so many mistakes. So this is, essentially, a crash course in building a fashion business out of a social media presence. TikTok makes it look easy. It's not. At the end of this course, you will present a business plan and show *one* piece that represents your vision for your brand at a final runway show open to friends, family, and industry colleagues. Those colleagues will help me select designs to be included in next summer's Revived by Mal collection, which will debut at New York Fashion Week—"

Wait.

Mal is choosing her favorite designs for a *collaboration*?

"—and if selected, you will be compensated according to industry standards for your designs, sit in on meetings with my team, and receive two tickets to Fashion Week in February."

Holy shit.

This summer is more than a chance to learn from one of my favorite designers. It's an opportunity to collaborate with Mal, a major step toward proving to my parents that fashion is more than just a *frivolous hobby*. If this summer can launch If the Shoe Fitz from a social media account to an actual clothing brand . . . maybe they'll take my dream seriously. Because it doesn't get more serious than debuting at Fashion Week.

I cannot wait to tell Dani.

The thought bubble enters my brain so easily, but pops when I remember how broken we are.

"I want to emphasize that this isn't *Project Runway*," Mal continues. "I don't find pitting artists against each other to be conducive to creativity. My team and I will select as many or as few designs as speak to us. We're looking to mentor and launch the next generation of designers. . . ."

Everyone starts taking notes on Mal's brand, her mission, what she and the team are looking for in a collaborator. I reach for my laptop, but I don't need notes. I've been following Mal since I was twelve, when Revived by Mal was just a weekly YouTube series where she created a new piece of art out of clothes sent to her by viewers. Today, Mallory Burton is one of the most successful queer designers in sustainable fashion.

She's everything I aspire to be.

". . . but I'm getting ahead of myself and quite honestly, I'm sick of hearing the sound of my own voice. I'm so excited to learn more about *you*, fellow designers, from your first assignment."

*Fellow designers.*

*Focus, Fitzgerald.*

For "Your Closet, Revived" we were asked to come ready to present a design that introduces us, using only existing materials from our closet. I finished mine weeks ago, inspired by how If the Shoe Fitz started: my sisters. They each have their own distinct style. Maya loves neutral colors and sustainable brands. Clara is bold patterns and loose-fitting fabrics. Tessa's classic capsule wardrobe is filled with mix-and-match staples that will never go out of style. I love combining their individual aesthetics and creating something that makes me feel like my sisters are always with me, so I designed a reversible blazer that would fit into any of their wardrobes. A black blazer from Tessa's high school debate era is the base, lined with a patchwork of colorful quilted Vera Bradley patterns sourced from Clara's endless tote-bag collection. Maya's influence is the extra wooden buttons that come with the oversize cardigans she lives in.

Tessa is practical and Clara is *not* and Maya keeps us all connected.

A story of sisters, in the form of a blazer.

I unzip my backpack and reach for my pink suede portfolio—

No.

No. No. *No.*

I don't have it. It's not here.

In my rush to transform myself from subway swamp monster to presentable chic, along with a solid but failed attempt to swallow the surprise that is Levi Berkowitz and the disappointment that Dani did not, in fact, greet me this morning with instant regret, I left my portfolio with my photos, my concept sketches, my ability to redeem my first impression on Mal, in my dorm.

Shit.

"Trevor, please kick us off," Mal says.

Purple Eye Shadow Goals—Trevor—stands. "Hey, everyone!"

I read the name tag stuck to the pocket of a mixed-print floral button-up.

*Trevor Anderson (he/him)*

My heart beats in my ears, loud. I'm sitting next to Trevor. Does this mean I'm next? I don't know what to do, how to explain to Mal that not only was I late . . . but I'm also unprepared.

It's so embarrassing.

"I'm from a tiny town in Texas where football is life," Trevor continues. "I loved going to games, but I hated playing. Every collision, I thought, *This is it*. But I'm fast, I'm good, and my dad was proud. So I played, even when it triggered intense panic attacks. It got pretty bad. My mom is a seamstress, and after every game I'd spend hours with her sewing machine. It was my therapy, you know? So that's why I came up with—"

He reveals his project, a floor-length, elegant A-line dress with a strapless black bodice and billowy skirt created entirely from football jerseys. I wouldn't touch polyester mesh with a ten-foot pole, but his execution is flawless.

"My relationship with football is complicated, but I wanted this homecoming dress to reclaim the parts of it I do love. And to acknowledge that it led me to my actual passion. Finally, these jerseys feel like *me*."

"I love this," Mal says, as everyone claps. "The contrast you created using a simple bodice? The story it tells? I'm obsessed."

I'm more than obsessed. I'm so blown away that I'm questioning how I'm even here.

Trevor glows from Mal's praise. I want that glow so bad.

Mal calls the name Lila Baker next, and I'm relieved that alphabetical order seems to be the way we're going here. It gives me a second to think on my feet, to improvise. Okay. I don't have my project. That's okay. Because guess what? Most of my outfit is upcycled. Sure, it's not as couture as Trevor's or as sentimental as the pantsuit Lila made out of her grandma's favorite dress, or as cohesive as my original project. But it *is* a versatile, everyday look that represents the aesthetic of If the Shoe Fitz.

All is not lost.

"Fitz," Mal says finally. "You're up."

I stand in front of my classmates, who are all a thousand times more talented and put together than I am, but I remind myself that I'm an actress as much as I'm a designer. I can convey confidence, pretend this is intentional.

"Hi, everyone! I'm Fitz and—"

Mal cuts me off. "Where's your portfolio?"

I do a spin. "I'm wearing it."

Mal raises her eyebrows, wordless.

"I have three older sisters—Maya, Clara, and Tessa. Growing up, their closets were my playground and I had so much fun reconstructing their hand-me-downs. Once upon a time, this jacket was Tessa's prom dress. These shorts were cut from Maya's mom jeans. And—" I don't have a Clara piece to complete the story. "—yeah! I love transforming clothes that have history into versatile everyday looks for today, and it's just a bonus that I get to feel close to my sisters when I wear them."

Eleven sets of eyes assess my performance.

. . . and call bullshit.

"The jacket is extremely well-constructed," Mal says, almost as a concession. Her eyebrows wrinkle. "I'm sorry. I'm just confused. You don't have your portfolio and I just learned more about your sisters than I learned about you. I've seen your work. I know you're talented. But . . . this wasn't the assignment."

"I . . ."

. . . don't know what to say. Mal has seen my work, thinks I'm *talented*, even, but that compliment is tainted by her massive disappointment in me right now. I can't process anything else, except for the cringe looks on everyone's faces.

"I'm sorry."

I sink into my seat as pressure builds behind my eyes and the class moves on.

As soon as we're dismissed, I exit before my tears surface, pissed at myself and this worst day ever that just keeps on keeping on. Outside, thick, humid air greets me. By the time I reunite with my air-conditioned dorm, I'm a sobbing mess of snot and sweat.

I drop my backpack at the door and notice that Dani's Docs aren't on the shoe rack.

She isn't here.

It's probably for the best. Otherwise I'd be knocking on her door to tell her how sorry I am and confess how much I need us to be okay, which is the opposite of *space*. Ugh. But I do need us to be okay. Of course I forgot my portfolio. I'm malfunctioning without her.

I close the door to my room and collapse onto my bed face-first, flipping off the portfolio that sure enough is on my desk.

"You look like shit," Em Rojas says, looking up from their laptop and removing an earbud. Em's bluntness is so jarring. Who tells someone that they've known for a week that they look like shit?

"Thanks," I say.

"Rough day?" Em asks.

"A massive understatement."

Em is from Central Pennsylvania and here for a creative

writing intensive at the New School for queer creators. During the roommate search, Em and I connected over a mutual obsession with *Big Brother* and very strong feelings about the best adaptation of *Cinderella* (unquestionably *Ella Enchanted*). But as it turns out, a shared interest in the same media does not a friendship make. They tuck their blue hair behind their ear, exposing the second set of fantastic eye shadow I've seen today—a smoky purple eye, with yellow and white accents, above black liner.

The nonbinary flag colors.

"Your makeup looks amazing," I say.

"Thanks." Em chews on their lower lip. "Dani wanted to practice. You know, for Pride."

"Right."

I swallow the emotion in my throat because Pride is this weekend and that's something Dani and I were supposed to experience for the first time together.

"I'm sorry. I've never, um, lived with exes before?"

I wave off their apology. "It's cool. It's temporary."

Maybe we can still go together. I can give Dani the space she needs to miss me this week and our whole reconciliation can happen during Pride. I'll find her in Washington Square Park and tell her that this hiatus is for her, that I don't need social media. I need *her*. It's the perfect place and the perfect amount of space.

Em nods, reinserting their earbud and resuming their show. This is how it goes interacting with them. To Em, we're strictly roommates, no need to exchange life stories or false pleasantries. It's fine. We don't need to be friends. But . . . Dani convinced Em to do their makeup and told them about the breakup. Clearly, they don't mind hanging out with her and crossing that invisible line from roommates to friendship. So. I don't know. It feels just a little personal.

Whatever.

I reach for my phone and instinct has me tapping for every app I willingly deleted. I can't even distract myself on CatTok. I really need CatTok right now. I don't know why I thought this would be easy. Without social media, without Natalie and Henry, and without Dani . . . I'm alone.

I don't know what to do with all this space.

So I open my laptop and type *Levi Berkowitz* into Google because I need a distraction and thinking about him and dissecting our subway conversation is the only thing that feels good right now.

Results include a sci-fi screenwriter, an obituary for a NASA astrophysicist, a web designer's portfolio. . . . The list goes on. There are too many Levi Berkowitzes—most of whom are over the age of fifty-five. He truly has the most Jewish grandpa name. I add plants to the search but only find Dr. Levi Berkowitz, professor of biology at Duke.

It's almost impressive, how off the grid Levi continues to be.

But Levi isn't in the Galapagos or Antarctica. He's *here*. Somewhere in this city of almost nine million people.

It's wild, our paths crossing again.

As little kids, we were inseparable. With Dad's night shifts at the hospital, Mom working late more often than not, and Tessa always studying or dancing, I spent more time at Levi's house than my own. I didn't mind. Levi had a Wii. We could play Mario Kart after we finished our homework and debate the merits of our favorite Sunchips flavors—Garden Salsa vs. Harvest Cheddar. Beyond the video games and silly debates, Levi was the first person who was ever really truly there for me. Whenever my sisters shut me out of their *big-kid stuff* conversations, his door was always open. He also had parents who ate dinner together every night, who always set a seat at the table for me, who I loved spending time with just as much. As long as I had Levi, I knew I would never be alone.

Then he left.

But now he's back.

I have to find him.

So I scroll, scroll, scroll, and it's a useless endeavor but a perfect distraction.

## SEVEN

*I* give Dani four entire days of space.

It's torture, but I'm determined to respect her boundary with a show-don't-tell approach. Let her see that I'm committed to taking this hiatus without her so I can eventually take the rest of it *with* her. So I move through the week on autopilot, distracted and frustrated because my broken self can't even absorb how amazing it is that three times a week, I'm breathing the same air as Mal Burton. Her program is designed to take us through the life cycle of a garment created with sustainable practices, so this first week has been all about spotting inspiration through sustainable sourcing. On Thursday, we meet the CEO of ScrapFAB, a nonprofit in Brooklyn that recycles and resells scrap fabric. I quietly listen to their presentation, swallowing my questions and opting to lie low until I get my shit together.

Every class this week, I arrive on time with my portfolio.

Blend in.

Until it's the weekend and I can initiate flight mode once more.

Friday night, I flee to Tessa's and take advantage of the spare key in my possession because at the dorm, Dani is everywhere—her "To Infinity and Blue-Yond!" O.P.I. nail polish on the bathroom counter, her *Waitress* hoodie draped over the couch, her bulk bag of dried mango from Costco in the kitchen cabinet. And the music. So much music. HAIM's harmonies are the backing track for study sessions. Avril and Alanis are for screaming at the universe on a shit day. Cardi B and Lil Nas X are the emotional equivalent to a Friday afternoon. Broadway soundtracks are for vocal exercises and audition preparation.

Dani's music is a constant.

Her gel nails are always tap, tap, tapping to a beat—at her desk, on her thigh, in my car. She's the only one who has—*had*—music privileges in my Subaru.

*Sorry*, she said, her cerulean nails fiddling with the radio when I picked her up for our first date six months and four days ago. *My therapist encourages me to sit in the silence sometimes, but I'd rather sit with Stevie Nicks and Bad Bunny, thanks!*

*Valid*, I said as Dani settled on an oldies station. *Imagine that dinner party? Iconic.*

*Julie Andrews would complete it.*

Dame *Julie Andrews*, I corrected. *Show some respect, Danica.*

Dani's snort-laugh filled my Subaru and wow, I lived for that sound.

I still do.

So anytime I hear it coming from the other side of her

door it's almost impossible to not run into her room and grand gesture too soon.

So crashing with Tessa?

It's just the easiest way to maintain space until tomorrow, when I'll be on a mission to find Dani at Pride and truly, properly apologize. I'll tell her I'm on hiatus and I'm so sorry that she ever felt like my photographer. I want to spend the summer with my favorite person. *Her.* It will resolve the way grand gestures do, with kisses and confessions and a happily-ever-after summer—and the euphoria in that moment will be worth these four broken days.

"Bitch," Tessa snarls at the dropped call on her laptop.

We're in our pajamas even though it's before seven p.m. and eating dumplings on Gertie, officially late to our Fitzgerald Sister FaceTime. We do these calls once a month, my sisters and me. I lowkey live for them, even when they're full of inside jokes that go over my head. It's the closest we have to being together all at once . . . when technology isn't conspiring to keep us apart.

Tessa's phone vibrates and Clara's name appears on the screen.

"Technology hates me," Tessa answers.

"Spectrum doesn't discriminate," Clara says.

Tessa groans. "Bennett took the router when he moved out."

"Broke your heart *and* stole your Fios?" Maya's voice asks off-screen.

"*Fuck* him," Clara says.

Tessa balances her phone against a whimsical cloud planter on her coffee table, so we're both in frame.

"A!" Clara squeals, the nickname only she calls me. She is a homemade crochet cardigan, oversize and colorful, her long blonde hair in pigtail braids. Crochet is her crafty thing—something I dabble in as well—but I'm not nearly as good as her. It doesn't come as naturally to me as working with a sewing machine does. "How's New York?"

"Are you okay, Fitzy?" Maya asks before I can answer. She enters the frame dressed in climbing pants and a tank top covered in chalk, her dark brown hair twisted in a messy topknot exposing her undercut. "Breakups suck."

I glare at Tessa. "You told them."

Tessa just reaches for her glass of pinot whatever and takes a sip. I haven't told Maya or Clara because telling all my sisters would make the breakup real and it's not. I mean, it is. But it's temporary. There's no reason to sound the alarm, when we'll be back together tomorrow.

"We saw your hiatus post and asked Tessa what was up," Maya says.

"Oh."

It's weird, hearing her mention my post so casually. My sisters were my first followers, but there's a difference between following and paying attention . . . and I guess I assumed they weren't. I mean. They don't comment on my posts anymore. Tessa has been so wrapped up in her research or with Bennett. Clara is balancing teaching full-time, a master's program, and a social life. Maya has a wife and a mortgage and babies' lives in her hands during her twelve-hour shifts as a neonatal nurse. It's comforting that just because they don't engage with my posts doesn't mean they aren't paying attention, but if they saw why didn't they reach out to *me*? I know my sisters are closer, but it's one thing to know that they talk without me and another to know that they check in with each other *about* me. That they still see my posts, not because they care about what I'm creating but to, like, *monitor* me.

"We should've just asked you," Clara acknowledges. "Sorry, A."

Maya says, "Forgive us and tell us everything."

All I've ever wanted is to unpack relationship drama with my sisters.

So I do.

And it's nice, catching up with them, even if the conversation revolves around an ex-fiancé and a (temporary!) ex-girlfriend. As far as relationship statuses go, my two oldest sisters are on opposite ends of the spectrum, as is their advice. Maya is a romantic who met the love of her life, Sarah Goldblum, during a freshman orientation event at UT Dallas's Chabad. Maya was there for the Brooklyn Bagels and in the most Jewish meet-cute of all time, Maya and Sarah reached for the last poppy seed at the same time. They split the bagel, Maya joined Chabad, and they've been Maya and Sarah ever since. Then there's Clara, who doesn't believe in monogamy before thirty as a concept and keeps assuring us that our pain is valid, but soon enough we'll feel liberated.

"What're you doing this weekend?" Clara asks.

"Not sure," Tessa says, then looks at me. "What do you want to do?"

"Oh . . ." It catches me off guard, this simple question. I just assumed Tessa's weekend was already filled like mine is. "Pride is tomorrow."

"Right! We should totally go."

"I kind of already have plans."

"Oh."

I feel bad, but tomorrow is too important to let Tessa crash, even if it would mean having my sister to myself for a whole Saturday for the first time in literal years.

"Sorry, I—"

Tessa shakes her head. "It's cool. Next weekend?"

I nod.

Maya changes the subject. "How are classes going?"

Because she doesn't direct the question to anyone specific, we all start speaking at the same time—Clara, Tessa, and me. The master's in studio art candidate, the PhD in neuro-something, and the fashion student.

"TAing a 101 class is more being a babysitter than an educational authority figure."

Clara raises her can of cider. "Preach."

"Babysitting is the worst," I add.

Tessa nods. "Someone showed up today in flip-flops and

I had to send them home. I mean, these kids don't even have basic lab safety down."

"We are glorified, underpaid babysitters, T," Clara says. "I still haven't recovered from Dante's inferno."

"What?" I ask.

"On the last day of school, one of my freshmen—Dante—lit a match to burn the edges of his paper and caused an impromptu fire drill, quote, *in the name of art*," Clara says. "It was traumatizing. Did I not tell you?"

She most definitely didn't. I would remember Dante's inferno.

"I maintain that you do not get paid enough for this shit," Maya says.

As my sisters vent about students, the number of hours they spend grading, and the bureaucratic bullshit that comes with academia, I listen and wait for a moment to casually mention Levi Berkowitz. *Hey! Remember my best friend? I ran into him on the subway and didn't even recognize him!* As much as I don't want my breakup to feel real is as much as I *do* want reconnecting with Levi to be real and not just, like, a subway fever dream.

I want to ask my sisters what they remember.

And I want them to help me find him.

"Do you—?" I start.

But then, Tessa blurts out, "Bennett called me yesterday."

I drop my chopsticks. "Tess!"

"Way to bury the lede," Maya says.

"His voicemail is bullshit."

Clara demands that Tessa play it, so she does.

*"Hey, T. Can we talk? I messed up, but I don't want to give up on us. I love you."*

"T? Since when does he call you that?" Clara snarls, protective of her nickname for Tessa as if it's, like, original.

Tessa shrugs. "What am I supposed to do with this?"

I swallow, sitting with the discomfort that I want to destroy Bennett Covington III's life for Tessa, but I would do literally anything to receive a message like that from Dani.

*It's different.*

"If he thinks my extra Bon Iver ticket is still his, he's a fucking idiot," Maya says.

"I'm creating a Goodreads page for his nonexistent book just to give it one star as we speak," Clara declares.

"I still need to tell Mom and Dad," Tessa says, her voice soft.

*"Tess."*

Tessa looks at me. "Do they know about Dani?"

I'm silent.

Tessa's eyebrows rise. *Thought so.*

"Mine is a break. Not a breakup."

"Does Dani know that?"

"She *will*. We can come back from this. It's not like anyone cheated—"

*"Fitz."*

Maya's *cut the shit* tone renders me silent and I'm ten years old again, about to be shut out of the room with the big kids for being too messy, too immature, too much. So I silence the emotions before they lead to a door in my face.

Again.

"Sorry," I say.

The subject shifts away from relationship drama and toward more surface-level updates for the rest of the call—feelings about the newest Taylor Swift album, podcast recommendations, and Clara showing off her latest thrift haul until Maya has to head out for her overnight shift at the hospital.

After we set next month's date and say goodbye, Tessa finishes her dumplings in silence. A forehead wrinkle appears between her brows. She's pissed. I am too. But I don't want this tension.

So I say, "I get why you haven't told Mom."

"It's not about telling—" Tessa starts, then pauses, considering her words. "Maybe it *should* be a breakup. You and Dani. Maybe this summer could be about figuring out how to be alone, for both of us. We are, um, notoriously bad at that."

"How introspective."

"It's not like we had the best example."

Is she wrong? Not exactly, but I'm not about to go there with her. Growing up with codependent parents who hyperfixate on work rather than admit that they'd be happier apart is a particular brand of trauma that I don't quite know how to articulate. I love my parents, but an example of sweeping romantic love they are not.

"I'm serious," Tessa continues. "It might be nice for us to have, I don't know, a Single Girl Summer?"

Um.

Does Tessa only want to spend time with me because she's now single? Is her idea of building our relationship . . . us being sad together? Like, Bennett is out, so I'm in? Seriously? No thank you.

"I'm good."

"I just think—"

"Tess. Maybe this is something you need to do. But Dani isn't Bennett. *I* messed up. I'm the Bennett in this situation. So stop acting like we're going through something together. We're not."

Tessa's eyes widen. "Understood."

She stands, brings her dishes to the sink, and retreats to her bedroom without another word. Angry tears sting my eyes as I lie on Gertie with a dramatic flop. Sometimes I can't help it—the filter drops and the mess that is me is exposed. But no one will ever engage with her. With *me*.

Maya says, *Cut the shit.*

Clara is silent.

Tessa walks away.

I wipe my eyes and open Instagram's shitty web browser. Type @iftheshoefitz into search. My first scheduled post has gone live, a shot of me in Rockefeller Plaza, a hand running through my hair in a pose that showcases the stack of Lola Chung bangles on my arm. I'm lowkey cringing at the reality that over the next two months, my main feed is going to become overtaken by just these sponsored content posts. I hope my audience isn't turned off by it. *No.* They know I'm on hiatus.

I scroll through the comments on the hiatus announcement.

> *fashionable_fiona: AHHH have the BEST summer*
> *ginalouisesews: cannot WAIT for the recap*
> *lunabluereads: love this for u!!*

It's fine. If the Shoe Fitz will not crumble due to a summer hiatus. I will not crumble due to a summer hiatus.

I read more of the comments, soothed by the scrolling, until I look up and notice the lack of light coming from under Tessa's door. I wish Gertie could swallow me. I hate sister tension. It makes the apartment stifling.

Whatever.

I'm going to grand gesture the shit out of tomorrow, so I won't even need to crash here again.

I cannot wait to prove how wrong she is about Dani and me.

## EIGHT

*I*'m surrounded by rainbow flags, absolutely fire fashion, and so much *love*. In the span of two minutes in Washington Square Park, I encounter a dance crew living their best life with speakers blasting Troye Sivan's newest song, a tribute to Marsha P. Johnson, and a dead ringer for Antoni from *Queer Eye*. I've never been around this many queer people and it's overwhelming in the best way.

Still, anxiety blooms in the pit of my stomach.

I don't know. It's, like, being surrounded by the queer community in this way . . . feels a lot more complicated than I want it to. I see the YOU ARE VALID pins with every identity's flag and I can't *not* think about all the comments on my posts that say I'm not valid.

*Bisexuality isn't real.*

*Pick a side.*

*I was bi once too.*

I pretend the biphobic comments don't bother me. Queer women and nonbinary representation in the mainstream fashion industry still has a long way to go. I came out online, in part, to show that we are here. I don't regret it—not at all!—but sometimes, I wish I'd protected that piece of me. Because it's one thing when queerphobic trash invalidate your identity. It's another thing entirely to experience biphobia from *within* the queer community.

As I am me, complicated queer feelings did not stop me from spending weeks perfecting my Pride look: a white cropped tee with a hand-stitched rainbow on the breast pocket, high-waisted denim shorts thrifted from Goodwill that I relined the pockets of with rainbow fabric, and Vans hand-painted with a swirling psychedelic—you guessed it!—rainbow print. It's simple but chic, giving room for my makeup to be over the top. No one can do a blended rainbow eye like Dani, but I gave it my best shot.

It's a travesty that my followers won't see this look.

But this isn't for Instagram.

It's just for Dani.

I lean against the fountain, my palms pressed against the warm marble. Parades are an anxiety trigger for Dani, so we'd planned on celebrating in the park, which isn't on the route but still close to the action. I don't know if that's still her plan, but I situate myself there so I have the best shot of spotting her if it is. I don't have much else to work with, since Henry straight up refused a temporary lift on my Instagram ban this morning, not even for the sake of checking out Dani's Stories.

I knew I chose the right friend to cut me off, but damn it.

Wait. Actually.

natalie
3:03PM

911
3:03PM

**Natalie Jacobson**
HELLO HI.
3:04PM

can u, idk, maybe possibly send me
screenshots of dani's stories?
3:04PM

FITZGERALD
3:05PM

your use of 911 has become . . .
way too liberal jfc
3:05PM

i just need to see if she's at pride!
give your lovesick bestie a break!!!
3:05PM

Natalie is weak. I love her so much. She sends a series of
four screenshots and three videos—photos of Dani and Em

getting ready, a close-up of Dani's purple and gray smoky eye makeup look, breakfast burritos from the Grey Dog, and the Washington Square Park arch. Yes! She's *here*.

One of the videos is a picnic basket in the grass, a blurry Pigeon Man in the background. Adrenaline coursing through my veins, I weave through the celebratory crowds, pushing toward the patch of grass on the west side of the park where Dani and Em are Pride picnicking near Pigeon Man, a Washington Square Park icon, always surrounded by dozens of pigeons. I love Pigeon Man. This is it. The grand gesture of grand gestures! My heart pounds *I love you, I love you, I love you* as I rehearse my apology over and over in my head. I pass a bench and so many pigeons, until finally a gingham picnic blanket comes into focus, and—

No. Dani's hand is *not* on top of Em's.

No. Her head is *not* resting on their shoulder.

No. She absolutely does *not* snort-laugh at whatever Em says.

No. No. *No*.

I swerve off course and hide behind a tree, my heart in my throat as I watch their easy back-and-forth. Em's nonbinary flag eye shadow perfection is a betrayal. Dani laughs and it kills me how beautiful she is, how not broken she looks, how maybe she doesn't want my grand gesture at all.

She doesn't even want space.

She just wants someone else.

I short-circuit, biting down on my lip so hard I taste metal on my tongue. Music, laughter, and all the joy that surrounds me morphs into white noise.

I back away because I'm not subjecting myself to any more of this. I make it as far as the fountain before my vision blurs and a sob escapes my throat, leaving me breathless at the spot where our summer started.

"I am that replaceable," I whisper.

Then I sit on the fountain steps and weep.

"Fitz?"

I'm not sure how long I've been weeping into a fountain in broad daylight when a soft tenor voice says my name like it's a question. A question, but also a terribly timed answer.

*Where in the world is Levi Berkowitz? Here for your Very Public Meltdown!*

Pressing the heels of my hands against my swollen eyelids, I choke out a laugh between hiccupped sobs. This has to be a joke. Levi here. Now. At this park. In *this* fountain. It's so nonsensical, I wonder what I did in a past life to deserve this. First, *No photos.* Now this. Neither is how I want to be reintroduced to Levi.

"Are you okay?" Levi asks, and because I don't have the energy to look up or words to describe what I'm feeling, I cackle-cry. A truly deranged sound. Snot drips down my nose and becomes one with the fountain. "Stupid question. You're obviously not."

Levi should back away and leave me alone in my misery. I mean, he just saw my phlegm.

But he doesn't.

Instead, he sits next to me, balancing a wicker basket with four small pots on his lap, and pulls a travel-size pack of tissues out of one of the pockets of his cargo shorts. The gesture is so unexpected and kind, it forces my eyes up, only to find Levi's hidden behind tinted Wayfarer frames.

I take the tissues. "Thank you."

A nose-scrunch and a wordless wave is Levi for *No problem!*, an act so recognizable it stuns me silent as I get my snot situation cleaned up. I know that I might as well be taking tissues from a stranger. I mean, we were tiny humans the last time we interacted, just developing critical-thinking skills and a more sophisticated vocabulary. So I can't even describe how it feels to still understand his wordless language.

"How's Eloise?" I ask.

Levi's mouth quirks. "In Gowanus, thriving in bright yet indirect sunlight."

"Is that Queens?"

"Brooklyn."

I nod. "Cool. So you're, like, a Brooklyn hipster now?"

Levi's mouth-quirk expands. "Nah. I just transported Eloise to an AP bio teacher there with a well-lit townhouse. I volunteer with this program that rescues plants and helps them find homes."

"Like a plant shelter?"

"Yeah. It's a huge problem," Levi says. "People abandoning plants after they have bloomed, or at the first sign of drooping leaves. It's maddening, how our planet's already limited resources have become integrated into throwaway culture, you know?"

I blow my nose. "People *suck*."

"Pretty much."

I nod at the herbs in his lap. Thyme, rosemary, and . . . okay, I am neither a plant expert nor a chef and can't identify the other two. "Is this another rescue mission?"

Levi shakes his head. "I hope not. For now they're an herb garden for these twins in my building that I sit for sometimes. Herbs are a great low-maintenance way to teach kids about plants. They're five, so their attention spans are all over the place."

"Stop. That's adorable—" I picture Levi plant tangent-ing to small kiddos and, well, I can't *not* smile. "The twins."

Levi, also. Objectively.

I'm not sure why I felt the need to clarify.

"Ella and Avery," Levi says. "They've been begging for a plant. Apparently, *TOMATO Talks* is all the rage right now."

"*TOMATO Talks*," I repeat.

"It's, like, *TED Talks*, starring an animated tomato."

"And . . . it's entertaining? It sounds deeply unsettling."

"It's a phase, but I'll take it. Better than *Paw Patrol*. . . ." His voice trails off and he looks at me, almost like, *Why are we talking about unhinged children's media right now?* "I'm sorry. I just. You're *here*."

"This is some truly cosmic shit," I say.

"Seriously! I mean, earlier this week, with Eloise? I never take the 1."

"Never?"

"I live on Avenue C."

Levi says this as if my mental map extends beyond the twentyish blocks between Washington Square Park and FIT. Oh, and the 1 train to Tessa! But Avenue C? Is that even real? I'm skeptical of all lettered avenues after learning that Avenue Q does not, in fact, exist.

"Meaning?"

"It's not my train."

"Plant Hero emergencies being the only exception."

"Exactly. What are you doing here?"

"Here, like, generally? Or here, single-handedly providing a secondary water source for this fountain?"

"Both?"

"Broadly, I am here, in New York, for this dream sustainable fashion program at FIT. Specifically, I am here"—I gesture at the fountain—"because I'm in love with a girl who said that coming here together for the summer was, quote, *a mistake*, and that she needs space. Said girl is currently holding hands with my roommate. So."

"Shit."

"It gets better! We all live together."

Levi winces. "Brutal."

"It's a shared suite, but still."

In a beat of silence, the humiliation that accompanies *I am*

73

*in love* settles in. I'm not sure what prompted me to word-vomit all over Levi Berkowitz—if it's emotional exhaustion, or the fact that Levi is a familiar stranger, or that his wicker basket of herbs for Ella and Avery is so disarming.

"I'm sorry. I'm totally trauma-dumping."

"You're not. Breakups suck."

"You keep catching me at the worst time."

Levi stands.

It was too much—the phlegmy tears and heartbreak monologue. *I'm* too much. Again. Now Levi, literally the only person I know who's here and can distract me from being crushed by all these feelings, is going to ghost me again in real time.

But he doesn't leave.

Instead, he nudges my foot with his and says, "Do you still like bubble tea? There's a great spot on St. Marks."

I nod.

Levi smiles. "Cool."

He holds out his hand and pulls me to my feet and we're so close, I have to look up to make eye contact. It's a new development. In my head canon, we're still the same height.

"You're taller," I say.

"You're not."

I laugh, *loud*, the sound surprising me. His hand is soft and warm and safe. I'm vertical now so I should let go. I don't. Instead, I squeeze his fingers, a question I'm not even sure how to articulate. His squeeze back is the exact answer I need.

*I am here.*

"Let's—"

Levi's sentence is cut off by a snort-laugh that triples the speed of my heart. My eyes shift toward the direction of the sound and of course it's Dani and Em, clumsily climbing into the fountain only steps away from where we stand. Is this, like, Dani rewriting her summer? Erasing the day we had here from her memory and redoing it with Em? I want to scream. I want to melt into the fountain and disappear. I want to know what is so funny.

Dani sees me.

Her smoky purple eyes look up, then widen at the sight of Levi's hand still warm in mine.

Honestly? I like the way it looks. I like that Dani also sees my fingers twined with someone else's today. I like the confusion on her face, the flicker of hurt before she looks away. Mostly, I like that it seems like she *cares*. That it might have been easy for her to say she needs space . . . but maybe she didn't consider what I would do with mine.

Dani's an incredible actress, but I know her. I love her. It's obvious how thrown she is.

It dulls my pain.

Sparks hope, even.

Because this reaction? I can work with it.

In fact, I want to lean into it.

So I look at Levi and say, "Can I kiss you?"

I don't think, I just say it. A true no-filter moment.

After a beat, Levi's eyebrows rise above his Wayfarers. "What?"

"Dani? The girl I'm in love with? She's here, sitting on the steps behind you with said roommate, who just launched a massive flirty splash attack and, I don't know. I want to exude big *I am moving on energy* too."

"By kissing me?"

"Exactly."

Levi's expression is impossible to read behind the sunglasses. How many times can I humiliate myself in front of this boy? Muttering "No photos" on the subway like I'm a C-list celebrity attempting to make a comeback on *Dancing with the Stars*. Confessing that I'm in love with a girl who doesn't love me back as phlegmy tears drip into the Washington Square Fountain. Asking if I can kiss him after a pity invite for bubble tea.

Oh my God.

I let go of his hand.

"Sorry. Please back away and delete this from your memory."

"Fitz."

"Delete this," I repeat. "And the next time the universe intervenes, let's just smile politely and protect childhood nostalgia because I clearly cannot stop making a total ass out of my—"

Levi cuts me off mid–backtrack babble, his lips pressing a kiss so soft, so tentative, so surprising against my mouth that it's an electric shock to my system. My arms drape around his neck and my fingers comb through hair too short to hold on to.

He cups my cheek with one hand as the other finds my waist. His finger hooks through my belt loop and there is, wow, nothing tentative about that. Or how Levi's teeth gently graze my lower lip. I melt into his kiss and it feels so good. Kissing Levi Berkowitz. Pretending I'm okay.

*I am kissing Levi Berkowitz.*

Holy shit.

What am I *doing*?

I pull away, my heart hammering in my chest, and look over his shoulder. Dani and Em are gone, but I hope she saw us. And I hope it hurt. I cannot be the only person who hurts. Because one kiss doesn't erase the pain—and at the end of the day, Levi isn't the person I want to be kissing. Even if it was, objectively, the hottest no-tongue kiss of my life.

My eyes shift back to him and I say, "Damn, Berkowitz."

Then I bro-punch his arm, because that's a normal thing to do.

Levi looks at me, his expression still indecipherable. Those Wayfarers! They're too powerful. I have no clue what he's thinking. But *I'm* thinking we can absolutely move on. We don't have to unpack whatever that just was. *Please don't make this awkward.*

"Yeah." Levi takes a step back. "So—"

He's going to make this awkward.

So I interject. "Are you still up for bubble tea?"

## NINE

*B*ubble tea obtained—Taro for Levi, Thai for me—we weave through the crowds and observe the commercialized Pride festivities along St. Marks Place: the tattoo shops offering ten-dollar rainbow hearts, the queer-owned record store offering twenty percent off TODAY ONLY!, the thrift store with a themed window display, packed bars with patrons spilling out.

My straw between my lips, I sip my tea as we wait for the light to change at First Avenue and notice a bi flag pinned on his tote bag. I feel the *twinge* because, like, of course we were two bi babies. I wonder what it could've been like in an alternate universe, Levi and I figuring out this piece of our identities together.

But he never called.

So.

"I've been trying and failing to find you online," I say. Maybe it's a red-flag admission, but I have a feeling that if the snot or the kiss didn't drive him away, neither will the light internet stalking. "It's almost concerning, how off the grid you are."

Levi's eyebrows scrunch, surprised. "You looked for me?"

"Yeah. Since the subway."

The real answer would definitely be too much. No way am I going to confess that I've spent years failing to find him or admit how much time I spent waiting for a call that never came.

"Well. I found you. Great time to take a hiatus, Fitzgerald."

Wait.

Levi has seen If the Shoe Fitz?

"You're on Instagram?"

"I have a plantstagram."

"What?"

Levi unlocks his phone, and just seeing someone's Instagram grid is a tiny boost of serotonin, but when I get a closer look at the bright plant-saturated feed that is @thymeisonmyside? It's literal sunshine. Each post is a before-and-after, Levi demonstrating how he finds and rehabilitates plants that are tossed too soon. Eloise is the star of the most recent post, the "after" shot showcasing her in an indirectly well-lit corner. The caption reads, *"Sunny days ahead in my new home. Currently in my ficus feelings about it."—Eloise (Ficus altissima)*

Oh my God.

He writes captions from the plants' point of view.

I scroll to the top of his profile and my eyes zero in on the 100K followers.

"You're a goddamn plant influencer."

"Am I? I didn't mean to be," Levi says, cheeks tinted pink,

his expression absolutely confounded by the concept.

"Do you have any brand partnerships?"

"No. I get some inquiries, but I just assume they're all spam."

I hand him his phone back. "You could absolutely monetize this."

He shrugs. "I just want to show people how to revive their plants."

Levi says this so simply, it cuts off the spiel I'm about to go into about engagement metrics and sponcon. I don't understand. He names the plants, writes POV captions that are quirky and original, and maintains a clean uniform aesthetic. Levi is good at this. How does someone so good at social media have no desire to capitalize on it?

"That's really cool, Berkowitz," I say instead. "So. How did you find me?"

"My friend—Adam—he's a fan," he says. "He wants a photo."

I swat his arm. "Too soon."

He laughs. "I'm serious! I mentioned the subway run-in and he pulled up your page in the unlikely chance that you were that Fitz. And. Well. You are."

We cross Avenue A and enter Tompkins Square Park. I'm not sure what to say next or how to pivot. How does one begin seven years' worth of catching up? Especially after a meaningless revenge kiss? And then learning that he's seen the much better version of me on the internet?

"I'm sorry," Levi says. "I'm trying to be chill. But kissing you? While you were that upset? It wasn't cool."

Oh my God.

"Berkowitz."

"Yeah?"

"I asked you to kiss me."

"I—"

"No. Listen. *I'm* sorry. I just used you to make my ex jealous. My motives are trash. In terms of who I am as, like, a human, I'm making the worst case for myself. Which sucks because I'm so excited to see you again."

I chase the no-filter admission with an aggressive sip of tea.

It's too saccharine.

Way too earnest.

So I swallow and add, "Wow. I'm also very much not cool."

"You're the first person I've kissed since Soph. My . . ." Levi pauses, scrunching his nose. "I don't know. Soph isn't my girlfriend. But she's not *not* my girlfriend? We're on a break. So when you asked, I thought, *why not?* Rip the Band-Aid off. It's been a month. But now I'm kind of falling apart even though it was the most platonic of kisses. Because it also was—"

"Hot?"

Levi laughs. It breaks the tension and the sound is so satisfying.

I can be disarming too.

"Hot," Levi confirms. "But it didn't mean anything."

I pause mid-step, my eyes widening. "Wait. You're not in love with me now?"

He makes a *ha* face at me as my faux shock relaxes into a smirk. I'm messing with him. He knows it. And yet, his eyebrows pinch ever so slightly as he struggles to formulate a response.

So I say, "We're both so obviously in love with other people, Berkowitz."

"Yeah."

"You're on a break? How long have you been together?"

"Three years."

I choke on a tapioca pearl, surprised by both the word "years" and the number in front of it. I can't even imagine it. I mean, I wanted a gold star after three *months*.

"Who initiated it?"

"Not me."

"Shit."

"Soph is in Denver for the summer. She asked for space the night before she left, because, quote, *We can't be each other's entire high school experience*. She doesn't want to have, um, any regrets."

"She said that?"

"Yup," Levi says, popping the *p*. "Total blindside."

"*Fuck* space."

Silence settles between us, so I finish my tea and take in my surroundings. We're meandering through a park I haven't been to yet. This one doesn't have fountains to cry in or fancy arches that attract tourists, just playgrounds and dog runs and massive elm trees that shoot out of concrete toward the sky, creating canopies that shade the pathways. We find an empty bench across from one of the metal playgrounds, and the sound of children's laughter as they run and climb and play takes me back to our playground days.

"So. You're not in Allen anymore," Levi says. A statement, not a question, and I feel my brow furrow, confused. The only posts that ever indicated where in the world I am were my most recent hiatus post and the sponcon shot all over the city because privacy and boundaries and all. He must notice because he clarifies, "Before we came here, we moved back for a minute. Just my mom and me."

"What?"

"Yeah. The summer before eighth grade," Levi says.

"I moved to Massachusetts that summer."

"Seriously?" Levi says. "We must've just missed each other."

"Must've," I echo, almost in disbelief.

Of course this is my life. Of course the moment I was so close to learning the answer to *Where in the world is Levi Berkowitz?* . . . I'm the one who leaves. That summer my parents didn't just move me 1,700 miles away from my sisters. *Levi came back.* I could've asked him why he never called. Told him how much it hurt that he never even answered the invitation to my bat mitzvah while that wound was still angry and raw. Our hiatus could have been a three-year blip, not a seven-year gash.

"Mom kept Grandma Jo's bungalow."

"On Bluebird Lane?"

Levi nods and memories of Grandma Jo resurface—matzo ball soup, crochet lessons, her magic garden. All until Grandma Jo's heart stopped weeks before the Berkowitzes left. A brutal double loss. I was inconsolable.

"I miss that house," I say.

"I did too."

"So Austin was temporary?"

"Extremely."

It's all so much to take in, but the way Levi says *extremely* has me processing the second piece of information. *Just my mom and me.*

Five words have never felt more loaded.

"Your dad . . . ?"

My voice trails off, unsure how to finish the question.

"He's in Nashville, teaching fifth grade and trying to break into country music."

"I'm sorry, what?"

Levi nods. "One of his songs went viral on TikTok last month."

"No way."

"Yeah. The cat jingle?"

"Shut up. Your dad wrote 'Purrfect Girl'?"

"He did."

"He's all over CatTok."

"Building a legacy as we speak."

We laugh in harmony with the playground children.

"Wait. So your parents are, like, doing long-distance? That must be hard."

"No." Levi shakes his head. "They're divorced."

I'm not that dense, I swear. It's just—my memories of David and Esther Berkowitz are a video reel, *love* always the throughline in every shot. Him, surprising her with her favorite slice of carrot cake from Lulu's just because. Her, sketching his profile on a paper napkin at dinner. Them, laughing, always laughing, the sound traveling from the kitchen to our ears, wherever we were.

I had never seen parents be so casually affectionate.

So *happy*.

"I'm sorry."

"I'm not."

There is zero hint of animosity in his tone. He means it. Whoa. I'm not sure my parents even *like* each other most days and I would still lose my shit if they ever got divorced.

"How's your mom?" I ask.

"She's living her best life, getting commissions for her art and teaching at Parsons."

"That's incredible."

"It is," he says, and the pride in his voice is so sweet. "She even has a gallery space in SoHo. It's just one corner, but it's a great location and sales have been steadier ever since she booked it, so things have been good. Really good."

"I love that."

I maintain a composed filter, but inside? I'm rattled by this influx of information, answers to so many questions except one: *Why did you never contact me?* I've waited seven years to ask that question and now that Levi is here, the words are stuck in my throat. I can't. I've embarrassed myself enough in front of him today. I can't admit that I've been holding on to this hurt. Nope. My red-flag quota has been hit for the day, the week, maybe even for the entire summer.

"This is a lot," I admit.

"I know."

"You live here."

"A few blocks east, technically."

"Do you love it?"

"I do."

"I want to," I admit.

"But?"

"Dani."

"Do you want to talk about it?"

Yes. No. I don't know.

"I went on hiatus for her," I say. "Because she thinks I'm only in love with my platform. It was supposed to be a grand gesture to show her how wrong she is. But now seeing her with Em—my roommate—is all kinds of confusing because, like, was everything she said about me and If the Shoe Fitz just a bullshit excuse? I don't know what to think."

Levi frowns. "She made you feel bad about your platform?"

"I can be a bit obsessive about it."

"Or . . . just passionate."

"Either way, she said all the photos and stuff were too much for her. And now I'm here, in this incredible fashion program that Dani found. *She* encouraged me to apply. *She* asked me to follow her here. The only reason I'm in New York is because of her."

Levi shakes his head. "You wanted fashion in New York before Dani. She may have handed you the application . . . but you're here because of you."

"You remember that?"

His mouth quirks again. "I remember the vision board."

Him bringing up the vision board so casually almost bowls me over. It hung above my desk, a corkboard filled with hand-sketched designs, a cityscape, yellow taxis, and every cliché I could think of to manifest my future New York life. When we were nine, Levi came back from a family vacation with the final piece, a postcard from a fashion exhibit at the Met. The vision board didn't survive the move from Allen to Lincoln intact, but that postcard is still, to this day, tacked to the corkboard above my desk.

"Okay. True," I concede. "But how do I untangle this city from her now?"

"You let an old friend show you all the local secrets."

"Yeah?"

"Definitely. How long are you here for?"

"Seven more weeks."

"Cool. I"—Levi is cut off by his smartwatch alarm—"am unfortunately on Ella and Avery duty soon."

"Oh!" I stand up and pull at the hem of my shorts. "Right. The herb garden."

"I lost track of time. You're okay to get home?" Levi asks.

"Preparing to crawl back into a fountain as we speak."

Levi's face morphs into concern. "Fitz."

"Kidding! I'll retreat to Tessa's."

"Wait. Tessa's here?"

"She lives uptown."

Levi nods, connecting the dots. "The 1."

"Exactly."

We exchange numbers before Levi walks me to the entrance of the L train on 14th and Avenue A, explaining that I will transfer at Sixth Avenue, which will connect me to the 1 via an underground walkway. It makes sense in theory, but in practice the subway is intimidating enough without adding a transfer to the mix, so I screenshot backup directions on my phone before I lose service.

We pause just a few feet away from the top of the subway steps.

"Thank you," I say.

"Text me when you're at Tessa's?"

I nod, mind blown by such a simple request. Text Levi. That's a thing I can do now. Then I take a step backward and attempt to salvage some degree of chill. "New York looks good on you, Berkowitz."

"Thanks."

"The cargo shorts, on the other hand . . ."

"Ouch." Levi covers his heart with his hand as I turn away. I make it down three steps, maybe, before he yells, "Wait!"

I spin around.

"Can I get a photo?" he asks.

He maintains a straight face for point-five seconds before he's laughing, and then we're laughing, doubled over like the playground children we used to be. An hour ago, I was sobbing in a fountain and now tears stream down my face from laughter and I'm not sure what that means or what this summer holds for us, but I do know the answer to *Where in the world is Levi Berkowitz?* is somehow, impossibly, right here with me.

## TEN

*I* let myself into Tessa's empty apartment and—once again!—whack my head on Henrietta the houseplant. I take a bag of frozen cauliflower rice out of the freezer and collapse onto Gertie, still reeling from the image of Dani and Em holding hands, the feeling of Levi's lips on mine, and the reality that my first Pride was spent not reuniting with the girl I love . . . but reconnecting with my first best friend.

Once Henrietta's hanging planter stabilizes, I notice that her leaves are beginning to yellow at the ends. She looks a bit sad.

*Me too, Henrietta. Me too.*

I snap a photo of the plant that's a metaphor for my life moments before the door swings open. Tessa is home with a shopping cart full of groceries.

"Hey," I say.

She eyes the frozen cauliflower pressed against my forehead. "What happened?"

"Your plant tried to murder me."

Tessa snorts. "Don't blame your lack of spatial awareness on Henrietta."

I stick my tongue out, then cringe because *ew*, that's the most kid-sister response. Tessa unpacks her groceries and the silence that follows feels like a needle scraping my skin because it's our first interaction since I snapped at her. Will she bring it up? Will we pretend it never happened? I'm not sure what I want in this moment, which response will lift the needle and which one will turn the scrape into a stab.

"How was Pride?"

The needle lifts.

"Fine! How was your day?"

"Chill," Tessa responds. "Just did some grading and grocery shopping."

"Cool," I say.

"You hungry? I'm feeling a falafel bowl."

I nod, standing up. "Do you need help?"

Tessa shakes her head. "I'm fine."

"Cool," I repeat.

She starts chopping a pepper and the rejection hurts more than it has any right to. Whatever. In this moment, I don't care if Tessa's not being honest with me. I'm not being honest with her, either. No way am I going to admit to her that she might be right about Dani. I can't even admit that to myself. And I'll choose this awkwardness over an interaction with Em that I'm so not ready for. So I deflate back onto Gertie and scroll through content that the Netflix algorithm is feeding to Tessa when my phone lights up with a new message.

Dani?

Nope.

**Levi Berkowitz**
Hey! Did you make it back to Tessa's okay?
6:46PM

Levi is checking on me.

I swallow whatever emotion is lodged in my throat and type without overthinking.

survived my first subway transfer!
6:48PM

thanks for checking x
6:48PM

He hearts the message, a move meant to signal *the end*. But I type, because I'm sad and Tessa is giving me nothing and if I'm going to sit in silence, I might as well do it texting Levi. Because that's a thing I can do now! So I send the photo of Henrietta to ask if he knows what's going on, what her yellowing leaves mean.

Hmm. How often is she watered?
6:50PM

i'm not sure
6:51PM

What's the current condition of the soil?
6:52PM

I stand up and go over to investigate, sticking my finger into the pot.

drenched
6:53PM

Thought so. Repot ASAP and let Tessa know that she's drowning her. She should let the soil dry out between waterings
6:54PM

"We need to repot Henrietta," I say.

Tessa looks up from prepping veggies, her eyebrows scrunched. "What?"

"You're drowning her."

"Since when do you know so much about plants?"

I shrug. "Since now."

Tessa doesn't push for a better explanation. "We'll do that tomorrow."

A week ago, I wanted to share the Levi news with Tessa. But now? I opt to keep him to myself, because if I start to talk about the series of events that occurred today, I won't be able to filter them and if my sister doesn't want to be real right now, then neither do I. So I return to my spot on the couch and we eat falafel bowls for dinner and watch the *Reputation Stadium Tour* on Netflix until Tessa crashes like the grandma she is.

I stand and bring our bowls to the sink. On the counter, sticking out of the single unpacked grocery bag, is a bag of Hot Cheetos.

Tessa *hates* Hot Cheetos.

My eyes well up.

Shit.

Not the sight of Chester Cheetah bringing me to actual tears. Okay. I guess it's not really Chester . . . but what he represents, and the hope that our relationship can evolve from filtered and fine into something that resembles, I don't know, actual friendship?

Ugh. I'm so lame. Also?

It's just a bag of Cheetos.

I wipe my eyes, then try and fail to wake Tessa up before taking the bed and texting plant questions to Levi until I fall asleep.

At least time flies texting Levi. Somehow it's Monday again, and I'm locking up Tessa's apartment. Back downtown I go. *Sour* blasts in my ears, complementing the snarl of metal on metal that is the subway slowing down between stations. I've timed my return with intention—Dani has improv classes, Em is at workshop, and our third roommate, Sloane, has a full-time production internship in cable news that keeps her so busy we haven't crossed paths—not once—since move-in.

So I enter an empty suite and for two glorious hours, I'm alone.

I blast *Harry's House*. A petty choice. Dani thinks Harry Styles is overrated. (And I still love her, despite that flat-out *wrong* take.) I flop stomach-first onto my bed, scrolling through notifications I missed on the subway. New texts from Levi, a missed FaceTime call from Natalie and . . . a missed call from my mom? Wow. For the first time in nine days, Diane Fitzgerald has entered the chat. Honestly, I am surprised it's so soon.

**Mom**

Just checking in! So used to keeping up with you on Instagram, this hiatus threw me for a loop.
8:30AM

How's fashion camp going?
8:30AM

I swallow a lump in my throat.

Of course Mom reduces a prestigious summer program to *fashion camp*. It's so typical, my parents' tendency to minimize my passion because it's not, like, saving city parks or premature babies. Also? Mom's only checking in on me . . . because I'm not updating Instagram? What? Social media is a highlight reel, and sometimes it feels like that's all I am to my parents, just a composite of highlights. It's easier to justify their all-consuming careers if they believe the reel is the truth.

i'm fine! busy, but everything is perfect.

9:33AM

Honestly, it is easier to *be* that reel for them.

Keep a filter on.

Because my parents love me.

But they don't get me.

I close the message and reach for my tablet on my desk, attempting to shake off those feelings because my first assignment for Mal's class is due tomorrow and I've had zero motivation. I need to put together a mood board with inspiration and rough sketches for a design that represents my brand. *One* design. What if I contain multitudes? And isn't the entire point of upcycling to be inspired by clothes? How am I supposed to come up with a concept when we haven't even sourced fabrics yet?

It's so hard.

An hour later, I'm still staring at a blank screen. I consider calling Clara, because she's the sister who understands all my *fashion is art* feelings, the sister who encouraged them with weekend thrifting trips, the sister who taught me how to sew and gifted me a vintage sewing machine that she bought at the estate sale where we found Gertie. It's a 1974 Singer, my most prized possession—and every single outfit I've posted has been made with its help.

I tap her name on my screen.

But.

I don't really want to tip off Clara that I'm anything other than fine on the fashion front.

Because if one sister knows, it's only a matter of time until they all know.

So I tap into my texts, returning to my only reliable distraction.

**Levi Berkowitz**
Hey! How is Henrietta?
8:47AM

too soon to say, but she's been repotted
and tessa is on a strict watering ban
9:47AM

His response is immediate.

Nah, she should be okay.
9:47AM

It looks like we caught it early.
9:48AM

After an education on the perils of overwatering, Levi and I didn't stop talking the rest of the weekend. He even sent me memes from *The Challenge*, a show that he still watches after I introduced him to it when we were kids. I remember feeling so cool that having older sisters gave me early exposure to MTV. I also remember the time we created a course inspired by the show in his backyard that resulted in broken pinkies. His actually broke, but I pretended mine snapped too so I could rock a matching splint in solidarity.

Dani and Sophie are topics too, but they come in and out of focus. It's actually kind of nice, commiserating with someone as lovesick as I am.

Levi understands.

It's so easy to talk to him, to ask plant-care questions and lose myself in a low-pressure conversation until a knock on my door brings me back to reality. Has it already been two hours? I guess I'm listening to "Music for a Sushi Restaurant" for the fourth time. Harry wouldn't lie to me. But I didn't even hear the door to our unit swing open. I tense, expecting Em. I know this is unavoidable, but it doesn't make it fun or easy.

"Hey?"

Dani's voice quadruples the speed of my heart. Of course it's her. Em wouldn't knock on the door to their own room. Oh my God. Does Dani think they're here?

She must.

"Not Em," I say.

"I know," Dani says. "Can I come in?"

Is this the end of space?

"Yeah," I say.

Dani swings the door open and my hope suffocates in a second of emotional whiplash as I process the picture that is her standing at my door with . . . a box full of clothes. My clothes—a black velvet crop top with fishnet sleeves, a reconstructed patchwork flannel, a pleated Britney skirt. So many pieces stitched together by me, all inspired by her nineties grunge aesthetic.

Now I can't even come up with a concept for a mood board.

I'm broken without her.

"Here," she says, thrusting the box in my arms.

I blink. "Oh. But . . . I made these for you."

"I can't keep them."

"Okay."

"I mean, that's weird. Isn't it?"

*No.*

"Probably."

Her eyes linger on the box. "Fuck, I love that flannel, though."

I bite my lower lip because she may as well have just said *I love you.* I want to drop the box, wrap my arms around her neck, and pull her lips toward mine. Remind her, remind me, what that feels like. Tell her I can erase the image of Em's hand in hers from my memory. Confess that I only kissed Levi as a reaction. Promise that we can still have a perfect summer.

But I've already exposed my heart to Dani.

With *I love you.*

With a hiatus.

It's her turn to make a move. I can't handle another rejection.

So I just toss her the flannel. "It's yours. Please, keep it."

She nods. "Okay."

"Cool."

I turn back to my blank laptop screen, expecting her to exit.

She doesn't.

"I saw you. At Pride?"

"Dani—"

"You looked good. Happy."

I did? Well. Hand me an Academy Award.

"You too," I say, an unintended edge in my voice.

"Em has been a great friend," Dani says.

I try not to analyze her choice of words and instead spin them back at her. "So has Levi."

"Levi," Dani repeats.

"He's an old friend," I say. "From Texas."

Her eyes widen. "Wait. Like, *Fitz origin story* Levi?"

I forgot Dani knows that story. That one snowy day after drama club, Danica Martinez asked me when I started going by Fitz and I told her about my first best friend who came up with a practical solution to there being three Avas in my class. *Fitz fits*, he'd said with a crooked smile. I loved it. It felt so much more me than Ava F. It still feels so much more me than Ava ever did.

"That's so cool," Dani says.

"It's been the best surprise."

I let the weight of this information settle between us, adding a layer of intensity to the kiss. It's unintentional, but I'm not mad about it. Let Dani believe what she wants. It's a perfect addition to the *I'm fine, your move* act.

Dani takes a step backward, then pauses at the doorframe and says, "I miss you."

Holy shit.

Did kissing Levi . . . actually work?

I drop the box on my bed and take a step toward her. "Me too."

"We were so good as friends, you know?"

"Friends." I take a step back.

Dani misses . . . my friendship?

"I'm not stupid. I know this"—Dani gestures vaguely, referring to the dorm situation—"is awkward. I know that friendship post-breakup is, like, a sapphic cliché. But it'd be cool if we could—I don't know, get there?"

It's been a week.

But I'm in character. I am fine. So I shrug and say, "We're cool. I just need space."

Dani blinks at her line thrown back at her. "Totally."

Then she scratches her nose, backs up, and exits, leaving me alone and so confused. She says she misses our friendship, but the way she looked at me? It was not a friendship look. I flop backward onto my bed and turn up the music, replaying our interaction on a loop, attempting to make it make sense from the look to the nose-scratch to—

Wait.

She scratched her nose.

Her tell.

Dani is acting too. She doesn't actually want to be friends. One fake kiss with Levi Berkowitz has Danica Martinez knocking on my door to debut her own *I'm fine* performance. It's a revelation that kind of changes everything. She's an incredible actress, but I know her. I love her. If this is her reaction to one kiss, what if . . . ? Oh my God. I reach for my phone, to text Levi because it's suddenly so clear. I need more than a hiatus to get Dani back.

I also need him.

## ELEVEN

*A*n hour later, I arrive at a cute ramen spot Levi suggested on the corner of University Ave and Waverly Place. I'm ten minutes early, so I grab a table along a wall with floor-to-ceiling window panels that are open to let in the summer breeze. I'm never early, but restless energy, a stubbornly blank page, and Dani's music propelled me from my dorm the moment our plans were confirmed. So I'm here, eating edamame alone and contemplating the best way to approach Levi with my idea when he arrives . . . by bike. Huh. Levi Berkowitz is a city biker? A surprising development. I mean. Drivers are impatient! Bike lanes barely exist here! Pedestrians jaywalk everywhere! Levi *risked his life* to meet me for ramen.

"Hey!" Levi says as he unclips and removes his helmet. "This spot is my—"

"You still love her? Sophie?"

I don't mean to cut him off, but I can't even pretend to be chill right now. He's silent for a beat, his eyebrows pinched together as he slides into the seat across from me. He unzips his backpack and pulls out a glasses case, switching out his sunglasses for regular frames. Levi is intentional with his words. I learned this in the lag between texts over the weekend, in watching the bubble appear and disappear with every message.

He's processing. Considering.

But it's so much more agonizing in real time, this response lag.

Finally, he says—no, *asks*, "Yes?"

"Berkowitz! So much buildup for . . . a question mark?"

"Obviously I am."

"Better."

Levi's eyes meet mine. "It's easier to admit behind a screen, you know?"

I do know.

"I—"

It's my turn to be cut off. Our waiter arrives before I can let the perfect plan tumble from my lips. I'm *so* pissed at Benny and his one-dimple smile as we both order vegetable miso ramen.

"Are you a vegetarian too?" Levi asks after One-Dimple Benny walks away with our menus.

"Yeah. As of, like, two years ago?"

"Cool." Levi smiles. "I went through a food-doc phase in middle school."

We're seriously shifting the subject to self-imposed dietary restrictions? Is Levi that desperate to pivot the conversation away from Sophie?

Ordinarily, I would explain that my vegetarianism was not triggered by subjecting myself to traumatic documentaries, but a more organic palate evolution. My family doesn't keep kosher in a traditional sense, but we never ate pork and I've never felt, like, a strong desire to try it on my own. I hate red meat. Fish is slimy. Chicken is okay, but I don't miss it. Once I learned about the environmental impact of meat production, making the switch just felt right for me. But I have to get this conversation back on track. Besides, plant influencer Levi being a vegetarian too is the least surprising development.

So I just say, "Those are, like, actual horror movies."

"Have you seen—?"

"Dani saw us. The kiss?"

I'm sorry to cut him off again, but we're losing the plot.

"I mean . . . you're welcome?"

"We talked. Well. First she returned a box of clothes I made her . . . but she kept the flannel."

"Okay?"

He's not following.

"She misses me! She literally said that. Then she tried to backpedal and clarify that she misses our friendship or whatever. But *then* she scratched her nose. It's her tell. Every time she'd come over my house and thank my mom for the delicious dinner? Or assured my friend Henry that his conversational Spanish is improving? She'd scratch her nose! She misses me. *Us*. And . . . I think it's because I let her think you and I are together?"

Silence.

Then, "Jesus, Fitzgerald."

His voice is soft, concerned. Not at all the reaction I'm expecting.

I ignore it, doubling down. "So what if we . . . I don't know. Pretend to be?"

Levi's forehead crinkles. "What?"

"What! You hate being on a break. I'm *so* lovesick for Dani I can't even create a mood board for class, never mind new outfits. We can both be sad about it all summer or we can try to get them back with a tasteful and flawlessly executed jealousy-inducing scheme."

Levi's nose scrunches. "Doesn't that seem manipulative?"

*Manipulative*? That's a harsh way to put it.

And wrong.

"Berkowitz! Oh my God. *No*. It's basic psychology. Reverse psychology, in fact. If Soph and Dani see that we've moved on, maybe the idea of losing us will make them realize how much they love us. We can't force them to feel jealous. If that's the result, it's just obvious that they still have feelings for us. Think of it more as a gentle nudge."

After another agonizing beat of silence, Levi's eyes meet mine. "You're serious."

That's not a no.

"We were already going to hang out, right? You'll show me around the city. We'll chill at my dorm in front of Dani. And we'll stage couple-y photos for your new personal Instagram account for Sophie. Easy."

"Easy," Levi repeats, his tone indecipherable. "Are you at least aware that you're plotting a rom-com?"

Levi has obviously never seen a rom-com.

"No way. Then it'd be us in the end, wouldn't it?"

Cue more awkward silence, as One-Dimple Benny with the impeccable timing sets down two bowls of ramen. Steam rises between us, filtering Levi's flushed cheeks. I cannot comprehend his hesitancy. Because I'm me, I reach for my soup spoon to fill the silence and immediately burn my tongue on the scalding broth. *Shit.*

"I know I kissed you," Levi says. "But Soph knows where I stand, so this plan? She'll see right through it."

"Will she? *She* asked *you* for a break. If anything, this will be evidence that you're taking it seriously. Also? Her Insta captions have been Taylor Swift lyrics for the past week."

"How do you know that?"

I reach for an edamame with an innocent shrug. "Did you know that forty-two people named Sophie follow Thyme Is on My Side? But only one has a photo of you hiding behind a plant on main? Sophie Sweeney. She's cute."

"But . . . you're on hiatus?"

"Sure, but public accounts are still accessible via Google."

Levi's expression is less stunned, more disturbed. "You are kind of terrifying."

Whatever. I'm a visual person. Sophie—*Soph*—isn't real until I see her. So I looked and saw all the fragments that make up @sophhsweeneyy. She's a red blunt bob, a smattering of freckles on cherubic cheeks, and cherry lips turned up into a sweet smile. She's on trend, dressed in midrise jeans paired with a sunflower tube top. She propagates plants, visits every pop-up exhibit at the Met, and is obsessed with her Yorkipoo, Nora.

Levi is still looking at me as if at any moment I could, like, stab him with my chopsticks.

"No one who captions all their posts with vague *evermore* lyrics is okay, Berkowitz," I continue, not even dignifying his reaction with a response. "It's obvious that Sophie is regretting her decision and too embarrassed to admit how massively she screwed up."

Levi scratches the back of his neck. "I don't know."

This is a much tougher sell than I was expecting. But what *was* I expecting? For Levi to still be the sweet boy who follows where I lead? I need to pivot. Levi's skeptical, but he still hasn't said no.

So I take a half step back. "Let's create an account. Just as an experiment."

"Right now?"

I nod. "We'll build your profile and blast it out to your close friends list on Thyme Is on My Side. You have one, right? We could create one, but that would be kind of awkward to add her to it."

Levi nods. "I have one."

"Sophie is on it?"

"She created it."

"Perfect. So. My proposition—"

"Proposition?"

"Just *listen*. After we blast it out, we wait. Eat our luke-warm ramen and just, like, enjoy each other's company. You can tell me about your latest plantscapades. Dani and Sophie will be off-limits. But if Sophie follows you by the end of the night? We keep the account up. We post cute boyfriend-girlfriend stuff. We do the thing."

Levi stifles a laugh. "Plantscapades?"

I kick his foot. "I'm serious."

"I know." Levi's mouth-quirk is back and it's so much bet-ter than his *she could murder me* face. "So does this mean your hiatus is over?"

"What? No."

I'm not sure who's more surprised by this response.

"You want to fake a relationship on social media . . . and not be on social media?"

"I mean. You have to be online because Soph is across the country. It's the only way she'll see it. I don't need to reactivate for this. If anything, Dani needs to see me still committing to this hiatus and proving that I can be in a real relationship *with-out* photos or social media."

Levi nods. Quietly considers.

I consider too. It's true, this reason to continue my hiatus. But there's also a piece of me that's a little relieved not to be online. Nothing about my New York summer is going accord-ing to plan. I have nothing to post. No new outfits or ideas to show off. I'm filtered on there, but I'm not a fraud. So being on hiatus right now means If the Shoe Fitz is one less thing to worry about.

Finally, Levi says, "And if she doesn't follow the new account?"

"We delete it and pretend this was never discussed."

His eyebrows rise. "Seriously?"

"I'll drop it," I say, holding out my pinkie.

It's juvenile, but instinct. It's how our deals were made.

"Okay," Levi says, wrapping his pinkie around mine, transporting me from this tiny ramen shop to the giant syca-more tree in his backyard. "I'm in."

Levi is in.

Before our pinkies even disconnect, I hold out my other hand. "Phone."

He unlocks his phone and hands it over. The weight of it in my hand? The power I feel right now? It's absolutely electric with possibility. I launch Instagram and tap *Create new account.* I consider a creative handle but since the goal is effortless discoverability, I settle on a basic @leviberkowitzzz. Simple. Effective. I type a planty password and just like that, Levi has an account.

Now, to craft a profile.

It's a skill I've been honing for years and it's effortless, the way my fingers *tap, tap, tap* to create Instagram Levi.

"Still he/him?" I confirm, before adding pronouns.

"Yeah."

"Cool." I keep the description minimal, just a plant emoji and @thymeisonmyside. Instagram Levi, like the real Levi, is not overly verbose. Instagram Levi will let the pictures speak for themselves. Then I open the camera, reposition the ramen bowls so they're off-center in the frame, and say, "Smile."

Levi's hand rises to cover his face *so* fast.

"Um. Did it not occur to you that this whole experiment involves photos? Of you?"

"Sorry." Levi lowers his hand. "Instinct."

It doesn't occur to me until this moment that there isn't a single photo of himself on his plantstagram.

"You hate this."

"I'm much better behind a camera."

"Okay. Well. Can I look at your existing photos, then?"

A camera roll is so personal, I may as well have asked to read Levi's diary. But he just shrugs. "Sure. It's mostly plants."

Of course it is. I exit Instagram and tap into his photos, filtering out the hundreds, nay, thousands of plant pictures. In most of the photos I'm left with, Levi is covering his face. Or they're blurry from him moving out of frame too quickly. Instinct, indeed. Damn, Berkowitz. He's not making this easy.

I scroll until I find a usable candid of Levi mid-laugh at some sort of botanical garden. His eyes crinkle at the corners and his hair is curled at the nape of his neck, much longer than its current cut. It's a semi-profile shot, a photo that obviously was taken without its subject having a clue, just at ease. It's perfect.

"This one," I say.

Levi's smile is sad. "Soph took that one. I totally forgot about it."

"Even better."

I set it as his profile photo, but we still need a first post. Hmm. I open the photo I snapped. It's blurry . . . but it's not a bad concept. It's not perfect. But it's real. It's *Levi*. Who is obviously, painfully, camera-shy. A new detail. But not necessarily a bad one.

"I have an idea," I say. "Can you hold your hand out in front of the camera?"

Levi complies. I snap a few shots. Since the sun has now set, the yellow overhead lamp casts an artsy shadow across Levi, his hand, and the exposed brick wall behind him. I am a visionary. Bless cameras with low-light capabilities. Satisfied with my work, I get my subject's approval. His face is artfully masked by his hand, so he agrees.

And just like that, @leviberkowitzzz has his first Instagram post.

Caption?

*this is me trying*

Because we see your *evermore* lyric and raise you a *folklore* moment, Sophie.

I complete the final step for now, sharing the photo and new handle via Thyme Is on My Side's Story to his close friends list.

"My face is on Instagram," Levi says.

"And your hand," I add.

Experiment initiated, I hand him his phone back and dig into my ramen. It's cold now, but I don't care. Five stars. As promised, I spend the rest of our meal listening to his plant-scapades, then any lingering awkwardness dissipates the moment we go down a reality-television rabbit hole. Content in our now-moonlit corner, we spend hours talking about everything and nothing until One-Dimple Benny kicks us out.

Before we part, Levi gestures at his notification-less phone. I shake my head. "This night isn't over yet."

"Fair enough." He buckles his helmet, then unlocks and mounts his bike. I hate that bike even more without daylight. It's incomprehensible to me that Levi is afraid of a *camera* and not, like, being hit by a car.

"Text me when you're home?"

He smirks. "Only to say I told you so."

Then he rides off, his laughter fading in the wind.

At six minutes to midnight, as I attempt to start Mal's assignment for the umpteenth time, frustrated that a girl with turquoise lips and perfect pitch has me so broken I cannot even come up with one idea, my phone glows with a notification.

A screenshot. *The* screenshot.

*@sophhsweeneyy requested to follow you*

Then, two words.

*I'm in.*

## TWELVE

*A* pillow to the face wakes me.

"*Shit*, Em!"

I groan and roll over, one hand palming the mattress in search of the incessant *cuckoo*. My phone in hand, I swipe left to snooze because sleep is good. Alarm is bad. Cuckoo clock? It's the worst. But it's the only sound that forces me up and vertical in fewer than three snoozes in the morning.

*Is it really—?*

My eyes pop open.

Nope. Too bright. I squint to adjust to the golden daylight filtering through the window. Shit. I fell asleep texting Levi. Didn't finish my assignment. Class is in two hours. I sit up and consider my unfinished sketch. It's *not* postable. That's a problem.

Because if it's not postable, it's definitely not presentable.

"*Fuckkk*," I whisper, rubbing my eyes and dragging my fingers down my face.

Em, now burrowed back under their blankets, extends one arm out and flips me off. So when the snooze is up, I let the cuckoo clock sing. Consider it retribution for their unwashed dishes in the sink, their pillow to the face, their hand being the last one Dani held.

But even *I* can only handle the cuckoo for so long.

When I turn it off, I see a new text from Levi.

**Levi Berkowitz**
Plantscapade. UES. 2PM. You in?
6:46AM

I can't explain what my heart does, seeing the word "plantscapade" on my shattered screen.

UES?
7:11AM

Sorry! Upper East Side. We could meet at Union Square? Figure we should probably discuss the terms of this arrangement?
7:12AM

I've never been a fake boyfriend before
7:12AM

I blink at the messages. In the span of seventy-two hours, Levi Berkowitz went from a long-lost friend to my fake boyfriend. I confirm plantscapade plans because we have less than seven weeks to execute this and there's no time to waste. While I wasn't making progress on my mood board and sketch last night, I created a template for our relationship content calendar. So today can double as a brainstorm sesh to fill it out with date and photo ideas. With each curated snapshot of us, Sophie will *so* regret the moment she broke my best fr—*Levi's* heart. And Dani? She'll see us together in real life so much that ignoring her feelings will kill her slowly, until she confesses that she loves me too, a declaration that will cure whatever is happening to me creatively and inspire designs that render Mal Burton speechless in the best way.

But until then? I cannot show up to another class unprepared.

*Improvise, Fitzgerald.*

I reach for my portfolio on my desk, thumbing through sketches for dozens of ideas that exist only in 2D—not yet stitched and constructed or queued for future posts. My favorite is a satin slip dress with a cowl neck and a slit up the front that is *so* nineties. So *Dani.* My eyes shift to the box she gave back to me. Instead of my sisters, lately I've been pulling inspiration from Dani's closet, designing my take on these vintage styles through sustainable and size-inclusive designs. My audience has been into it.

*Oh.*

I can present this.

It's so different from the blazer I meant to present last week . . . but that's the entire point. I submitted a portfolio inspired by my *why*—my sisters, who each have their own unique style. But I've never had a brand that's identifiable by a singular aesthetic. That shows I can breathe new life into anyone's closet. Choosing this dress will show my versatility as a designer to Mal.

It's perfect.

So I start pulling images for a mood board to match.

I arrive to class (two minutes!) early and take my usual seat between Trevor and Lila. Trevor's eye shadow matches his teal high-top sneakers today. Lila is in a black utilitarian shirtdress and scuffed combat boots. Their animated conversation comes to an abrupt halt with the scrape of my chair against linoleum. I'm so awkward. Why are these chairs so heavy?

Mal flashes a kind smile my way before she begins her lecture. I don't deserve it, but it feels like the opportunity for a second first impression. I open my laptop and immerse myself in taking notes, asking questions, being an actual student of fashion.

For the first time, I feel like I'm doing the thing I came here to do.

"Cool skirt," Trevor says during the break.

He gestures to my denim midi skirt with embroidered daisies. Clara taught me how to embroider and it's always been one of my favorite ways to upcycle. I love getting lost for hours in hand-stitching, the intricate details I can create, how it adds personality to almost any basic item.

"Thanks," I say. "I'm obsessed with your makeup."

Trevor's eyes widen. "She speaks!"

Lila slides a ten-dollar bill across the table, wordless.

I am the worst.

"Sorry. It's . . . been a week."

Trevor snatches the bill, waving away my words as he reapplies cherry ChapStick. "How long?"

I raise my eyebrows. "What?"

"When my ex dumped me, I didn't leave my bedroom for two weeks."

Is it that obvious?

"Eight days."

"Damn," Lila whispers.

They pass another ten to Trevor and I swallow, so embarrassed that they're betting on if I will speak, my relationship status, and who knows what else. How much broken disaster energy did I radiate last week? A lot, clearly. I need a rebrand. Now.

"It's more of a hiatus than a breakup."

"Insta imitating life?" Trevor asks.

"Um—"

I'm cut off by Mal bringing the break to an end. "Okay. I, for one, am so ready for our first crit session. Every week, crit is an invaluable opportunity to receive feedback from your fellow designers. Remember that today we're presenting rough drafts. Perfection is *not* required. Rather, during a presentation I want you to ask yourself three questions. Is the narrative of this brand clear and compelling? What differentiates the piece from competitors? And is it sustainably scalable? You may not be able to answer that last question yet, but by the end of week four, you will. And remember, participation in the crit is not only encouraged, but also required."

Mal continues to set critique guidelines and expectations, then asks for a volunteer to go first. My hand shoots toward the sky without hesitation. It's meant to convey confidence, that I'm not as thrown as I am by a casual reference to my hiatus and last week's flop. Delete it from the main feed. When Mal says my name I stand and set up, connecting my tablet to the projector.

"Y'all! I am so excited to share a design for a closet staple inspired by silhouettes and textures that defined nineties fashion, but made for today—"

Presenting is easy as long as I pretend there's a camera in front of me, like it's just an IG Live. I share the mood board, my inspiration, and speak to how the versatility of the design will resonate with my audience. Honestly? With a little more work I *would* post this.

I finish the presentation, my pulse spiking as Mal examines my design.

"Thanks, Fitz." Her tone is neutral, her expression unreadable as she opens up the floor to student feedback.

Immediately my design is deconstructed by eleven pieces of contradictory feedback. It's a lot to process, a critique in real time, to my face. Compliments are sprinkled throughout, at least—on the detail in my sketches, on the potential of the outfit, on the swatches I added this morning to show a variety of fabric combinations. I try to hold on to that.

But then Lila raises their hand. "It looks like an Instagram ad."

Their tone? It's not a compliment.

"Can you elaborate, Lila?" Mal asks.

*Please don't.*

"Sure." Lila pulls out their phone and opens Instagram to show everyone one, two, three ads for outfits that are, admittedly, a similar vibe to my design. "See? Every brand is targeting me with their version of this dress. I don't see a unique voice or point of view. I just see an influencer chasing trends."

Um.

I have no clue why Lila is coming for my throat like this.

"I mean, if the shoe fits . . . ," someone behind me mutters under their breath.

People snicker.

And that's the moment it hits me, *truly* hits me, that these people are not my audience—they're my *peers*, all with platforms and social media presences of their own. I'd been prepared for critique on my clothes, but not on, like, my entire identity as a creative.

"Harsh," Trevor says.

But Mal agrees with Lila. "I see a well-conceived, on-trend dress. Last week, I saw a well-constructed, on-trend outfit. But . . . I still don't see *you*, Fitz. In your next crit, I'd love it if we could see a piece that shows us who you are as a designer. Don't make something Instagrammable. Make it for yourself."

I nod, unable to even formulate a coherent question. Like, aren't I here because my looks are Instagrammable? How is this suddenly not the goal? It does not compute. I sink into my seat, Mal's words ringing in my ears as the now-familiar pressure builds behind my eyes.

Even at FIT, I don't fit.

rip off a piece of caprese baguette and pop it into my mouth, then chase it with an iced vanilla latte as I people-watch from the Union Square steps and process my first crit. It's a weird combination, balsamic and coffee, but so is just about everything I see. I can't believe I'm surrounded by so many jeans, cardigans, and combat boots in the middle of summer. Do people not have sweat glands here? As I consider this, a Burberry trench coat crashes into a walking Lululemon ad. Clearly, in this city, fashion defies weather logic. Or I have a sweat problem. Because I'm in a loose white linen tank and a skirt and still possibly dying from heatstroke. I swallow and wipe sweat from my forehead . . . removing my right eyebrow in the process.

Shit.

I locate my pencil and reapply my eyebrow before Levi arrives to whisk me away on a plantscapade, which might temporarily pause the brutal highlight reel from class that runs on a loop in brain. Online, I can filter criticism. Solicit feedback from trusted friends and block out the rest. So I didn't expect to even be fazed by it. It's what I signed up for and it's necessary to evolve as a designer. But Mal called my designs *Instagram-mable*. I'm not sure what to do with that critique or these feel-ings. Because I believe in my brand and that I shouldn't have to lean into any one aesthetic or be any one thing.

I'm fixating so much that I overfill my eyebrow, so the right one is both too thick and too dark compared to the left. With a paper napkin, I remove both and start over. But the scratchy napkin texture irritates my skin, so my thick blonde brows are now tinted red with inflammation.

Cool.

I'm terrible at shaping eyebrows even when I'm not melt-ing. Only Dani can make them look perfect. Only Dani—

"Hey!"

Levi's soft tenor voice is the antidote for an incoming Dani spiral. Just in time. I look up from my compact and note the same khaki cargo shorts, this time paired with a long-sleeve navy shirt. Sleeves. In ninety degrees. How? I want to cry. It's what I aim to lead with, until my eyes meet his worried frown.

"Are you—?"

"Sensitive skin." I stand, toss my backpack over my shoul-der, and head toward the subway entrance, so ready for this plantscapade to distract me from both my fashion feelings and my Dani feelings.

"Are you sure? It looks, um, like an allergic reaction."

I snort. "Charming."

"Concern *is* charming!"

"Sure, Boyfriend."

Levi's neck flushes and I have to stifle a laugh as I swipe my MetroCard. It's a small victory when the turnstile lets me in on my first try. Levi isn't so lucky. He swipes once, twice, then proceeds to *walk right into a locked turnstile*. Ouch. The third time's the charm and Levi is finally in, but clearly still flustered.

This isn't going to work if he falls apart over just that word. *Boyfriend*.

It's not even real. Also? It's weird for me, too! I've never had a boyfriend—fake or otherwise. I've crushed on boys of the unattainable-celebrity variety. Initiated a kiss with the Paul to my Corie Bratter just once outside of the scripted one in *Barefoot in the Park* sophomore year. But I've never dated anyone who identifies as a boy. I've never been in a hetero-presenting relationship.

Huh.

I follow him to the platform, unsure why I'm feeling some kind of way about this revelation. But I swallow it.

I need to be filtered, fun, *fine*.

We board a too-crowded Q train and being a sweaty sardine is quickly becoming my least-favorite New York thing. We're immediately pushed toward the middle of the car and it's too crowded to talk, too crowded to *think*. I just clutch on to the metal handle for dear life, but balance is futile and with each abrupt stop, I crash into Levi's shoulder.

We take the train to its penultimate stop at 86th Street and when I get out I can breathe again. The station is a surprisingly grandiose welcome to the Upper East Side—so bright, so modern, so absent of weird smells.

"Our rescue is just around the corner," Levi informs me as an endless escalator takes us up, up, up. "Millie was left in the dark for two months while her family went on a European tour. When they got home, they severely overwatered her."

"A tour?"

Levi nods. "As if they're, like, seventeenth-century aristocrats."

"Millie deserves better," I declare, wondering if everyone in this neighborhood is on some sort of Grand Tour. It's quiet uptown, the residential streets sprinkled mostly with parents pushing strollers in pointy-toed mules and puppies I want to pet so bad. It's a muted, neutral color palette, so opposite from the loud mixed prints and texture that define downtown.

It may as well be another city.

A ceramic llama planter greets us on the second-to-last step of a gorgeous redbrick townhouse on 87th Street between First and Second Avenue. On its back is Millie, the sick rattlesnake plant, her leaves drooping and browning along their scalloped edges. Levi picks up the llama, his brow furrowed as he punctures the soil with his index finger, then examines each leaf.

"Root rot," he diagnoses.

"Is that . . . deadly?" I ask.

"Sometimes. Seems to be early stage," he says, placing

Millie in a canvas tote bag. "But I won't know the extent of the damage until I give her a proper examination. You hungry?"

I blink, my eyes shifting toward poor Millie in her little tote gurney. "Do we not have an examination to conduct?"

"Millie isn't flatlining."

"But she's in *pain*."

"Plants don't have nociceptors," he says, so matter-of-fact. "Okay?"

"Even if she's in pain, she can't feel it."

I've never wanted to be a plant before, but that actually sounds pretty nice right now—to not feel, to just *be*.

Convinced her quality of life will not be hindered by a food detour, we walk just a few blocks south, to Bonjour Crepes & Wine, which sounds about as authentic as the French representation in *Emily in Paris*, but Levi swears the orange chocolate crepe is a revelation.

Inside has a cozy coffee-shop vibe. Dark wood tables. Low lighting. Every item is written on a chalk menu. We split the revelatory crepe, and honestly? I'm not sure what an authentic crepe is supposed to taste like and I don't care. Much like *Emily in Paris*, this shit is incredible.

"It's not strawberry-lavender jam," I say. "But it's close."

Levi's eyes meet mine. "Nothing is strawberry-lavender jam."

"Except Disney World."

Levi laughs. "Right."

Grandma Jo's strawberry-lavender jam was legendary. A

county fair award winner. A top-secret recipe. The best thing my tiny taste buds had ever consumed. So every present or activity or really anything was measured against that jam. But what was most special about it to me was that when Levi whispered the secret ingredient in my ear when we were six years old, I knew he trusted me. It made me trust him, too.

I carve a piece of the crepe with my fork. "So that was a plantscapade?"

Levi nods. "People message Repot and Rehome—the non-profit I volunteer at—to pick up their ailing plants. We nurse them back to health and either return them with care instructions or find them a new home."

"I need to workshop a new word," I tease. "'Plantscapade' implies adventure! Drama! Daring rescue! My eyebrows are more dramatic than this plantscapade."

He assesses them. "They've calmed considerably."

"Still."

"I don't know. Every time I pick up a plant, I get to discover something new about this city. Calliope, a fern, brought me to Pomander Walk, a street with cobblestone houses straight out of a fairytale. Blake, a monstera, showed me a walking bridge at the west end of 145th Street that leads to this massive recreational park on top of the Hudson. Now, thanks to Millie, you're eating Bonjour Crepes on the Upper East Side. Is this not adventure?"

I swallow, grateful the low lights hide my blush because maybe he's right—that adventure can be quiet moments, too. And after all these years we get to have them again. Not make-believe adventures in his backyard. Quiet ones, but real ones.

"It is," I concede, forcing myself not to say any of that.

"To Millie, your first plantscapade!"

Levi's mouth-quirk blooms into a full smile as he raises his water. We clink glasses, laughing, and I kind of love that he's now so attached to this ridiculous word—*my* ridiculous word.

"Okay," Levi says. "So how exactly does your plan work?"

"I'm so glad you asked, Berkowitz." I unzip my backpack, pull out my laptop, and open the content calendar I created. "I started brainstorming date ideas and content that builds into a cute date-y narrative. We have history, so I think leaning in to nostalgia will aid in the authenticity. Like, we *have* to go to the Met because I still have that postcard you gave me, the one from that costume exhibit?"

His eyebrows rise. "You do?"

I nod. "From the vision board. I don't just, like, throw things away."

"Hence the upcycling."

"Exactly."

"I don't know how I feel about that," Levi admits. "Using our past to curate our present."

"Why not? It's the content we need for Sophie to buy that we're real."

"Is it?"

"Totally," I assure him. "We'll do three posts per week to start, then work our way up to daily posts. You need to be somewhat active when we're not together, too. Post plant content, musings, whatever else you're into. It'll look weird if your feed is *only* us."

Levi looks at me as if he already regrets agreeing to this plan.

"These are some date ideas," I continue, turning the computer toward him. "I don't want to be too prescriptive. I mean. You're the local. But I think we should block date days in our calendar and sketch out the first two weeks of posts. Then next week we outline week three. And onward."

His eyes scan the screen. "You made a spreadsheet for this."

"Of course I made a spreadsheet for this! We're on a deadline, Boyfriend."

"Right." Levi nods, absorbing the spreadsheet that will soon be populated with our fake dates. "So. What are the rules?"

"Rules?"

"Yeah. Do we commit to this for the whole summer? I mean, we can't expect Soph and Danica to be on the same timeline here. If this even works at all. Because how do we explain this to our—"

"Whoa! Berkowitz," I cut him off. "It's a six-week fauxmance. At the end of the summer, we share an amicable breakup post. Admit that we jumped into something too quickly on the basis of childhood nostalgia and say that we're better as friends."

Levi's eyebrows rise again. "You already have our breakup post outlined?"

I nod. "It's in the spreadsheet."

"Right."

I start a new tab and type TERMS OF THE FAUXMANCE into the first cell because Levi's right, we do need to clarify how we're doing this. If this is going to work, we need to be on the same page. Full stop.

I draft a contract of sorts, dictating as I type. "A six-week arrangement after which a mutual 'We're better as friends' breakup post will be sent one week before I (Fitz) leave New York." I pause and look up, my eyes meeting his. "Is that cool? I want Dani and me to still have some time together before I have to go home."

"What if it works sooner?" Levi asks.

"I *love* the optimism. Obviously, we'll post sooner in that case." I resume typing, adding that addendum. "What else?"

"No posting photos without verbal consent from both of us," Levi says.

"Okay. But you can't reject a photo just because you're in it."

"I won't."

I type Levi's rule.

"In terms of physical contact—?"

I cut him off, choking on my water. "Oh my God. Berkowitz. I swear, I will never ask you to jump me in a fountain again.

I'm, like, not even one for massive PDA. Plus, I'm almost positive Dani saw that kiss, so just your presence will be *more* than enough. I recommend maybe, like, hand-holding for Instagram purposes, but you should control that narrative. So—"

I'm babbling.

"—kissing, no. Hand-holding, optional. In all situations lead with consent."

Levi's mouth quirks. He's enjoying this, me being the flustered one. "Got it."

Other rules and guidelines are added to the spreadsheet. Levi will adhere to my post frequency suggestions. He'll also conveniently hang out at my dorm at least twice a week and before the scheduled dates in order to get in that crucial face-to-face time in front of Dani.

"Anything else?" I ask.

Levi shakes his head. "I don't think so, but let's make the terms amendable, just in case. You?"

"I'm good, Boyfriend."

We seal the deal with a clink of our glasses, but *boyfriend* still feels weird on my tongue. Maybe the more I say it, the more natural it will feel. It needs to feel natural. Believable. Maybe I just need to focus less on the word in a romantic sense and more on the *friend*. Because it's still somehow so easy, being Levi's friend.

"So. How soon can we start?" I ask.

"I'm free tomorrow," Levi says. "Or Friday, if you'd want to come to Shabbat—"

I cut him off. "Tomorrow is perfect."

The idea of Shabbat with Levi—one of the only people who never made me feel like I wasn't Jewish enough because my family isn't observant—is way too much, way too soon. I don't want to admit to him that I don't Shabbat anymore. Nope. I want cute, filtered, fun nostalgia. Engaging with complicated Jewish feelings that scrape at old wounds is not part of the plan.

"Let's meet at the Met," Levi suggests. "There's actually a temporary exhibit I've been meaning to check out."

"Cool," I say.

I'm surprised that Levi seems to frequent the Metropolitan Museum of Art often enough to know its exhibit schedule. He hated being dragged to art museums when we were kids. It forces me to reckon with the reality that as familiar as he feels, as easy as it is to be his friend . . . there's still so much I don't know about him. But there's something exciting about that too. I can't wait to learn more about who Levi Berkowitz is now.

Tomorrow, our fauxmance begins at the Met.

But until then, Levi and I linger in the air-conditioned creperie, drawing out our plantscapade day, and it doesn't occur to me, not once, to take a photo.

## FOURTEEN

*A* mere twenty-four hours later, I'm at the Met with Levi and it's surreal to stand on the granite steps, to be in a space where so many iconic looks debuted. I mean, the Met Gala is my Super Bowl. Watching the red carpet and judging the looks with my sisters is a core memory. Maya is a stickler for adhering to the theme. Clara is drawn to the loudest, most avant-garde outfits. Tessa is the defender of the classic gowns. It's still the one day a year when our group chat is the most active, sending screenshots and commentary and flailing over Zendaya.

A not-so-small part of me wishes I were here with Tessa, affectionately dragging her when she inevitably gravitates toward the most basic silhouettes on display at the Costume Institute. But being here with Levi and making our childhood postcard a reality is still a good reason. Today he's cargo shorts (*always* cargo shorts) and a black polo, while I'm casual day-date attire—a floral print bodysuit and upcycled denim shorts, with an oversize white button-up that combats the chill of central air and can easily be tied around my waist in the outdoor humidity. Our outfits don't clash . . . but they don't do each other any favors, either. That's okay, because today I'll just be a photo credit on a post, not *in* any posts.

It's way too soon for that.

I follow him as he moves through the museum with purpose and before my eyes this museum transforms from a postcard passed between nine-year-olds to a space that Levi Berkowitz can navigate without a map. He leads us toward the temporary exhibition hall that's currently displaying Kyler Coates, a sustainable artist who makes animal garden sculptures out of landfill trash.

"Oh. I've heard of her," I say, somewhat relieved that this exhibit isn't too out of my depth. "My mom is trying to get a Kyler Coates piece installed in Boston Common."

"Cool."

It's the sixth word he's said to me today, after "Hey" and "Ready to go inside?" and I'm not sure how to ask if he's okay. If *this,* us, the plan, is still okay. What if he says no? I couldn't handle that.

So I don't ask. I follow him into the exhibition room filled with intricate, to-scale animal sculptures shaped out of landfill items—a butterfly woven out of plastic bags, a bottle cap and button deer, bunnies carved out of Styrofoam. At the center of the space is an elephant created from tech trash—vintage printers, monitors, CDs, et cetera. An endangered species created with extinct technology pulled from a landfill. It feels profound, this elephant. And cool. So I open my camera and start snapping photos from various angles because the exhibit is the perfect place to start collecting the content that'll launch our plan into motion. For the last shot I capture Levi reading the elephant's informational placard, his back to me, positioned to illustrate the massive scale of the sculpture.

It's a perfect photo.

When I lower my phone, Levi turns toward me and says words seven and eight of the day. "You good?"

I nod. "Are you?"

He shakes his head no, then exits the Kyler Coates exhibit without saying word nine.

I follow him out the museum exit.

Down the stairs.

Into Central Park.

He's so fast that I regret my shoe choice, brand-new platform sneakers that are destroying my heels in real time.

When something bothers Levi, words have to be extracted from him. He's always been the stew-in-silence type, even when we were little, a direct contradiction of my entire essence. Small Fitz felt so *loudly*. I'd run over to Levi's house, all messy tears after an existential crisis over *Finding Nemo*, after my first B-plus on a report card, after Tessa snapped at me over not instantly grasping the concept of photosynthesis. Levi knew how to be there for me because I told him what I needed—hot chocolate with a scoop of fluff, cuddles with his cat, Monet, a Mario Kart tournament. But Levi? I had to learn how to be there for him—to bite my tongue in order to give him the quiet he needs to process, to wait for just the right time to gently nudge and assure him that he can tell me, that I'm a safe space for him.

"Berkowitz!"

He pauses finally, then turns to face me, wiping his cheek. His eyes are red and it makes me feel like I'm eight years old again, ready to take down Aaron Schroeder, the second-grade bully who pushed Levi off the tire swing. It doesn't matter how much time has passed or how many questions I have. It's muscle memory, this protectiveness I still feel toward him.

"We're off to a shit start if us hanging out reduces you to tears in less than ten words."

Levi snorts. "It's not you. It's—"

I cut him off. "Save it for the amicable breakup."

Levi laughs and it cracks something open in me, this ability of mine to still know what he needs.

"Soph loves the Met," he says as we sit under a tree that's a species I'm not even going to pretend to know, our backs pressed against the trunk. I count his words. We're up to seventeen, an improvement. "We'd been looking forward to that exhibit forever. So being there without her? It was just a lot."

"I get it," I say.

"I don't even *like* the Met," Levi continues. "Or I didn't. I don't know. I'm not one to search for meaning in stolen art that's in a museum by way of violent colonization. But Soph loves it here. So I go with her and then the temporary exhibitions are usually kind of amazing? I'm a hypocrite."

"Oh my God, I felt the same way when I started getting into musicals because of Dani. Like. Do I believe Broadway is classist and inaccessible? Yes. Will it stop me from weeping over the *Les Miserables 10th Anniversary Concert* soundtrack? No. But now any Broadway soundtrack reminds me—" I don't finish the sentence because I don't want to make this about Dani and me. "Maybe moving forward, we veto dates that remind us of our people? Even if it leans into our history?"

"Probably a good idea."

"Although, our first post being at one of Sophie's favorite places is kind of savage. As a move, I respect it."

"It wasn't a *move*," Levi insists, running a hand through his hair. "I just like Kyler Coates."

"Okay."

"Anyway, we didn't take any pictures."

I hold up my phone. "*You* didn't take any pictures."

"Hey! What about rule two?"

"I believe that rule is about the posting of photos, not the taking of them," I say with an innocent shrug.

"We need to amend that rule."

"Absolutely not."

I open my photos and show Levi some of my favorite shots to see if he's cool with posting any of them, because even if it wasn't, like, a premeditated *move*, I can't imagine that Sophie won't feel some kind of way, seeing Levi experience one of her favorite places and artists without her. She won't see how hard it actually was for him—how quiet he got inside, the abrupt exit, the tears that followed. Nope. All she'll see is what she missed.

"But you're not in any of these," Levi says.

My eyebrows rise. "You move fast, Berkowitz."

His neck flushes. "I just mean—"

"You think I would be making my Insta Girlfriend debut in uncoordinated attire?"

"No?"

"Of course not!"

I text him the photos I want him to post, and to distract from our sad relationship feelings we work on a photo dump of the Kyler Coates exhibit that doesn't do the sculptures justice, but absolutely works for our purpose. I even convince Levi to use the photo I took of him with the elephant sculpture.

"For the caption, just tag me as the photo credit. Like. Camera emoji, colon, @iftheshoefitz."

"That's it?"

I nod. "We let the pictures speak for themselves. Verbose captions don't feel like *you*."

There's a beat of silence and it makes me wish I could delete and rewrite those words because of their implication. I have to keep reminding myself that there's a difference between knowing who someone was and who they *are*. I'm not the Fitz that Levi knew anymore, either. I don't feel so out-loud now. Except in fountains. But that was an anomaly. I thought I was alone. I'm losing the plot. I just mean, like, who am I to declare what does and does not feel like Levi?

"Unless you're pretending to be a plant," I add.

Levi laughs, the sound releasing the tension in my shoulders, because while I don't think I'm qualified to state what is or isn't Levi, it still feels so good to be a person who can make him laugh. Sure, time has passed. We've changed. But we're still wired to understand each other and there's a safety in this that I haven't felt . . . well, since we were ten. And I like that now we get to use that for a common goal. Something to help both of us.

Levi types the caption, *my* caption, then looks at me. "We're really doing this?"

"If you still want to," I say. "I do."

"Me too."

"Cool."

"I just want to confirm before it's real," Levi says.

"Fake," I correct.

His shoulder nudges mine. "You know what I mean."

I do, so I confirm again and with one tap on a screen, our fauxmance becomes real.

## FIFTEEN

On Friday, I'm once again on the 1 en route to Tessa and ready to talk.

*Really* talk.

Being able to be there for Levi at the Met? It felt good. I want Tessa to know that I can be there for her, too. She just has to let me be. I don't know. I want to ask if we can go to the Costume Institute together, just us. I want to *talk* to her. I don't want to go home at the end of the summer feeling like the closest we've been in literal years is also the furthest away we've been emotionally.

I'm going to say that out loud.

But first, cookies.

I purchase a dozen snickerdoodles from the Insomnia Cookies by Tessa's apartment as soon as I'm off the subway. We're obsessed with them—Maya, Clara, Tessa, and me. I eat two on my walk to Tessa's and they're soft, warm, cinnamony perfection. Using the spare key—*my* key—to enter Tessa's building, I groan at the staircase that hasn't yet become any less painful to climb.

As I catch my breath at the top, Tessa's distinct cackle sounds in the hallway.

Does she have people over? Is Bennett here? *No. Do not backslide, Tessa! Not tonight. I'm here with snickerdoodles and I have nowhere else to go and I do not have the emotional bandwidth to deal with Bennett Covington III—*

"Also? He's a plant murderer! Henrietta is on fucking life support."

So Bennett the cheating plant murderer is definitively *not* on the other side of the door.

Okay.

I unlock the door and push it open.

"Fitz!!!"

Tessa is crisscross on Gertie facing me, earbuds in, computer balanced on her lap. A half-empty bottle of pinot whatever is on the table, which explains the multiple exclamation points in her voice.

She removes an earbud and inhales. "Holy shit. Are those snickerdoodles?"

I snort. "You're—"

Tessa giggles at her screen. "I'm trying! I told y'all she'd make an appearance. One sec."

She disconnects her earbuds and that's when I hear them, the *y'all* on Tessa's screen.

Maya and Clara.

And now? I almost wish it *were* Bennett.

"Fitzy!" Maya squeals.

"Come join the Fuck Bennett party!" Clara shouts.

Join? *Crash* feels like a more accurate descriptor. But I put on an unfazed filter as I hand the snickerdoodles to Tessa and take the empty space on Gertie. On the screen, I see my other sisters are also together on Maya's pink velvet couch. Maya is leggings and an oversize *Speak Now* tour tee. Clara is a pink terry-cloth sleep set that matches the couch. Both are also clearly wine drunk like Tessa.

"We just added 'plant murderer' to the cons list," Maya informs me. Of course she's making a list. Maya is Dad's daughter through and through—and this includes their enthusiastic belief in contingency plans and pro/con lists.

"Bennett Covington III: puppy hater, compulsive toe cracker, shit writer, and plant murderer," Clara says, reading the list in a truly abysmal British accent.

I reach for a snickerdoodle. "Are there any pros?"

Tessa sighs. "The sex."

Laughter fills the apartment in three-part harmony. Maya throws her head back, her septum piercing reflecting the light, then orders Tessa to open "the Tinder" immediately and start swiping. Yes. *The* Tinder. Clara refers to dating apps as *a necessary evil*, her accent shifting from posh to cockney. While Tessa swipes, their attention shifts to me.

"Fitzy! How is FIT?" Maya asks.

*Try real.*

"Honestly—"

"Fuck!" Tessa yells, throwing her phone across the room.

I jump off Gertie on a rescue mission. "*Tess*. What are you doing?"

"I *matched*."

Clara drops the accent. "Yes!"

"What do I do?" Tessa asks.

"You don't break your phone! Jesus," Maya says.

I hold my breath when I see it facedown on the hardwood floor. A precarious position. But when I pick it up, I find that despite the dramatic moment, her phone is okay. Just a shattered screen protector. *Phew.*

"Send us pics!" Clara demands.

Tessa grabs her phone from my hand. "He *messaged* me."

"Because you matched . . . ," I say as Tessa takes a screenshot of his profile and sends it to my sisters.

"Oh. He's *hot*," Clara says.

Drew Carnegie—Tessa's match—is a Generic White Guy with a Strong Jaw. Seriously, he looks like he belongs on the "college football player to *The Bachelor* lead" pipeline. I skim his profile over Tessa's shoulder.

Maya frowns. "He . . . radiates Republican energy."

Tessa cackles. "What does that even *mean*?"

"His suit pic, his crew cut, his name literally being Andrew Carnegie . . ."

"*Drew*," Tessa corrects.

Clara snorts. "Not every white man in a suit is a Republican, Maya."

I shrug. "True. But the American flag lapel pin is—"

"He has a cat named Dolly Purrton!" Tessa exclaims.

"Holy shit," Maya says.

While my sisters enable Tessa to pursue rebound sex with Bennett 2.0, I . . . eat another snickerdoodle and exist around their chaotic energy. I'm always around it, never a part of it. It's impossible to even finish a sentence without being cut off.

So I reach for the pinot whatever.

Just to, I don't know, be a part of it.

But Tessa confiscates the bottle before I even take a sip.

"Plenty of drinks of the nonalcoholic variety are in the fridge."

"Seriously, Tess?"

"A glass of wine isn't going to kill her, T," Clara says.

Tessa shakes her head. "I do not serve alcohol to *children*—"

Pressure builds behind my eyes as Tessa and Clara debate if I'm allowed a sip of the pinot whatever as if I'm not right here. Honestly? I'm over this attempt to force myself into a wine-induced conversation that I wasn't even invited to. It's so *desperate.*

I stand. "Whatever. I'm exhausted anyway."

I retreat to Tessa's bedroom, closing the door between us. I flop onto the bed and reach for the remote on the night table to turn on *Project Runway*, my most comforting comfort show. I love the retro seasons from, like, the mid-2000s, even though I have to cringe at the sometimes ageist comments directed at the older designers and the not-so-subtle body shaming of the early aughts. Christian Siriano? His side bangs were a moment. Growing up, my sisters and I would all watch it together. So I watch it whenever I miss them. My sisters. But right now? I shouldn't miss them.

Tessa is so close that not even a door and turning the volume up can block out her cackle. But it feels like they're all in Texas, the three of them together, a unit.

And I'm in Massachusetts, totally alone.

A rogue tear slides down my cheek and I wipe it away with one hand as I rummage through my purse for my phone with the other because I need more than old episodes of *Project Runway* to distract myself from how much it *hurts*, this confirmation that my sisters have these separate calls without me. And for this one to be a Fuck Bennett Covington III Party—excuse me? No one has accumulated more creative insults for that asshole over the last seven years than me. Also? I am the Fitzgerald sister who is actually *here*.

With snickerdoodles.

Whatever.

Phone retrieved, I open my content calendar. Let my sisters have each other. *Dani* is my person. Instead of trying and failing to bond with someone who still sees me as a child, I need to refocus on the person who actually sees *me*. The online fauxmance seems to be going well so far. Sophie liked the Met post minutes after Levi pressed send. A small victory. So next up, we have to work in some subtly curated opportunities for Dani to see us together, in person. Just like our online relationship arc, the idea is to start small. First up in the spreadsheet is to have Levi stop by the dorm before we go out when I know she'll be home. Then, see a show at the Public while Dani is working the ticket counter. Later this summer, we'll work up to chill hangs in the dorm.

I'm about to text Levi when a new message comes in from him.

**Levi Berkowitz**
Hey! Are you free Mon? It's
not blocked off on the spreadsheet.
9:30PM

*Levi referred to the spreadsheet.*
Another victory.
Before I can type a response, a second and third message appear.

I have a plantscapade near the high line
9:31PM

could be a good spot for another "date" if you're down?
9:31PM

Google populates a park in the sky on the west side of Manhattan.

now THIS is a plantscapade that screams
adventure
9:32PM

i'm in! can you swing by my dorm after?
9:32PM

i'm pretty sure dani will be home
9:32PM

I type *pretty sure* as if I don't have her schedule memorized.

Can do!
9:37PM

I kind of love that Levi is reaching out with his own date ideas, that he's getting into this too. Sure, we already have a schedule to adhere to, and this isn't on it, so I'll have to rethink this week's post. But that's not a huge deal. Levi's obviously riding the high of Sophie engaging with his first photo and wants to maximize our content.

It makes sense.

And it's time to hard-launch our relationship online *and* in-person.

# SIXTEEN

O n Monday, Levi and I stroll among the flowers on an abandoned railroad line that has bloomed into something beautiful. Situated on the west side of downtown Manhattan, the High Line is a promenade in the sky that stretches twenty-two blocks along Tenth Avenue. We're elevated thirty feet or so above concrete streets and there's so much to take in: the open-air art installations sprinkled throughout the walking path, the colorful murals painted on facades, the stunning cityscape architecture.

"Now over five hundred plant and tree species thrive here, all sustainably sourced . . ."

And, of course, the plants.

Levi is in full Plant Nerd mode, name-dropping botanical species like this is AP Bio as I take in the views and scope out the perfect backdrop for our first couple photo. A section of the path briefly transports us from the city to a small forest full of leafy green trees, dense shrubs, and wildflowers. Perfect. We snag a wooden chaise near it to share and then unwrap Lenwich sandwiches for our sunset picnic. An adorable fake date.

". . . and most are locally grown, too. Fun fact: more than half of these species are native to America."

"Cool." I snap a photo of our sandwich spread. "You should be a tour guide."

"I am."

"Seriously?"

Levi nods. "Once a week. It counts toward my community service requirement for graduation, but I'd still do it for fun. I get to introduce people to this unique space and reveal that its existence is, in some ways, a happy accident. Because this structure would've just been demolished had no one discovered the wildflower garden. . . ."

As we eat, he details the history of this park in the sky, and it's so endearing to listen to Levi Berkowitz, the tour guide. I can't even keep a bamboo alive, but I swear, I could listen to him talk about drip irrigation and composting all day.

". . . and I'm rambling," Levi says, finally pausing to take a bite of his veggie wrap. "Sorry."

"You're not."

"A deep dive on sustainable irrigation systems is not a part of the usual tour."

"Their loss."

Levi's mouth quirks. "It really is. Anyway, being here for a not-date felt somewhat on-brand for you, too."

"Yeah?"

"It's what you do, take something anyone else would discard and turn it into something beautiful."

Oh.

Feeling a blush blooming on my cheeks, I turn away from his eye contact and unzip my backpack in pursuit of my water bottle. Is that really how Levi sees If the Shoe Fitz? Is that how he sees me? Because after experiencing this place, calling me the architect of my own sort of High Line is the nicest thing anyone has ever said about what I do, like, to my face. But I'm also not sure what to do with this compliment and how lovely it feels that he sees what I'm trying to do and how much it sucks that Dani doesn't—

*No.*

Dani found my summer program.

Dani is the reason I'm here.

Dani supports me, my clothes, my passion.

Obviously.

The clothes were never the issue. My priorities were. But I'm on hiatus now. If Levi sees that, then Dani's definitely going to realize she's wrong about me—that I *am* more passionate about my craft than growing my platform and just like her, I'm an artist too.

I sip my water, swallow, then change the subject. "Does Sophie love this stuff as much as you?"

I bet she does. I bet this is a spot they frequent to do their homework, to watch the sunset, to just be. I bet he's content to be here with me, but he wishes he were here with her. I understand. In an alternate universe, I'd be here with someone else too.

Levi shrugs. "I don't know about love, but she's a plant parent too. I'm . . . taking care of them while she's out of town."

"Wait. Stop. She demoted you from boyfriend to plant sitter?"

Levi scratches the back of his neck. "I offered."

"Berkowitz!"

"What? It's not Delilah and Petunia's fault."

I snort. "She did not name a petunia . . . Petunia."

"She also has a fish called Fishy."

There's a non-zero percent chance Levi is a fish sitter, too.

Golden-hour light starts to cast a sepia filter over the skyline as the sun sets over the river. It's gorgeous. Super romantic. Perfect lighting for the photo we still need to take. Is this progress, having to remind myself to get a photo before we lose the light instead of obsessing over it the whole time? Is two weeks off social media already transforming me into the girlfriend that Dani wants me to be? Soon we'll be back together and roaming the city, our perfect summer back on track, and I can even bring her here. She'll ask me to pick a direction and I'll choose west. I cannot think of a more perfect day.

I stand. "Photo time!"

Levi groans. "Can't I just post one of you?"

I shake my head. "No way. The next post needs to be our first couple photo. It's—"

"—in the spreadsheet."

"Exactly."

Earlier today, I video-chatted with him to make sure our

outfits wouldn't clash, and he let me style him to coordinate with my simple cream off-the-shoulder maxi dress and gold accessories. His closet isn't tragic. It turns out that Levi Berkowitz has solid instincts. It's just his execution that leaves something to be desired. I stayed true to his khaki heart but got him to swap the cargo shorts for chinos and the primary-color polo for a deep-green button-up, the sleeves rolled up to his elbows. He pushed back at first with "I look like I'm going to a bar mitzvah" until we layered the button-up over a graphic T-shirt and left it unbuttoned.

He still looks like Levi.

Just elevated.

In addition to elevating his style, I've also been brainstorming creative solutions to work around his camera-shyness, to make sure he's comfortable. I pose us off the main path, the west side streets our backdrop, and explain the concept to him—that our backs will be facing the camera since that seemed to work well at the Met. He won't have to worry about what to do with his face. Instead we can concentrate on creating a sense of intimacy through our body language.

He nods. "I can do that."

"Perfect," I say, then step in front of two NYU sweatshirts. "Excuse me, do you mind taking a photo of us?"

"Oh. Sure!"

I hand his phone to the student with chipped lime nails and cherry-red lips and I wrap my hand around Levi's wrist, pulling him toward our perfect backdrop. Despite his verbal consent to this photo and best efforts, Levi's stance is stiff and awkward. We don't have time for awkward. We have, like, ten seconds tops because I can't hold these strangers hostage. Also, the sun is setting. The skyline will only retain its golden glow for so long.

So I say, "Fishy is a shit name."

Levi laughs. "I was pushing for Bubble Fett."

"But that's . . . so much worse."

"It's a *Star*—"

"I get it, Berkowitz. You're a basic *Star Wars* bro."

"This is my truth."

It's a few seconds of fish name banter, but it's enough to make him forget about the camera until Chipped Lime Nails returns his phone to me. I swipe through the five photos and I *see it*, the exact moment when I make Levi Berkowitz laugh. We are partial profiles in that one, and damn it, my bridge bump is visible. I should've kept my gaze fixed straight out toward the city. But . . . Levi is at ease in this moment, his mouth-quirk visible, and I'm not sure we'll be able to replicate it. Besides, it's not like this is a photo for If the Shoe Fitz. It's a photo for Levi's page, a rare photo of him that will show Sophie what she's missing. So I let the bridge bump go, selecting the photo and playing with the filters to emphasize the sunset lighting.

"Why do you hate being photographed so much?"

"When a camera is pointed at me, I forget how my limbs work?"

"Oh! You just need to learn your angles."

"Also, I have never taken a good school picture."

"Those are always the worst."

"Mine are traumatic."

"Well, consider this exposure therapy."

I assess our work. If I came across this photo on my feed, I would see his mussed hair and half smile and think, *Cute.* I would never suspect that he's camera shy. Or that the people in this photo are just friends. I would only see couple goals. Maybe even be a little jealous.

Perfect.

I turn the phone toward him to show off the final result. "See? You don't have anything to be embarrassed about. Objectively."

Levi looks at it, his eyebrows lifting. "I don't hate it."

"Is that consent to post?"

Levi nods, so I post our sunset photo as the sun retreats in real time.

We're now Instagram Official.

"So. What now?" Levi asks.

I don't think he literally means this minute, but I answer as if he does. "A lesson on angles."

"Now? But . . . aren't we losing the light?"

"So there's no time to waste," I say, handing his phone back to him. "I have self-conscious moments too, you know. Taking tons of photos and learning what worked for me was the only way I got over it enough to be able to post anything at all."

"Seriously?"

"Pretty much every time I post a new outfit."

"Why? You're so talented."

"You don't have to—" I swallow the end of that sentence and try to accept the compliment. "It's not about the clothes."

"But. You're—"

"I just mean, I get it. Cameras are intimidating."

I show him how I manipulate my posture, from the tilt of my chin to the arch of my back. How photos start to not feel so scary once you're confident in your poses. It's not about, like, changing my body to conform to patriarchal beauty standards. Fuck that. I like my body. It's more about how understanding camera angles empowers a subject in front of a lens. Certain poses exude confidence. After the photo shoot, I swipe through the photos and point out the differences these subtle shifts in body language make.

"See?"

Levi shakes his head. "Not really."

"Berkowitz!"

"You seriously think some of these pictures look . . . bad?"

His eyes meet mine, his expression so serious—and I'm not sure how to respond to his earnest bafflement. So I roll my eyes, then insist that we practice basic poses until the sun recedes into the river and the path illuminates, lit low along our feet. He's an excellent student, asking questions and taking mental notes and seeming to actually care about this area of expertise of mine until we lose the light. We then stroll east, exiting this park in the sky en route to my dorm, en route to Dani.

I have exactly one mile to become Levi Berkowitz's girlfriend.

*It's what you do, take something anyone else would discard and turn it into something beautiful.*

*You're so talented.*

*You seriously think some of these pictures look . . . bad?*

I let his words loop as we walk toward her and it's almost too easy to get into character. If Levi is this good at being a fake boyfriend, I can't help but wonder why Sophie would ever want a break from having him as her real one.

One mile later, we're at my dorm.

When the elevator opens at my floor, I hold out my hand. "Ready, Boyfriend?"

"No," Levi says, but he takes it and follows me down the hall to my suite, where I know Dani will be on the other side of the door. Whereas I will take any opportunity to not occupy this shared space, Dani lives here. Like, leaves-dirty-dishes-in-the-sink-and-has-outerwear-draped-over-every-available-common-room-chair lives here. As we get closer, I hear a familiar dance break and it's all but confirmation that she's home.

"Is that . . . 'Seize the Day'?" Levi asks, his voice low.

My eyes widen. "Are you a theater kid?"

"I just help out with set design. *Newsies* was our spring musical."

"You're a theater kid," I confirm, obsessed with this new detail about him.

We enter the suite. The music is so loud Dani doesn't hear us, so we find her dancing in the kitchen with a Swiffer in her hand. Dishes are drying on the counter and the entire common area smells like lemon cleaning solution. But . . . Dani *hates* cleaning. She told me in a soft confession in my car the week before our New York departure. *I am a slob*, she whispered against my lips. *Please don't hate me when my shit is everywhere*. I shook my head. *Never*. I meant it. I still do. That night, I also learned that she'll only clean to songs with a dedicated dance break that denotes, for her, an actual break. Now I'm witnessing a dance break in real time.

It's so cute.

Until she spins toward us and screams.

*"Shit."*

Dani, no longer oblivious to our arrival, jumps backward and slips and falls on the Swiffer-slick floor. I abandon my plan to keep hold of Levi's hand for as long as possible and run over to her because what if she hit her head or landed on her wrist? I'm here to bruise her heart. Not, like, seriously injure her.

"Are you okay? We didn't mean to—"

Dani stands up, refusing any assistance, and pauses the music. "I'm fine. You just scared the shit out of me."

"Sorry! I—"

I short-circuit the moment I process that Dani is wearing the flannel.

My flannel.

Dani knows I'm here on weeknights. And we just talked about this shirt. So. Is she wearing my flannel on purpose? Does she want me to see her in my clothes? Oh my God. She totally does.

Levi covers my unraveling by introducing himself with a tentative wave. "I'm Levi."

"Danica," she says.

"So sorry we—"

I don't hear whatever polite small talk Levi is engaged in with Dani. I'm too fixated on the flannel, until Levi's fingers twine together with mine. *Good move, Boyfriend.* It centers me, the warmth of his palm, and brings my attention away from the flannel and back to the conversation.

"—on the subway, actually," he finishes.

Dani's smile is forced. "It's so wild that the two of you randomly reconnected here. I couldn't believe it when Fitz told me."

Levi's eyebrows rise and I see the question. *You know who I am to Fitz?*

But instead of asking, he just nods and repeats, "Wild."

"Cosmic shit, it is," I say, back in character, and I squeeze his hand, a wordless *thanks* for getting this meet-awkward back on track. "Being reunited with my first best friend."

"I missed her a lot," Levi says.

He says those five words so earnestly, I almost believe him.

"Anyway. We'll leave you—"

"I'm about to head out to meet Em for dinner, so the place is yours."

Now it's my smile that's forced as Dani puts the Swiffer away, then picks up her keys off the common room table and steps into her Adidas slides by the door. I'm almost convinced, but before she clips a fanny pack across her body, she scratches her nose and I'm vindicated. Dani was clearly in for the night. Meeting Em is bullshit. I mean. She was *cleaning*.

I let her go.

The moment she's out the door, Levi releases my hand.

"I have no clue what just happened," Levi admits.

"*Progress*, Berkowitz."

"Really?"

"The idea of spending time in the same space as us is so nauseating, she made up an excuse to flee."

He processes this and I *see* the moment it clicks. "She cares."

I nod. "She *cares*. Great work, Boyfriend."

"You too."

Performance over, Levi shows me a new comment on our post from Sophie that says *missing that view.* For the rest of the night I am floating. Because this fauxmance plan of mine?

It's working.

For both of us.

## SEVENTEEN

*I* ride the high from my interaction with Dani all the way into my next week of classes, positive that this beginning to our getting back together arc will inspire something. The week begins with a field trip. Tuesday morning at eight a.m., Mal meets us at the Sixth Avenue L train to usher our cohort across the East River to ScrapFAB's warehouse in Williamsburg for a tour of the facility and the opportunity to source fabric for our projects. It's exactly what I need, to be out in the field among the textures and colors of recycled fabrics that have the potential to become something beautiful.

"Most textiles come to us through take-back programs," Charlie Calhoun, a cofounder of ScrapFAB, explains as we walk through a room with rows of industrial washing machines. "Brands like Revived by Mal partner with us because we have the infrastructure to take used garments and prepare them for resale as fabric that can be purchased in bulk."

"I've been a ScrapFAB partner since I decided to scale," Mal says. "Now, I'm able to mass-produce my designs while staying true to a closed-loop business model."

Oh.

I've only ever made one-off upcycled designs and I'm nowhere near scalable—I don't even sell my clothes yet. I'm still learning, experimenting, perfecting my craft. But when I'm ready to open an online shop, these are things I need to consider. What will I do if two people want the same shirt and I only have enough material for one? As Charlie rattles off statistics about textile waste, I take notes on my phone. *Scale.* It's wild to be even thinking like this. That I'm here, learning how to do that, because Dani encouraged me to apply.

It makes me love her even more.

When we enter the fabric room, it's not at all what I expect it to be. I anticipated the organized chaos of a thrift store. Piles of clothes sorted by color and texture. Me, rummaging through them in search of inspiration. It's a gift of mine, the ability to find garments where the bones are good, to be able to *see* their potential to transform into something original and new. It's how I've always upcycled.

But this warehouse?

It's a sustainable Jo-Ann Fabric—rows and rows of shelves with rolls of textiles in a variety of colors and patterns.

Trevor's eyes widen. "This is what heaven looks like."

But when I take in the size of the warehouse, the number of choices in front of me, potentially so many wrong choices that could end my career before it begins . . . I couldn't disagree more with this take. And when Mal explains that we're allowed to source five yards of fabric for our project, covered by the program fees, I'm once again in my worst nightmare, overwhelmed by the endless possibilities in front of me.

*Think.*

*Do not start panic-grabbing.*

*Stay away from the satin.*

"Fitz! You good?"

Trevor stands in front of me, his arms full of gorgeous fabrics. I look around to see everyone perusing the rows, comparing swatches, sourcing with intention while I'm on the verge of a panic attack.

"Yeah," I lie.

"You typically do thrift flips, right? If you need someone to bounce ideas off, I can—"

"I'm fine."

It comes out colder than I intend. I'm not sure why Trevor is being so nice to me but the snap in my voice has all but guaranteed that this unsolicited kindness will stop. He looks almost hurt as he nods once and then walks away, combat boots loud against the concrete floors.

I pivot and search for something that speaks to me, but I don't see any outfits in these rolls of fabric and the impostor syndrome is real. How is this so easy for everyone else? Am I even a designer? Or just a stylist who upcycles? How can I select fabric without a vision for this project? What if I choose wrong? I don't—

"Fitz?"

This time, Mal's voice interrupts my spiral.

"ScrapFAB has a retail space on Lorimer Street."

I'm not sure why Mal is telling me this. "Okay?"

"You can always use your fabric credit there, when you're ready to source."

Not Mal calling out my total inability to source fabrics in real time.

*Filter on.*

I grab the first fabric I see. "Thanks! But that won't be necessary."

Mal's eyes meet mine. "It's okay, though, if it is."

She stays in place for a beat to give me an opportunity to speak, to ask for help.

I don't.

I return to my dorm that afternoon with five yards of a midnight-blue galaxy-print jersey blend that I have no clue what to do with. I drop my keys on my desk, flop onto my bed, and scroll through Netflix in search of something to take my mind off the field trip. I settle on *Legally Blonde*, an early-aughts rom-com that my sisters introduced me to and I've since memorized. I don't even make it through the opening credits, though, because the song playing over them could not be more wrong. Today was not a perfect day.

Everything did go wrong.

I hit pause and pick up my phone, realizing I left it in *Do not disturb* during my commute back to Manhattan, and when I disable the setting, my phone vibrates with notifications.

Levi.

Levi.

Tessa.

Levi.

I read their messages.

Two of Levi's texts are plant photos, and the third is a screenshot with the details for our next not-date, a painting class. Another activity that was Levi's idea, and I'm obsessed because not only can we tie it into memories of finger-painting blank canvases in his backyard, but it's also an activity with an end result meant for a photo. When I look closer I see he booked it for Saturday. July 10. My birthday. I don't know if he forgot or if this is intentional.

I read the message from my sister before I can obsess over that.

**Tessa**

Hey! Do you have any birthday plans this weekend?

12:31PM

Tessa is oblivious to how much walking in on her chatting with Maya and Clara *hurt*. Of course she is. It's not like I told her how I felt. But seeing that she reached out to me this time to make plans? It dulls that hurt. Maybe there's hope for us yet. I reread Levi's paint date confirmation. It's a two p.m. class. Perfect.

day plans with a friend, but
free for dinner?
4:07PM

Thai?
4:08PM

perf
4:09PM

My shoulders relax, letting go of tension that I wasn't even aware I was holding. I'm not one to look forward to birthdays, but I'm relieved because my emo Cancer sun self would absolutely have stewed in sadness if I were to spend mine alone. Even if Levi doesn't remember that it's my birthday. Even if I'm still hurt by the confirmation of Fitzgerald Sister FaceTime sans me. Even if neither of these plans are an off-Broadway show and dinner in Little Italy with Dani, which is how I envisioned celebrating turning seventeen. It's okay.

More than okay, considering the alternative would be a birthday spent trying to figure out what the fuck I'm supposed to do with this fabric.

## EIGHTEEN

C abbage and peppers would never be planted together."
Levi frowns at the whimsical painting of a vegetable garden that we're meant to replicate. He's so
perplexed by the sample's inaccuracy, so *serious* about its mis-
representation that he hasn't even started. Leave it to Levi Berkowitz to find a way to turn a paint class into a plant lesson.

I laugh. "It's just a painting."

"The cabbage will inhibit the peppers' growth."

I tie a smock around my waist. "No vegetables will be
harmed by the painting of this picture."

"But—"

Levi's dissent is cut off by Lilith, the artist employed
by Muse Tribeca who will be guiding us through painting
this (inaccurate!) vegetable garden for the next ninety minutes. Lilith is willowy, with turquoise hair and piercings all
the way up one ear. At the end of their spiel, they ask if we
have any questions and I expect Levi to raise his hand and
ask why the fuck the peppers are next to the cabbage, but he
doesn't, likely due to the family of three seated at our table

that includes a small child wearing a pink tiara.

I mix colors on a palette, following Lilith's instructions to create various shades of dirt brown and sky blue. I try not to be intimidated by the blank canvas in front of me. It's *not* the same as a blank page in my sketch pad or a roll of untouched fabric. A paintbrush is in my hand, not a pencil. I don't have to think or create something original. I just have to follow Lilith's step-by-step instructions.

So, brush in hand, I paint.

"Cool hair!" the kid in the pink tiara says to me.

I touch the faded ends of my ponytail, which are overdue for a touch-up. "Thanks! Cool crown."

"Thanks!" Pink Tiara smiles at me. "It's my birthday."

I respect a birthday crown moment.

"Hers too," Levi says, nodding at me. He was the first person to send a text at 12:01 a.m., and it felt so good that he remembered.

"No way!" Pink Tiara squeals. "This is kismet! Kermit the Frog taught me that word."

"How old are you?" I ask.

"Eight. Did you know—?"

Pink Tiara's dad cuts off the question. "Tabitha. You have to listen to Miss Lilith, okay?"

"Sorry! She's a chatty one, our Tabitha," Tabitha's mom says with a chuckle.

"Oh! Me too," I say.

*Our Tabitha.*

It scrapes at my heart, the tenderness in these strangers' voices toward their child, nothing like when I talked to my parents this morning during their brief window of togetherness. Dad had just returned home from the hospital. Mom was about to head off to brunch with friends. They butchered "Happy Birthday," then asked about Tessa and fashion camp. I gently reminded them that FIT is a big deal.

"There's actually a final runway show for friends and family to see what we've worked on all summer," I told them. "Mal, the instructor, is going to choose her favorite designs for a collab with her brand."

"Is it in the calendar?" Dad asked.

We have a shared family calendar. That's how we communicate. Via calendar notifications. Dad's shifts at the hospital, Mom's community fundraising events, my extracurriculars. If it's not on the calendar, it doesn't exist.

"No—"

"We'll try to make it," Mom said.

"Try?"

"Of course we *want* to make it," Dad said.

"*Of course*," Mom emphasized. "Add it to the calendar and we'll circle back."

It doesn't feel great, being reduced to a calendar event. I try to imagine my parents taking me to a place like this on my birthday, together, but I can't. One or both of them would be working. We'd do cake the day before or the weekend after or whatever day best fit their schedule. I'd say I understand. Of course a meeting with the city council about the park budget or assisting in the delivery of triplet preemies are more important than my birthday.

Objectively.

But Tabitha's parents look at her like *nothing* is more important.

I swallow the emotion in my throat and refocus on my canvas as Lilith articulates how to layer the paint step-by-step in a soothing manner that radiates Bob Ross energy. I add another swipe of blue paint, swirling my brush to add texture as demonstrated. While I'm waiting for my sky to dry, my attention shifts away from my canvas and toward Levi.

"What? Do I already have paint on my face?" Levi asks.

"Already?"

"You know it's pretty much inevitable."

"Part of your creative process," I say, remembering the mess of color all over him after a finger-paint day.

Levi nods. "Exactly."

I laugh.

Then pick up a paintbrush and . . . swipe soil into the sky instead of a cloud.

Shit.

I picked up the wrong flat brush.

Instinct has me wipe the brown splotch away with the pad of my thumb before it dries, but it just spreads the soil even more into the sky. Great. I must salvage this before Lilith circles back this way, so I add more blue, but that doesn't help either. It's, like, the more I try to fix it, the *worse* it looks, and now half of the sky is streaked with brownish splotches.

"Shit," I mutter, out loud this time, because not only is it unfixable, there's also no way that I'll be able to post this on Levi's Instagram. We need a post. It's the entire reason we're here. Not because it's my birthday. We just happen to be collecting content *on* my birthday. Content that I ruined just like I ruined—

Levi's voice pulls me out of the spiral. "What's wrong?"

"I messed up," I whisper.

"I'm sure you didn't."

"Berkowitz. It's bad."

He peers over to look at my canvas, his eyes widening. "Whoa. What happened?"

With Levi's verbal confirmation that it *is* as bad as it looks, I stand and bolt for the restroom because not only have I ruined today's content, I'm seconds away from bursting into tears on my birthday in front of an eight-year-old on *her* birthday. Once I'm alone in the single gender-neutral restroom, I press the heel of my hands to my eyes, so frustrated that I can't even make something beautiful when I'm following someone else's instructions. Tabitha is eight and has a garden more put-together than I do. Painting is supposed to be chill. Fun. Low stakes. So much for a cute canvas for Instagram.

A few minutes later, someone knocks.

Well. Hiding is no longer an option.

I wipe my eyes, open the door, and return to my station . . .

to find a blue sky, the brown streaks somehow erased.

Levi looks at me and as promised, blue paint has dried on his chin. "I fixed it."

"I just . . ." I swallow, touched but still embarrassed. "Thanks."

I take my seat. It's not perfect, my sky. It's a shade darker than the example, the paint thicker than it's supposed to be. But there's zero indication that it was once shit brown. I reach for a paintbrush to start on the vegetables, as if I didn't just have a semipublic meltdown.

Levi seems down to forget it, but Tabitha isn't. "You have to let the paint dry longer first," she says, painting a tomato. "Just so you know. For when you mess up again."

*When?*

"I messed up too, " Tabitha adds humbly, pointing to a wonky carrot. "But I'm eight."

Shit, Tabitha!

Levi snorts. "Also? It's not that serious."

"Well. It resembles a garden?" Levi says when we exit the art studio half an hour later, canvases in hand.

I shake my head. "I was roasted by an eight-year-old."

"Kids are brutal."

"I can't post this."

"Why not?"

I snort. "Next to yours? It'll look ridiculous."

Levi not only fixed my mess, but he also created a work

that's inspired by the example but with a level of detail and realism beyond it. Also accuracy. Instead of inhibited peppers, a tomato vine is next to the cabbage. It's incredible. I knew Levi was artsy. Esther, his mom, taught him how to hold a paintbrush before a pencil. But I had no clue that in these last seven years, Levi Berkowitz evolved from the best doodler I knew into lowkey Picasso.

"Well. I told you to not put the peppers next to the cabbage."

"Berkowitz."

Levi pauses midstep. "If you agree to post the paintings, I will also post something that I'm bad at."

"So my painting *is* bad."

Levi ignores me. "It's the sort of activity that would even require video evidence."

My eyebrows rise. Wait. Levi will let me take a *video* of him? An Insta Story will totally make our "relationship" seem more believable. But seeing how he reacts to a camera, it seemed so beyond off the table to even ask. He's never not surprising me.

"I'm intrigued."

"And I already regret this," he says, then starts walking in the opposite direction.

I'm not sure what it says about me that I'm living for the truth that Levi Berkowitz is bad at mini golf. Bad is an understatement. He's *terrible*. Seriously. A putter in his hand is a safety hazard. By the sixth hole at Pier 25, he is on his fourth ball—two have sunk into a body of water and one flew over the gate and rolled away onto the pier. I manage to get the promised video evidence when ball four jumps the fence and Levi sheepishly walks away to ask for a fifth.

"You're the worst," he says when he returns.

I point my camera at him. "You did this to yourself."

Part of Hudson River Park, Pier 25 is home to Manhattan's only outdoor mini-golf course. New York is so much more than the tourist spots everyone knows. I knew that but it's different experiencing it, learning that it's also parks in the sky and mini golf on piers. It feels like I'm just beginning to scratch the surface of the contradictions woven into the fiber of this city. Like how is it possible that from this mini-golf course, there is a jaw-dropping view of the Freedom Tower? I snap a photo, but it doesn't do it justice.

Not at all.

I turn back toward Levi in time to document him setting up his shot, bending his knees and adjusting his grip on the putter.

He swings and . . .

He misses.

Actual tears stream down my cheeks, that's how hard I'm laughing.

"Are you messing with me? Trying to make me feel better?" I ask.

"I promise I'm not."

He swings again, even more determined, and this time he connects with the ball, sending it shooting off the course and into the bushes. An honest improvement.

Soon it becomes clear that the strangers around us are either frustrated with or invested in Levi, the worst mini golfer in Manhattan. At one point, when he hits his ball and it lands *in the next hole*, people actually applaud. It's a moment.

I keep score and at the end it's 61 to 102. Not my best, but a respectable score *and* I finish with the same pink ball that I started with. We return our putters and I swear I've never seen a mini-golf staffer look so relieved to see two people leave.

Levi stuffs his hands in his pockets. "Was that fun for you?"

"Incredibly."

I snap a photo of the scorecard, holding it out in front of me and angle the camera so our shadows are in the photo. Aesthetics-wise, it will look so good on main next to our High Line photo.

We find a patch of grass to sit on in the park along the pier and I'm content to just eat birthday ice cream, but Levi is determined to collect on my half of the bargain. I suppose I can stomach posting my painting if it's the second photo in a set, so people will only see it if they swipe. Maybe. As we lay our canvases side by side for the photo, I wonder how it's possible for him to be okay with being so bad at something with so many people watching. I'm not sure how to accept my bad like Levi can, how to love my acrylic vegetable garden for what it is.

"Fitz?"

"Yeah?"

"Are you okay?"

Levi asks in his soft, tentative way that cuts through my bullshit banter and makes me feel so seen, so *embarrassed*. My cheeks heat. But if Levi can put himself out there for me like that, I owe him an honest answer.

"I thought a paint class would be impossible to mess up. I mean. On the website it said 'suitable for ages seven and up.' Then I did. And I just keep messing up . . ." I pause, snapping my hair elastic against my wrist. Then exhale and just say it. "I'm not exactly thriving at FIT. Creatively speaking."

"Oh."

"My designs are 'Instagrammable.'"

Levi frowns. "That's not a good thing?"

"Not in this context. It means derivative. I chase trends, when I should be creating them."

"No pressure."

"Right? At the end of the summer, there's a runway show that is a huge opportunity. Everyone else is already sourcing fabrics for their designs and I don't even have *a* design. I've *never* been blocked like this, Berkowitz. I'm blowing it because I'm heartbroken and distracted and everyone in my class is so much more talented and . . . I don't know what to do."

Levi considers what to say next, his brow furrowed.

"You're putting a lot of pressure on yourself, Fitzgerald."

I shrug, unsure how to respond because Levi says *pressure*

like it's a bad thing. I don't think that's true. I'm here, in New York, at FIT *because* of this pressure—to level up my craft, to grow my audience on social, to not submit a portfolio that was anything less than perfect. Pressure isn't the issue.

It's that I've stopped being able to perform under it.

"Sometimes art takes the time it takes," Levi continues.

"I'm kind of on a deadline."

"I just mean—"

"It's fine. I'll figure it out. But thanks! For fixing my sky and for almost getting us banned from a mini-golf course. I needed a win."

"You're welcome. Happy birthday," he says, not pushing it further, then hands me a card.

A memory floats back to me that reminds me it's not just a card. It's a *Levi* card that will probably include incredible doodles and a ridiculous birthday pun, like all his cards do. Did. Who knows if he still does that? I was ten the last time I got one, the week before he left. He drew two adorable cartoon bubble teas and wrote, *Happy Birthday, Best-tea!* So dumb, but I loved it so much. It also made it even more confusing when he never called. That is *not* best-tea behavior. Still, it's in a box under my bed, as is every other stupid birthday pun card.

I open this new one to see . . .

A ficus.

Wait. Not just *a* ficus.

Eloise.

Above her, it reads *HAVE AN UNBE-LEAF-ABLE BIRTH-DAY* and it takes every ounce of my restraint to not burst into tears.

"I love it. Thank you."

"You're welcome."

"It sucks that my card box is at home. It would've been such a cute post, this with all your cute kid drawings."

His eyebrows rise above his Wayfarers. "You still have those?"

I nod. "Just like your postcard. I don't throw memories away."

Even the ones that leave a bruise. I'm not a person who likes to let things go, be it clothes or cards or *people*. And when I moved away from my sisters and the only home I'd ever known, it felt more important to hold on to things than ever. Sometimes the people tied to these memories are a massive disappointment—my sisters for excluding me from calls, Levi for never calling at all. But somehow I think it would hurt worse, to throw them away.

Levi swallows, then crumples his ice cream cup and looks at me. Really looks at me. Then he says, "I have a confession."

"What?"

"Your eyebrows are blue."

It's the last thing that I expect him to say.

"Berkowitz!" I laugh.

I open my phone's camera and examine the situation. Sky-blue paint indeed covers my eyebrows and I cannot believe I've been walking around the city like this. I should be mortified. But honestly? I'm kind of rocking it. Paired with the retro Keith Haring shirt I'm wearing, it feels more like a creative choice than a mistake. Is there a metaphor here? I don't know. But I do know that one of the many things I appreciate about Levi is his ability to read between the lines, to take my cue, to not force conversation. He just looks at me and knows what to say. Whatever happened, we still have that.

Levi Berkowitz is a fixer of paint mistakes, a disaster of a mini golfer, and now, as our laughter fades, a comfortable quiet.

"You should come to Shabbat next week," Levi says after a beat. "Soph's friends want to meet you."

I frown. "Soph's friends?"

"*Our* friends," Levi amends. "Soph was the first person I met when I moved to New York. She introduced me to her friends, who are now my friends too. I love them—Adam and El—but I've kind of been avoiding them this summer because I don't know how to navigate friendship with them during this break, especially when they were *hers* first and I'm just . . . ."

"An extra appendage?"

Levi nods. "Exactly."

"I get it," I say. "I love my friends too, but they've known each other since, like, kindergarten, and there's just no competing with that kind of history, you know?"

He looks at me. "I know."

And the way he's looking at me, I can tell we're thinking the same thing, that we are each other's history.

*So why didn't you call?* I want to ask.

But I also don't want to ruin my birthday with the answer. So I don't.

"Anyway," Levi continues. "They've been seeing the posts and want to meet you. So Shabbat? Thoughts?"

"Won't that be . . . I don't know. Awkward?"

"Possibly," Levi admits. "But it's also face time around people who will report back to Soph? I can't avoid Adam and El forever and I feel like introducing you to them will only make us seem more believable. Oh, and don't worry about the services. It's a Reform synagogue. Queer friendly. Pretty chill. My mom would also love to have you for dinner after, but no pressure."

"I'm free. I'll come," I say, before I can change my mind.

Even if I'm not a Jewish person who Shabbats anymore, I tell myself I can be one if it means seeing Levi's mom again. Esther Berkowitz is the person who made the best after-school snacks, who bought me my first sketch pad, who I once upon a time brought all my loud feelings to without judgment.

He smiles at me. "Cool."

I reach for my phone to add Shabbat to the spreadsheet and see I have so many missed messages from Natalie and Henry, but also Tessa. I look at the time and—

*"Shit."*

I pop up to my feet because I'm thirty minutes late for my birthday dinner with my sister. I'll be over an hour late by the time I get uptown. She's going to be so pissed. Levi says to go, that he can handle the photo and will send me the draft before he posts anything. It's a testament to how panicked I am that I trust him and sprint with my painting toward the subway. Ten minutes later, while seated on a train and sending a string of apology messages to Tessa at each stop, my phone vibrates with screenshots of the draft post from Levi—our mini-golf scorecard, our vegetable garden canvases, and a candid of me on the mini-golf course, bent over laughing. I don't remember him taking that.

I'm about to pick it apart when I read the caption:

*HBD to my first best friend*

I look at the photo set that Levi curated of my birthday again and all I can think is, *Maybe you're still my best friend.* And while this date was very much fake, these feelings—*friendship* feelings—are definitely not.

## NINETEEN

**W**ho's Levi?"

This is how Natalie greets me a few days later when I answer her FaceTime call, with a question that mirrors her most recent text I never answered. Her mouth is pressed in a line. Her energy right now? It's giving the same as Tessa's energy when I showed up an hour late to my birthday dinner.

She's pissed.

"Fitz?"

I consider my response to this question. How I want to handle this situation. On the one hand, I can't wait to tell Levi that Dani mentioned him to my friends. But on the other, I now see that I got so wrapped up in our exes' reactions to the fauxmance . . . I didn't consider, not once, how this fake relationship would intersect with my real ones.

"Oh!" I say, settling on keeping my voice light, breezy, casual. "Oh my God, Nat, it's such a New York story. Levi's an old friend. I haven't seen him since he moved away the summer after fourth grade . . . and, well, he lives here now. We legit bumped into each other on the subway like a meet-cute in a Nora Ephron movie."

Natalie cocks an eyebrow.

It reads: *Still pissed.*

"He's, like, my Henry," I continue. "Or *was.* I don't know what we are now."

She frowns. "I'd never use Henry as a rebound. So."

"Whoa! Harsh. I'm—"

"Also? If that's all this is, why did I hear that you kissed him from Henry, via Danica? Remember Danica? The girl you went on hiatus for? Wait. Why are you even still on hiatus if you're over her?"

"Because I'm *not,*" I admit, letting the rest of the words I've been holding back spill from my lips. "I only kissed Levi to make Dani jealous. He has a girlfriend. Well. They're on a break. So we figured if we're going to hang out anyway then why not make it seem like we're together to make our people jealous?"

"You think that will work?" Natalie's judgment is obvious from her tone. Um. She's in no position to judge me. Natalie Jacobson has executed some pretty unhinged schemes in the name of love and a school musical.

"Considering you're asking me about Levi? Yeah, I think it already is."

Confirmation that this information has infiltrated my friend group is a major development. I mean. You're not over someone if you're going out of your way to talk about who they're kissing.

"Fitz!"

"What?"

"That still doesn't explain why I'm only learning about this *now*. You're on hiatus from social media . . . not your friendships."

There's no judgment in her voice anymore.

She's hurt.

"You're right."

Natalie's expression softens. "This makes so much more sense. I'm sorry I jumped to conclusions. I just miss you and I love you and I want to hear about major news of the kissing variety from *you*, okay? Even if—no, *especially* if—it's because you cast yourself in a rom-com."

"Henry can't know."

Natalie agrees. "Obviously."

I nod at my phone, processing that I told Natalie the truth and it could very well blow up in my face. Is Natalie even capable of keeping a secret from Henry? I've never asked her to. But he's too close with Dani and I can't risk putting him in the middle of this and sabotaging a plan that's very much working.

As if Natalie is reading my mind, she says, "You can trust me."

So I choose to.

Besides, Natalie keeping me posted about Dani is a great way to gauge how well the fauxmance is working.

"Thanks, Nat."

"Always," she says. "So, tell me more about Levi. You reconnected on the subway?"

"I didn't even recognize him. I thought he was, like, a follower."

*"No."*

I tell her the whole story, from losing him on the subway to finding him again in the fountain.

"—and the kiss was impulsive, but being around Levi? Scheming together in the name of love? It's the only thing that feels good right now."

"Besides FIT, right?"

"Of course."

Okay, that's a blatant lie, but I can only confess so much truth. Classes this week focused on some best business practices for launching a brand, from ethical distribution to website setup and SEO, everything I wanted to learn. Yet I came out of all of it as uninspired as ever.

I'm trying to internalize Levi's advice.

*Sometimes art takes the time it takes.*

I just wish it could take less of it.

"Levi was actually the first person to call me Fitz," I say, changing the subject.

"How have you never mentioned him?"

"I don't know. It was so long ago."

I brush off the question. I prefer to keep those memories tucked in a box under my bed because they end with how *lonely* I was after he left. Without him, I was a girl named Fitz who didn't fit. Not with her too-loud colors and feelings, her unapologetic opinions, her crushes on girls, boys, everyone.

"Can I Insta-stalk him?" Natalie asks. "Please?"

"Sure. He's a pretty popular plant influencer, actually. Thyme Is on My Side is his handle."

"You both have pun handles? Stop it," she says as she taps her way to his page. "Okay, this is adorable. But it's all plants! Where is *he*? What's his last name?"

I swallow. "Berkowitz. But his personal account is private. So."

"He's Jewish too?"

I nod. "He invited me to Shabbat tonight."

Natalie drops her phone, the picture going black as it collides with the bedspread. "You never Shabbat."

"Well, I do tonight and I'm meeting his friends. What am I supposed to wear?"

Her eyes widen as the video resumes. "You're asking *me* for fashion advice?"

"*Shabbat* fashion advice," I clarify. "Just to, like, fit in."

"How observant is he?"

I repeat Levi's descriptors. Reform, queer friendly, pretty chill. Natalie lives for this opportunity to guide me through a fashion crisis . . . until Reid beeps in. We haven't settled on a full outfit, but of course, she has to go.

It's fine.

Shabbat services start in an hour, so I tear apart my closet, alone, until I settle on a mauve pleated maxi skirt paired with a lightweight cream sweater, and flat floral mules, inspired by an eleventh-hour Pinterest rabbit hole. It's neutral—neither too casual nor too formal. A look that conveys, *I am Jewish enough to be here.*

At least thanks to clothes, I can always, *always* look the part.

Due to a weather catastrophe and navigational difficulties, I'm late.

This time it's not entirely my fault. It started to pour the moment my mules stepped out of my building and touched the pavement. So like any reasonable human, I ran back inside to grab my umbrella. But I knew walking would only result in showing up to Shabbat looking like a drowned rat. So to the subway I went, but . . . to the subway everyone went. I missed my stop at First Avenue, unable to squeeze through damp bodies before the doors closed. So then to Brooklyn I went. By the time I turned around and resurfaced, the sky had cleared as if it had never rained at all.

After dropping my umbrella in a metal bin at the door, I step inside the sanctuary. Levi is in the third row chanting along to "Lecha Dodi" with the congregation, an empty space beside him. I move toward it, grateful that there are other stragglers coming in with me. Once close, his botanical kippah comes into focus, the same one he wore when we were kids.

It fits now.

I step into the empty space beside him and whisper, "I'm *so* sorry."

"You didn't miss much," he whispers back, waving away my apology. "I'm just so happy you made it."

And that's it.

He doesn't make me feel bad or insist on an explanation like everyone else does.

Levi is just happy that I'm here.

I, on the other hand, am unsure how I feel about being here. My family doesn't do Shabbat—or religion in general. I'm pretty sure that resisting religious institutions is one of the few things my parents have in common. Mom grew up Conservative Jewish. Dad was raised Irish Catholic. I am both. I am neither. It depends on the day, the context. I am Jewish, but my name is not. I am Catholic, but I begged for a bat mitzvah. My sisters all had them because at that point in Mom's life she was still trying to please Grandma Dee. By the time it was my turn Mom was over it, but I still wanted one.

I sit and reach for a siddur. I don't chant because no one needs to hear me sing, but I do follow along during the service, whisper the blessings as past Shabbats with Levi's family resurface in fragments—the sound of my giggle every time Levi's kippah slid off his head, the glow of lit Shabbat candles back at Grandma Jo's bungalow, the taste of her homemade challah. Levi sings the entire service beside me, his childhood voice replaced by a smooth tenor. It's good. Levi's voice. Shabbat.

"I haven't been since I used to go with you," I blurt as soon as the service concludes, like it's a confession.

Levi closes his siddur. "Oh."

"I think I missed it. Grandma Jo made the best challah."

He nods. "She did."

"Remember the bake-offs we had?" I ask.

"As if the trauma of jalapeño challah isn't burned into my brain."

I laugh. "Challapeño! A delicacy."

"Hello? Earth to Leviii," a voice to his left sings. "Do we have to introduce ourselves or . . . ?" Honestly, I was so focused on the services, on the memories, I didn't even notice the sets of eyes watching our interaction. The first set belongs to a light-skinned Black kid donning the most incredible pink pinstripe trousers. The second set sits below the pierced eyebrow of a white kid slaying a black sleeveless maxi dress and scuffed Docs.

"Meet Adam and El," Levi says.

Right. His friends.

The whole reason I'm here.

"Elodie Sweeney," Eyebrow Piercing says, extending a hand. Sophie's cousin, according to the primer Levi gave me over texts. "It's so nice to confirm that you are, in fact, real."

"I love you," Adam blurts.

"He means If the Shoe Fitz," Elodie clarifies.

It will never not blow my mind, this kind of recognition. "Thanks! Your pants are incredible."

Adam blushes. "Really? Because I made them! Well, flipped them. Like you."

Elodie claps Adam's back. "A-plus job playing it cool, Greene."

He laughs. "I deserve that. Sorry."

I wave away his apology. "I short-circuit whenever I'm perceived in real life. You're not talking to the epitome of cool, I swear."

"It's true. Fitz assumes everyone wants a picture with her," Levi teases.

"Hey!" I don't think, I just smack his arm with my clutch. "Some people do!"

"I do," Adam admits.

Everyone laughs as we exit the sanctuary and congregate in a small function room for the blessings over grape juice and challah that kick off the oneg. And that laughter is like the serotonin boost that comes from every like on a post I'm unsure of when I press send. So I can relax.

Somewhat.

"So. How'd y'all meet?" I ask.

"Soph introduced us," Adam says. "A friendship forged when she matchmade us via *Fiddler on the Roof.*"

"She got rush tickets," Levi clarifies.

"A true Yente moment," Elodie says.

"Been pretty much inseparable ever since," Adam says.

"Pretty much."

It's a lot to process, this super-Jewish friendship meet-cute, the way Adam casually name-drops Sophie, reminding me that Levi's people are hers, too. It's so easy to be with him when we go on plantscapades and exist in our bubble built on nostalgia and Sophie is just an account on the internet. It's not as easy at East Side Temple, where I'm dressed in a sweater that makes my skin itch and resisting the urge to pull out my phone to look up what "yente" means. It's just a word, but it feels like a reminder that I don't actually fit.

Not at Shabbat.

Not in Levi's real life.

Suddenly, it's so much, being here with them.

Adam says, "Okay, seriously, I really would love a photo?"

"Of course!"

I may not know what a yente is, but I do know how to pose for a photo. It's such a relief, and at least Levi is a buffer.

Until he says, "Be right back."

And then disappears into the crowd.

I try to stay in my element as Elodie snaps shots of us in various poses.

"I *love* these," I declare as we flip through them after.

In my favorite shot, my arms are wrapped around Adam's torso because he's, like, a whole foot taller than me. It's not a model shot, but I'm learning to appreciate more candid photos for what they are and a part of me misses this. Capturing a moment in time that's just for me or my friends. Still, I tell Adam to tag me because although I don't miss the pressure to post when I have nothing to say or share these moments that could just be for me, I do miss the tags, the small digital connections I've made with my followers, and I want to have that with him when my hiatus is over.

After Adam tags me and posts, someone says his name and he's pulled into another conversation, leaving just me and Elodie.

"You just made Greene's life," she says, her voice flattening now that it's just us.

"I'm glad," I say, choosing to ignore this shift in energy. But my eyes scan the room, searching for Levi.

"Levi's had a rough year, between his dad and Soph, you know?"

I blink. Is this a test?

Elodie smirks, as if satisfied that I don't know. It creates a fissure in my filter. But when Levi returns, double-fisting tiny cups of grape juice, he either doesn't notice the tension or chooses to ignore it. He offers a cup to me and I take it, wordless as Adam returns to our circle. He says something that makes Levi laugh, but I'm not sure what. My heart is beating loud in my ears, Elodie's words looping in my brain. Levi hates social media, but he filters too. I don't know him anymore, even if it feels like it. Not like Elodie. Or Adam. Or Sophie. Shit. I don't even know what a yente is. I don't belong with them. I—

Levi interrupts this spiral, wrapping his hand around my wrist to pull me to a quiet corridor.

"You okay? You look paler than usual."

"What's a yente?" I ask.

Levi's mouth quirks, surprised. "Yente is a character in *Fiddler on the Roof*."

"Oh."

Dani had been introducing me to musicals, but we hadn't made it to *Fiddler* yet.

"She's a matchmaker. But a *yenta* is, like, every stereotypical Jewish mom on network television. People think yenta means matchmaker, because of Yente. But that's not true! A matchmaker is a shadcham. And—"

"Berkowitz."

"Yeah?"

"Don't leave me again, okay?"

"I won't."

Levi's hand is still on my wrist, his fingers pressed against my pulse. We stay like this, as the once-quiet hallway becomes an echo of blessings led by the rabbi and her wife. But even with Levi it's still too much. Shabbat with my former best friend. Current fake boyfriend. My filter cracks. So I focus on the rhythm of the prayers, the repetition of Baruch ata Adonai until the beat of my heart steadies and he drops my wrist. As we raise our tiny cups over whispered prayers and spoken promises, the panic subsides, making way for embarrassment that crashes into my rib cage.

And for the rest of our time at East Side Temple, Levi doesn't leave my side.

It's me who slips away, mortified, without saying goodbye.

## TWENTY

*I* make it three blocks before his name glows on my shattered screen. I hide the notification and focus on the slap of my mules on wet concrete as I follow the blue line on my maps app toward the subway. I swipe my MetroCard while a train approaches the station and my heart pounds *get away, away, away* in my chest. Away from prayers I know in a language I don't understand. Away from small talk with people who are not mine. Away from the boy who saw my filter crack and held my hand through words that will without a doubt keep me up at night.

*Don't leave me again, okay?*

Fuck. What was *that*?

I exit the subway and make a snickerdoodle stop at Insomnia as another apology for being an hour late to my birthday dinner. I blamed it on the clothes, on being so absorbed in my work that I lost track of time because it was a better excuse than the truth. She said she understood. Dinner was fine.

We're *fine*.

But we'll be better after snickerdoodles.

I enter an empty apartment. *Working late,* reads a Post-it note on the kitchen counter. It's lowkey triggering. As Mom and Dad exist on opposite schedules most days, they communicate any household updates via Post-it notes as if it's still the nineties and we don't have these magical devices called cell phones.

Whatever.

I eat a snickerdoodle, sink into Gertie, and sit in silence for maybe five minutes before it's too loud. So I call Maya, my most Jewish sister, because maybe she can remind me how to be Jewish so I don't feel so out of place the next time I'm in a temple. *Next time.* It surprises me that I think there will be a next time, that part of me wants there to be. Because I think I missed it. Shabbats with Levi. Even if I don't know all the Jewish things that Levi and his friends do, I can learn, and then I'll fit—

"Fitz?" Maya answers on the final ring, concern in her voice. "Is everything okay? I'm at Shabbat."

"Oh." I completely forgot that Maya would likely still be at services because time zones. "I'm fine. Sorry! I was actually . . . just at Shabbat too."

The background noise softens to a dull hum, like maybe Maya stepped outside. "Really? Wait. Are you becoming more observant?"

"I don't know. I went with a Jewish friend and it felt good, but also so confusing?"

"I'm sure. Mom was so over Shabbat by the time you came around."

"Exactly."

"Didn't you used to go to services sometimes with the Ber-kowitzes?" Maya asks.

"Yeah. I remember the prayers and stuff. It's not about that. . . . It's more about, I don't know, the cultural stuff? I was the only one in a conversation who didn't know who Yente was."

Maya snorts. "Even if Mom was the most observant Jew, she'd still hate musicals and you wouldn't know that."

"True. But . . ." My voice trails off and I take a beat to consider what it is that I'm trying to say. "I guess I just didn't feel like I belonged tonight. I need a crash course on How to Be Jewish."

She laughs at this. "There is no crash course on How to Be Jewish. You *are* Jewish. But I get it. Being with Sarah was super intimidating at first. We'd hang out and she'd make a summer camp reference and I'd wonder if I was Jewish enough to be with her. But I just kept showing up to services. I was willing to learn. You can too, if this is important to you."

It feels like it is, even if I can't quite articulate why.

"Okay."

"Listen, I have to run or I'm going to miss the oneg bless-ings, but we can totally talk about this more another time. I'm here for any and all complicated Jewish feelings—and I know Sarah would love to chat it out too. But every Jewish person I know has felt either too much or not enough. It's the universal Jewish experience."

"Thanks, Maya."

"Of course! Love you, Fitzy."

Maya hangs up and while I'm still not sure if the mild panic attack was the result of complicated Jewish feelings or even more complicated *Levi* feelings, it felt good to talk some of it out with her. I miss talking things out with Maya. She's the best at that. So it must be about the Jewish feelings. It *must* be.

As I'm attempting to form an explanation text to Levi, the apartment door swings open and Tessa spots the *I'm sorry* on the table. "You can't just buy me snickerdoodles every time you fuck up."

Um.

Maybe we're *not* fine.

"I mean," she continues. "You can, but it doesn't just change the fact that I'm kind of pissed about your birthday."

I blink. "What?"

Tessa drops her backpack on a chair, then gets peanut butter from the fridge to slather onto a snickerdoodle. "I'm trying to spend actual time with you . . . but it just feels like you're using me for a place to crash. Which *sucks*."

Excuse me? I'm the one who comes uptown every weekend, even on *my* birthday. It's not like she ever comes down to me. *She's* the one busy with weekend labs, or talking to our sisters, or going on rebound Tinder dates. I said no to Pride, but every other weekend I've been here.

*I* am the one who is trying.

"That's not fair, Tess."

She holds up one hand and pinches the bridge of her nose with the other, cutting me off. "Forget it. I had a shit day and my head feels like it's going to split in half and I'm a bitch when I have a migraine."

"Go lie down," I order.

Because even though I want to talk about this, once her attitude fades I see the pain on her face. Tessa was diagnosed with migraines in high school, after Maya and Clara had already moved out. Mom and Dad knew they would probably be at work at some point when Tessa had an episode, so I had to learn what to do. Dad taught me, walked me through the science so I understood what works and *why* it works. Ice has a numbing effect. Heat can reduce muscle tension. Caffeine can help, but just a little. It's been a minute since I've been with Tessa during an episode, but I still know what to do. So I prepare a cold compress and a cup of coffee.

"Thanks," Tessa says, sipping the coffee in bed.

"Sure."

"Sorry I snapped at you."

"It's fine, Tess."

We say good night and I close the door behind her. Nothing shuts down sister bickering faster than one sister being in actual, physical pain. But part of me wonders what would've been said, if we hadn't been interrupted by a migraine. Would I have called bullshit on Tessa?

Probably not.

Still. She believes she's trying to spend time with me. I'm

definitely trying to spend time with her. How can we both want the same thing and still feel so off? Where is the disconnect coming from?

I don't know.

I flop onto Gertie to ruminate on this, but see that Levi is three missed calls and too many texts on my shattered screen, and their tone is progressing from confusion to concern to actual panic. Oh my God. Levi has me, like, starring in the next episode of *Dateline*. As the *victim*. I . . . am a terrible fake girlfriend.

> sorry i bailed
> 9:26PM

> i forgot a tampon because i am an actual
> human disaster!! and then i just, like,
> really needed to lie down
> 9:27PM

> i must've crashed. don't hate me!! cramps
> are an asshole!!
> 9:27PM

> can we reschedule dinner? I feel AWFUL
> bailing on esther! & u!
> 9:28PM

With a terrible fake excuse. My period cramps *are* an asshole. Just not currently.

OH.
9:30PM

that's it??
9:31PM

> . . . do you have a uterus, berkowitz?
> 9:32PM

Jesus, Fitzgerald
9:32PM

You just LEFT. I thought there was an emergency!
9:32PM

> there WAS! a uterus emergency!
> 9:33PM

Why do I send Levi back-to-back texts with the word "uterus" in it? Why is it so much easier than typing the truth? Maybe because it shouldn't be so easy for him to crack my filter. And I can't let it happen again.

Well. You could've told me that you felt shitty
9:35PM

Is there anything you need? I can run to a duane reade
& swing by your dorm
9:35PM

What?
I ghosted him. Flaked on his mom.
Yet he's offering to go on a pharmacy run for my nonexistent period cramps?

honestly? i just need to curl up in
bed with a heating pad and
project runway reruns
9:36PM

OK. Feel better!
9:37PM

See you Sunday?
9:37PM

uterus dependent!
9:38PM

I need to stop texting. I need to stop thinking. Over-analyzing every interaction with Dani has me way too in my head with everyone else too.

So I set my phone to silent and put on *Project Runway* until I crash. But I can't stop one thought from making its way in. Even though my filter cracked, when Levi saw it, saw *me*, he didn't pull away.

I did.

# TWENTY-ONE

**S**unday is a new kind of plantscapade—not a rescue mission, but a delivery route. I spend the afternoon following Levi around the West Village and collecting content of us bringing now-healthy plants to their forever homes. Sometimes it's a brand-new home with a seasoned plant parent. Other times it's returning a plant to its prior (murderous!) owner after a brief lesson on best practices to avoid a repeat offense. Levi says that Repot & Rehome always gives people the option to get their plants back . . . but I'm skeptical of returning plants to the people who are the reason they needed to be rescued.

"What if they just end up hurt again?" I ask, after we return a monstera to an apartment on Cornelia Street.

"I had the same thought at first, but it happens less often than you'd think. In most cases, people want to learn and do better by their plants. Everyone deserves a second chance, right?"

I can't really argue with that.

After delivering six plants to their hopefully forever homes, we get bubble tea and sit on a bench in Abingdon Square, a tiny park nestled on the corner of 12th Street and 8th Avenue that's less square and more triangle. Not even a quarter of an acre, yet home to more than forty species of plants, according to Levi.

"It's one of the oldest parks in the city," he says in his tour-guide voice that I'm growing fond of. "The land was fenced off in the 1830s, but the landscape design wasn't executed until the 1880s. The architects also worked on Prospect Park."

I snap a photo of the park for our next post. "You are a whole encyclopedia of plant and landscape knowledge, Berkowitz."

His neck flushes pink. "Am I rambling again?"

"Yeah, but it's cool. I'm into it."

"It *is* cool. It's kind of my dream, to be a landscape architect and create spaces like this."

"When did plants . . . ?" My voice trails off as I consider how to best phrase what I'm trying to say. "I guess I don't remember plants being such a thing for you."

"They weren't."

I nod. "So when? Tell me your Plant Boy origin story."

Levi shrugs. "Somewhere between Allen and here. We moved around a lot and I couldn't take people with me, but I could take plants? I don't know if that even makes sense."

"It does."

"Yeah?"

I nod. "It's clothes for me. Before I moved, my sisters all

came home the same weekend to help clean out the house. So much of their stuff was sorted into donate and trash piles and I just panic-grabbed as much of it as I could pack. I always loved fashion, but I didn't get serious about it until that first summer in Massachusetts and . . . now *I'm* rambling, but I guess what I'm trying to say is that I get it, needing an antidote to loneliness."

Levi looks at me. "That makes sense."

"What?"

"I was never lonely in Allen," he says.

His eyes meet mine, his expression so serious as those six words hang in the air between us. I need a beat, so I sip on my tea. Maybe I'm still tender from Shabbat, but he can't just say shit like this when *he's* the one who left and never contacted me. But he isn't the one who fled on Shabbat. And I'm pretty sure he won't flee now. So maybe it's time to finally just ask.

"So why—?"

I don't get to finish the question that has been eating away at me since recognizing him as the subway pulled away, because out of nowhere, the sky splits open. It's not cute rain that we can co-opt for another curated romantic moment. It's a bone-soaking downpour that wasn't predicted by my phone when I quadruple-checked the forecast. We run into the grocery store across the street, drenched, and I regret my fashion choices because my very white tank top . . . is quickly becoming a very see-through tank top. Maybe it's not as dramatic as I think it is?

Nope! I catch Levi averting his gaze so fast it pretty much confirms that I could be arrested for, like, indecent exposure or something.

He unzips his backpack and holds his rain jacket out to me. "Here."

Of course, Levi Berkowitz is prepared for a flash flood at any moment. I take the jacket, put it on, and zip it all the way to my chin, attempting to play it somewhat cool. "You're a hero."

He scrunches his nose and waves off my words. "Summer showers are becoming more unpredictable."

I nod, ignoring the pink tint of his cheeks. "I will never slander your cargo shorts again."

"You are a shit liar."

"So do we just wait this out?" I ask, ignoring him.

Levi frowns at his phone. "Wait out a flash flood warning in effect until midnight?"

"Seriously?"

"Let's just book it to the L and figure it out from there. It's not too far."

It should be a five-minute walk, but my footwear choice—white platform sandals—is less than ideal for booking it or dealing with massive puddles at every street corner. It's impossible to avoid them all. Ugh. And if ruining these shoes isn't enough of an indication that the universe hates me, when we finally do arrive at the L station, it's caution-taped off due to planned service changes.

"Fuck," Levi mutters.

"What now?" I ask.

Levi takes my hand. "We run."

Rain is *so* much cuter in the movies.

We spend the next ten minutes fully sprinting all the way across town along 14th Street, not stopping until we reach my dorm and the elevator doors close behind us. Once inside, Levi releases my pruning fingers and removes his streaked glasses. I don't run on principle, so catching my breath once the adrenaline wears off? It's a struggle! Water drips from everywhere— our backpacks, our clothes, our hair. I watch it puddle at my feet as the elevator takes us up and note that my once-white sandals are now concerningly brown.

"What did I step in?"

Levi's nose scrunches. "I promise you don't want to know."

*Ew.*

Levi and I were planning on hanging out at the dorm tonight in the hopes of more face time with Dani anyway, and at least a flash flood means she can't run out this time. I didn't envision being this wet as part of the plan, but I'm not about to let that ruin the best opportunity we've had yet. As we get closer to my suite, I hear familiar piano notes and the cackle-snort that cracks my heart in half.

"Is that *Shrek: The Musical*?" Levi asks.

"You're two for two, theater kid," I say.

I push open the door to my suite to see Dani, Em, and two

unfamiliar faces sitting in front of the television in the common area, their backs to us, absolutely losing their minds over the pro-shot of *Shrek: The Musical*. It's so reminiscent of our movie musical nights, and I'm not sure if I want to scream or cry or throw up knowing that Em has definitely received a dissertation on Sutton Foster's career now.

"You're missing the *best*—"

I drop my backpack on the floor and the sound cuts Dani off midsentence, causing everyone's eyes to shift from the television screen to me.

"Already seen it," I say.

Dani's eyes flick down to my fingers intertwined with Levi's and she bites her lip. "Oh."

"You're not Cal," someone wearing thick charcoal eyeliner and bangles up to their elbows says.

"Nope! I'm Fitz. Em's roommate."

I choose my words with precision because saying "Dani's ex" out loud would make it real. Besides, "roommate" sounds cool, unaffected, disinterested, exactly what I'm going for. Bangles introduces themself as Nina with a small wave and the other person, who's leaning hard into Y2K fashion in a tube top and low-rise jeans, is Yelba. Em introduces themself and their pronouns to Levi, who offers a tentative wave before doing the same.

"Sorry to interrupt! We were caught in the storm and sought the closest refuge."

Dani shrugs. "Fitz. It's cool. This is your room too."

Now she's the one who's cool, unaffected, disinterested.

I swallow. "Well, Levi is going to wait out the storm here with us."

Dani nods, now fully in character as *chill roommate*. "Okay."

"Okay," I repeat.

Dani is still looking at me and I swear there's this *energy* between us. But then Levi releases my hand, and I miss while trying to grab it again. It's awkward. We're awkward. It occurs to me that the first introduction only felt like a success because Dani left before I could melt into an awkward puddle of feelings. Curating a photo for Sophie to see from over a thousand miles away is a million times easier than acting out a full scene in person.

"Well. I need to go peel myself out of this dress. I'm, like, so wet."

"Same," Levi says.

Excuse me while I throw myself back into the flash flood.

Dani fixes her attention toward the dance break on the screen while Nina and Yelba look at each other with expressions indicating that this is going about as well as I think it is. Em reaches for an open beer can on the table and takes a long sip, but then stands and walks up to us.

"I have clothes that should fit-ish," they say.

"Oh." Levi waves off the offer. "You don't have to—"

But Em is already halfway to our room. We follow behind them and I'm mixed emotions. Em is the person between Dani and me. Em is the roommate who has been indifferent to my existence from the moment they claimed the bed by the window. Em offering dry clothes to Levi is too nice. . . . There has to be a catch.

But there doesn't seem to be. Em opens a dresser drawer and pulls out a pair of black joggers and a Harry Styles T-shirt. Damn. Em is a Styler? In another universe, we're besties.

"Thanks," Levi says.

They shrug. "It's chill."

Em leaves us, returning to Dani and closing the door behind them.

"Smooth," Levi says.

I throw a towel at him. "Shut up."

Levi's laughter infuses some levity into this awkward situation. "What are we doing?"

"A shit job. You let go of my hand."

"You were cutting off circulation," Levi retorts, before checking his phone.

His screen indicates three missed calls from his mom. It prompts me to check my phone and I find unread texts from Tessa, checking that I made it back to the dorm safely before it started dumping rain. *Also, you still make the best coffee*, she texts last, the closest I will get to a thank-you for taking care of her the other night. Not that I need one. We're sisters. So I just let her know that yes, I'm at the dorm and safe, while Levi returns his mom's call.

Esther answers on the first ring.

"Hi, Mom. Sorry. I'm safe. Yeah, I'm with Fitz. Hold

on—" Levi removes the phone from his ear and turns speaker-phone on. "Yeah. You're on speaker now."

"Ava Fitzgerald, you still owe me a dinner."

"I know."

Esther's voice is the best sort of familiar.

"It's a mess out there," she says.

"Yeah," Levi says. "I'm going to miss curfew if it keeps up."

"I would say so."

"I'll be home as soon as the rain dies down."

"It isn't going to anytime soon. The warning has been extended until the morning."

"Shit," Levi mutters.

"Honestly, I'd feel so much better if you'd just stay put for the night."

"I can't just crash—"

"We have a couch," I interject.

Levi's eyebrows rise. "Are you sure?"

"Nope! Go swim home."

He makes a face, but with Esther's seal of approval it's decided that Levi Berkowitz is spending the night.

Here.

He goes to take a shower first and I shimmy out of my soaked clothes the moment I'm alone. I wrap myself in a fluffy pink robe that matches the faded ends of my hair and try to wrap my mind around how this night has leveled up to a whole sleepover. Not our first. But the last time? We were ten. Activities included sneaking M&Ms from the not-so-secret hiding spot in the pantry, swing-jumping competitions, and playing make-believe.

A decade later, we are still playing make-believe.

Someone knocks on my door.

*Dani?*

But it's just Levi. "I'm all set."

I open the door, frustrated at my heart for daring to hope. Levi takes a step through the doorframe, smelling like my lavender soap and dressed in Em's clothes, but then he freezes, looking at me as if I'm not wearing the *least* sexy bathrobe. Figures! He's only in character when no one is looking.

"I'll be quick."

Levi blinks. "Cool."

I push past him, hopeful as I close the bathroom door behind me and step into the shower that whatever energy just passed between us can be recreated so Dani can see it. Hot water scalds the skin I'm rubbing raw with a washcloth and I exhale. Showers are a safe space. No filter necessary. In here, I can acknowledge to myself how hard this is. Admit to myself that our entrance was not my best performance. Possibly worse than the time I threw my two left feet into a dance audition for the school musical.

But Levi staying over is a second chance.

We have an entire night to play make-believe.

I can do that.

I exit the bathroom, scrunching my hair with a microfiber towel in my striped shorts and a ribbed tank-top set that I know

Dani loves. I'm composed, confident, and in-character until I walk in on Levi thumbing through the pages of one of the sketch pads on my desk. The one where I create the earliest concepts for outfits. The roughest of drafts that no one ever sees.

"Berkowitz!"

Levi jumps back. "You scared me. Fitz, these are—"

"Private."

I swipe the pad out of his hands and clutch it to my chest, pissed because my sketch pads are for me to brainstorm, to experiment, to let my proportions be off, and just create *badly* first. It's the only space I can let myself draw without judgment because it's for my eyes only. If a concept is shit? No one will ever know. If I didn't have this space, if I thought someone else would look at my works in progress? I would never be able to start or finish anything at all.

Levi takes a step back.

"You're right. I'm sorry."

I blink, super disarmed by his immediate apology because this boundary I set?

Most people call it an overreaction.

My parents.

Tessa.

Dani.

I had a similar reaction when I caught her looking through my sketches the week before AP tests. We were taking a study break. I wanted Hot Cheetos. Dani asked for Cool Ranch Doritos. When I returned to my bedroom with the requested snacks, I found her with that same sketch pad and, um, kind of freaked out. It wasn't cute.

I can still hear the hurt in her voice.

*Seriously? You don't trust me with this?*

I didn't know how to explain to Dani that it wasn't about *trust*. It wasn't about her at all. But Levi seems to get it without me explaining.

"Thanks," I say, and in a weird way, his apology makes me *want* to hand the sketch pad back to him, to tell him more about this creative block that I can't seem to escape. But then I think about our conversation at the oneg and before the storm and how it feels so good opening up to Levi Berkowitz until it doesn't. And besides, it would be a waste of a forced proximity moment, to spend any more of this night with a door between Dani and us.

"We should . . ." My eyes shift toward the door.

"Right."

"Maybe try to look at me like I'm still wearing that hideous robe?"

I exit the room before I can see Levi's reaction. He follows me and we crash the *Shrek* watch party that's still happening. We take a seat on the empty end of the couch and share a blanket, a brilliant create-a-sense-of-intimacy-without-too-much-touching hack if I do say so myself.

"How do you feel about movie musicals?" Nina asks us.

Levi shrugs. "Not all are created equal."

Dani nods. "So true."

Levi gestures at the screen. "It's, like, why can't they all just be released like this?"

"Yes!" Dani agrees. "Democratize Broadway and save us from shit adaptations."

"*Cats* was the last straw," Yelba says.

"It was *Dear Evan Hansen* for me," Levi says.

My eyebrows lift. "You said you just helped out with set design."

Levi shrugs. Add *musical connoisseur* to the list of new things I'm learning about Levi Berkowitz tonight, right next to his ability to respect boundaries and wear the hell out of a pair of joggers. Objectively.

But I think I liked the idea of Levi being a theater kid more than the reality of it, because as a result Dani is definitely paying attention to Levi, but her focus is his every opinion about adaptations, and it's as if I'm not even here. I reach for a tangerine seltzer and pop the tab as Levi asks her if she's seen anything on Broadway yet. She tells him about her internship at the Public and that means something to him. He shares tips for rushing shows that mean *everything* to her . . . and we've officially lost the plot.

I sip on my seltzer as Levi shifts from ranking the worst movie musicals to a critique on Broadway elitism that makes these theater nerds swoon. Even *Em*. Who isn't into guys *or* theater. He doesn't even pause to allow me to enter the chat. *Levi*. Less musical theater discourse! More looking at me like I'm still wearing the fluffy bathrobe!

He doesn't.

Instead Dani looks at me and smiles. "He can stay."

Shit. She's not supposed to *like* him.

*Shrek: The Musical* ends and I have to do something before this hang disperses.

"I—"

My words are cut off by booming thunder.

Then?

The power blows.

"Fuck!"

"Shit!"

"Seriously?"

When five minutes pass and it doesn't flick back on, Nina and Yelba return to their suite to smoke weed as there is, quote, *nothing else to do*. Em and Dani start to clean up the mess of snacks and beer cans on the coffee table by cell phone light, while I think of a way to salvage this. What do people do without electricity?

Before I can come up with something, Dani yawns and moves toward her bedroom. "Choosing an internship that starts at seven a.m. has made me so lame."

What?

Dani and I used to stay up texting until two a.m. on school nights.

Em snorts. "Theater kids. When the show is over, so is the party."

"Seriously," I mutter.

"Sloane is out of town on an assignment, so I can take her bed," they offer.

Before the idea of Dani and Em sharing a room makes me short circuit, Levi says, "No way. I'll take the couch."

"You sure?"

"Positive. I won't wear your clothes *and* kick you out of your room."

"Chill," Em says, then leaves Levi and me alone in the common room darkness, lit only by the glow of our phones as rain continues to pelt the windows in a relentless downpour. Fuck this rain. I retrieve a pillow and extra blanket from my room, stubbing my toe on the doorstop because why not add *maim a toe* to the bingo card of what has gone wrong tonight. I limp over to the couch and sit on the opposite end, so there's a cushion between us.

"Good job," I whisper, sarcasm heavy in my voice.

"Thank you," he says, ignoring my snark.

"You were *peak* theater kid! Why? She's not supposed to like you, Berkowitz!"

"I don't know. I guess I thought playing up the theater thing might make her more jealous? If she knows we have that in common it might make her believe that I'm actually your type."

That . . . makes sense.

"Got it. But let's work on the execution? Next time it'd be cool if you seemed more interested in *me* than an oral history of *Cats*."

"Obviously, you haven't read it. I mean, it's *as told by the original cats.*"

This earns him a pillow to the face.

He stifles a laugh. "Sorry!"

I turn off my phone flashlight to conserve the battery.

Without the artificial light, I can't see anything.

There's a beat of silence as we both adjust, then Levi says, "Actually, I *am* sorry. For looking at your sketches without your consent. I feel awful."

It's the last thing I'm expecting, a double down on the apology.

"It's okay, Berkowitz."

"It's not. I should've let you show me them yourself."

"I wouldn't have."

"Why not?"

"I don't show people less than my best," I whisper.

I'm not sure what it is about this darkness, why it makes me brave enough to say the honest, unfiltered truth to a boy I know so well, to a boy I barely know at all.

"That sounds really fucking exhausting," Levi says, returning my honesty in his soft, tentative way.

It *is.*

But I don't know how to be any other way. It's who I am. Perfect grades. Perfect clothes. Perfect Fitz. But if I'm a person who never shows people less than their best . . . how is it possible to still feel like my best is never *enough*? I don't know. I'm not sure how to articulate this in a way that makes sense, so I don't. I stay quiet and it stretches on for so long I think Levi has fallen asleep.

Until he asks, "Have you always been this hard on yourself?"

No.

Maybe.

Yes.

I wrap my arms around my knees. "People like the perfect picture."

"Maybe," Levi concedes. "But most people also know that the perfect pictures aren't real. I mean, If the Shoe Fitz is just a version of you. Right? You're still a real person behind that perfect persona and even if your followers *think* they know you, they don't. And that sucks for them! Because you're—" He cuts himself off. "Sorry! I don't know why I made this about social media. As you may have picked up on, I ramble when I'm nervous."

"I make you nervous?" I joke.

"Incredibly."

It's another whispered confession in the dark, this one his. I understand completely. Levi is nostalgic yet new, and he makes me nervous too. As a kid, I wasn't a perfect picture around Levi. I was my messiest truth. And he left. I know he didn't choose to leave me, but he never contacted me . . . and that *was* a choice. But now he's here and this friendship we're rebuilding feels as good and as *easy* as it used to be. I don't want to fuck it up. So I bury the question I almost asked in the park yet again because I don't want to be too messy. I don't want him to ghost me.

I don't want to ever wonder where in the world Levi Berkowitz is again.

## TWENTY-TWO

*A* door slam wakes me the next morning. I'm on the couch alone, a blanket covering me. Last night comes back to me in pieces. Levi in joggers. The storm. Our conversation in the darkness. After, Levi chose a new murder-mystery comedy from the Netflix algorithm and extended an earbud to me. I scooted closer to watch the movie on his tiny phone screen, tucking my legs up on the couch and whispering predictions only to fall asleep before the murderer was revealed.

I fell asleep.

On this couch.

With Levi.

Who is now gone.

I stand, rubbing the crick in my neck, and look at my phone as I walk to the kitchen. At least there's a text from him.

**Levi Berkowitz**
had an early plantscapade—
thanks for letting me crash!!
6:07AM

Two exclamation points?

Oof.

I open the fridge.

"Levi's nice."

I nearly drop my phone at the sound of Dani's voice. She leans against the threshold of the tiny galley kitchen, dressed in distressed jeans and a T-shirt with the Public logo on the breast pocket. Her eyelids shimmer gold and match her nails. I swallow hard. No one should look so good this early in the morning. I don't. I'm a messy bun and a chin zit. I reach for the water pitcher so I can look away, then close the fridge.

In my hoarse morning voice, I say, "Thanks for being cool with him crashing."

Dani's eyes meet mine. "I wasn't."

"Oh."

Those two words make me forget why I'm in the kitchen. My brain grasps at straws until I remember the pitcher in my hand. Water. I came into the kitchen for water. I open a cabinet, but even on my tiptoes all the glasses are on a too-high shelf. So Dani steps toward the open cabinet and with her longer reach hands a glass to me. She's just, like, right here, so close I can smell her cherry-vanilla perfume. It evaporates every logical brain cell I possess, that smell mixed with that confession.

*I wasn't.*

She loves me. *It's working.*

But then Dani takes a step backward. "How's FIT?"

"Great!"

My not-yet-finished revision for tomorrow's workshop would beg to differ. While everyone else is beginning to share their partially constructed designs, I'm still stuck at the concept stage. But creative block, impostor syndrome, and the pressure I feel every time I breathe the same air as Mal Burton is not sexy.

"Great," Dani repeats.

"How's your internship going?"

"It's incredible," Dani says, unscrewing the lid on her water bottle. "I mean. Honestly? It's mostly admin. But I also get to sit in on workshops and watch how shows are built from the ground up. It brings back memories of *Melted*. Of . . ."

Her voice trails off.

"Us?"

Dani nods.

Holy shit.

"We were magic onstage. You know?"

"I know."

Dani fills her water bottle as I chew on the inside of my cheek, chew on her words because to me, it was *all* magic— our chemistry on and offstage, our ability to make each other laugh over everything and nothing, our dreams taking us to the same destination. Dani chose me and I chose her back and *that* is magic. She's my person. I am hers. Or I can be. I can be a fun, low-maintenance girlfriend who doesn't spend all day taking pictures. I can do long-distance. I am ready to go the distance for her.

"So. Levi. You two are . . . ?"

I bite my lip.

*It's working.*

"Does it matter?" I say instead.

"It's just surprising."

"What does that mean?"

Dani snorts. "He looks like he walked out of an L.L. Bean ad."

"So?"

Do I tease Levi about his cargo shorts every time I see him? Yes! Is anyone else allowed to? Fuck no! But also, does she seriously think that I'm, like, that superficial? Do I come off as someone who judges romantic prospects based solely on their visual aesthetic?

"Also, Levi is so *nice*," Dani says, her voice low as she takes a step toward me. "Since when do you like nice guys?"

My breath hitches. "I—"

And then Dani's mouth is on mine, rough and hot with desire. She tastes like bubblegum ChapStick and it's muscle memory to wrap my arms around her neck and weave my fingers through her hair, pulling her closer, closer, closer. She opens her mouth, deepening the kiss, her fingers on the hem of my shorts and it's so hot. I've missed this, her, us. So much. I love her so much.

But she breaks the kiss too soon.

Eyes wide, she takes a step back.

Says, "Fuck. I'm . . . so sorry."

Then Dani pivots and exits the scene without another word, leaving me dizzy and breathless and absolutely floating. Because our plan?

It's definitely working.

Or maybe not?

I don't know. It's now Thursday, four days after the storm that resulted in a kiss that has resulted in . . . nothing. Dani is avoiding me again. If I'm in the suite, she's hiding out in her room. If I knock on her door to try to talk, she's always on her way out to a show, to dinner, to a friend hang. It all feels very one step forward, three steps back.

And it's created an environment that's impossible to focus in.

So when Mal calls my name for today's crit, I have nothing to present.

She asks to speak to me after class and really, I should've seen this coming. But even though Levi's words resonated a little in the darkness, in the daylight I'm not ready to stop showing people less than my best. Today, that meant not sharing anything at all. I'd rather disappoint Mal with nothing than show her another "Instagrammable" design.

When class is dismissed and we're alone, Mal pushes her glasses up the bridge of her nose and says, "Explain."

Her tone makes me think maybe *this* disappointment is worse.

"I'm sorry."

"Your apology is appreciated, but I want an explanation."

If I'm being honest, even if the kiss hadn't happened, every time I open my sketch pad, every time I try to be someone worthy of taking up space here . . . I just can't. Minutes become hours and at the end of each session I end with what I started with.

Nothing.

"I just ran out of time."

"Ran out of time?" Mal studies me from her desk, then her expression softens into genuine concern. "You're burnt out."

*No.*

I repeat, "I ran out of time."

Mal presses her lips together. "Crit is for sharing works in progress. Running out of time isn't a valid excuse. Can I see some sketches? You must have something that you can show me."

I shake my head. "I don't."

"Fitz. You're talented or you wouldn't be here, but you have to be able to handle criticism. I'm not here to validate you or let you coast. The entire point of this program is to grow. Do you even want to be here? I can't tell—"

"I want."

"Then why are you blowing this?"

Her tone is so gentle even though the words are harsh. In it I hear an invitation to open up, to be honest.

I open my mouth to speak, but no words come out.

I can't.

So Mal continues, "I want sketches for three designs on

my desk on Tuesday. You still have time to get it together for the final runway show. I can help you, but only if you let me help you. If you can't deliver something, I'm going to have to disqualify you from participating. Please don't make me do that. It's just three sketches. And they don't have to be perfect, they just have to exist. Okay?"

I nod, but I'm already spiraling.

*Three?* I can't even do one.

But if I can't present at the final runway show? If my parents see that this entire summer culminated in *nothing* . . .

No.

That's not an option.

So I need to fix things with Dani. *Now.*

On my walk home, I sign into Levi's Instagram, correct in my assumption that he didn't change the password I gave his account when I created it. I scroll through our carefully curated page. It's some of my best work. We look adorable, Levi and me. Maybe Dani needs to see this. She needs to look at these perfect pictures and feel like I'm slipping away. If one group hang made her kiss me, imagine what all these photos could do.

I may be on hiatus for her . . . but Levi isn't.

So "Levi" sends Dani a follow request.

It's time to double down.

## TWENTY-THREE

S o. Drew Carnegie was a total flop. A six-pack does not an interesting conversationalist make."

Tessa and I are eating dinner at a trendy Mexican spot near Columbia's campus. I skip Shabbat because I owe Tessa a dinner where I'm present and on time. I want her to know that I'm not just using her for a place to crash. So I'm here, listening to her deconstruct every Tinder date she has been on in the last week.

"He opened with questions about my stock portfolio. Asked if it's diversified."

"Is that a euphemism?"

"No! He's an analyst at Vanguard. I'm, like, I barely have a 401(k)."

"That feels like a mistake to admit."

Tessa nods. "It was. By the third drink, he started to mansplain the difference between stocks and bonds."

"Gross."

"I know. Like. I know how to invest. I'm just a broke PhD student who can't afford to."

"Key distinction."

"Exactly."

"So. Did you . . . ?"

She shakes her head. "No."

So far, Tessa has ended each date after three drinks. Some for legitimate reasons. Asher, a talent agent, mentioned he was in an open relationship and spent the entire date talking about his girlfriend. Elliot, a novelist, described his debut as "Ernest Hemingway meets Jack Kerouac." But then there was Graham, a middle school science teacher who at least pretended to be interested in Tessa's brain research. And Nate, the buff vet tech with two floofy Goldendoodles. He was my nonproblematic favorite. When I remind her of this, though, Tessa repeats the same excuse.

"Nate lives in Brooklyn, so it will never work."

"Work? It's a rebound, Tess."

"You sound like Clara."

I shrug, but of course these dates have already been deconstructed with Maya and Clara. Likely via video chat. I swallow a sip of horchata while my phone vibrates three times on the table. *Levi, Levi, Levi.* We haven't seen each other since the storm, but we have another date planned for tomorrow and the stakes feel higher, now that Dani and Levi follow each other. Still, I'm supposed to be present with Tessa. So I silence my phone and flip it facedown.

Tessa asks, "Who's that?"

"Just a friend."

"A *friend*?"

"I—" I cut myself off before I can deflect the question, my initial instinct. Since I showed up outside her apartment, our conversations when we're together have almost exclusively revolved around the implosion of our relationships. So part of me is like, are we not more than this? I didn't know it was possible for two sisters to fail the Bechdel test so hard. But I think Tessa opening up about her post-Bennett dating life is her way of trying.

And I want to try too.

"Do you remember Levi Berkowitz?"

She looks at me like, *duh*. "Of course! You were attached at the hip."

"Well . . . he lives here?"

"Seriously?"

I nod. "We've been hanging out?"

Why am I speaking in questions? I don't know. Maybe because "hanging out" feels like both an overstatement and a massive understatement.

"Y'all were the *cutest*. Wait. Define 'hanging out.'"

I shrug. "He's just been showing me around the city."

"Where?"

"Um. The High Line, an art studio in Tribeca, mini golf on the pier—"

"Oh my God. You're rebounding with Levi Berkowitz."

I shake my head. "We're friends."

"He took you to the High Line."

"Levi's just super into plants."

"Righttttt." Tessa's eyebrows rise suggestively as she dips a chip in guac. "Condoms are in the top drawer of my night table."

I choke on my horchata. *Tess.*

"What?"

"It's not like that."

"Yet you are blushing."

I throw a chip at Tessa. It bounces off her cheek and, like, cracks open giggles that cannot be contained. Even if we're only capable of failing the Bechdel test, it's kind of all I ever wanted as a kid, to talk about relationship drama with any of my sisters. So many of my memories are hushed whispers. My sisters together in the bedroom that Maya and Clara shared. Maya closing the door on six-year-old me, saying it's just "big-kid stuff." In so many ways, I still feel like that little kid at the door begging to be let in.

But tonight we're on the same side of it.

After our giggles subside, the rest of dinner is more than fine.

It's good.

"We should do this more," Tessa says, unlocking and pushing open her apartment door.

"For sure."

After slipping out of my shoes, I check on Henrietta, pleased to know that Tessa seems to be listening to my watering advice. Her eyes meet mine and she smirks. *Levi's just super into plants.* I know Tessa is noting this and connecting the dots, as if it's additional evidence that we're more than friends. But honestly? I'd rather Tess think Levi and I are a thing than be on the receiving end of her judgment if she knew the truth.

"Have you seen the new Tom Holland rom-com?" she asks.

"Tragically, no."

"Wanna watch?"

First dinner, now a movie? Is this an actual sister date?

I nod, attempting to keep my tone chill. "Sure."

We change into our pajamas and then Tessa makes popcorn on the stove, like Maya used to before the Met Gala. I choose my favorite corner of Gertie and catch up on the messages from Levi because I still have not-date plans to confirm with my not-rebound before I silence my phone for the night and watch movies until Tessa falls asleep.

**Levi Berkowitz**
So! Sunday
6:32PM

I know we had uptown plans
6:32PM

BUT. Can we go to Brooklyn instead?
6:33PM

> where? why? details?
> 7:46PM

> that is just such a subway commitment
> 7:46PM

Levi's answer is immediate.

> It's a surprise! But it'll be worth it
> 7:47PM

> Trust me
> 7:47PM

I do. Trust him.

So I confirm plans, ignoring the way my stomach flutters at the thought of him planning a surprise for me and how much I like it. Whatever Levi's surprise is, it's for the sake of a cute Instagram post to get Sophie's attention. Obviously. But it's still real friendship, not a rebound like Tessa says. Like, if I'm ever brave enough to show my rough sketches to anyone, I think it will be to him. It's hard to want to show less than my best when everyone in my life is exceptional at what they do. My sisters. My parents. My friends. *Dani.* I want to be seen as exceptional too.

I want to be taken seriously. That's why I take my platform so seriously.

But.

Levi already takes me seriously exactly as I am.

"Ready?" Tessa asks.

My eyes snap up from my phone. "Yeah."

Tessa sits on the opposite end of Gertie. She holds out a bowl of popcorn, M&Ms mixed in, and presses play. I heart Levi's last text, then put my phone facedown on the coffee table. Within ten minutes, Tom Holland's character *dies* and Tessa screams *This is not a rom-com!* at her television, prompting another round of the giggles from both of us. As we laugh I note the romance novels that now line the built-in bookshelves, replacing Bennett's pretentious-as-fuck collection. Tessa has a lot of feelings about romance, the genre, but also whatever is going on with Levi and me. I let her tease me as we tune out this not-rom-com.

Let her be my big sister.

Because it feels so good to just *laugh* with Tessa—and it makes me hope that one day she'll see the version of me that Levi sees too.

## TWENTY-FOUR

*I* meet Levi at the 14th Street F train platform, spotting his cargo shorts in the crowd. They're olive green today, not his typical khaki. He has wired earbuds in and is reading a book and the image is, like, a perfect candid for that Instagram account that features hot dudes reading on public transportation. Objectively. I approach him, but he's so immersed in his book that he doesn't notice. What is this riveting content? I look at the cover. *The Hidden Life of Trees.* Of course.

I tap Levi's shoulder and he closes the book. "Hey! Excited to leave the Manhattan bubble?"

"I don't know why I am. So . . ."

"Well. You should be."

"Berkowitz."

"What?"

"Tell me!"

Levi shakes his head, his lips pressed together to keep from blurting out the surprise as he unzips his backpack and puts his book away. Not telling me? It's killing him. We both know it. As kids, never did I open a present from Levi Berkowitz and not already know what it was. He will crack. He always does.

"Nope."

"I promise I'll act surprised for Instagram."

His eyes snap up to meet mine. "Fitzgerald. Not everything is for Instagram. Okay?"

I swallow. "Okay."

A train approaches the station. I look toward it, processing Levi's new-to-me ability to not spoil the surprise. He offers me an earbud after we step onto the Brooklyn-bound train and I take it. He's listening to *MONTERO* and I kind of love that Levi is listening to Lil Nas X while reading about the secret life of trees.

It's a surprisingly short ride. Not even time to come up with a guess as to what Levi planning a whole surprise that isn't for Instagram could be about. In just six stops, we exit at York Street and are greeted by the view of an overpass that slices through the Brooklyn sky.

"Welcome to DUMBO," Levi says, as we walk parallel to it.

"DUMBO," I repeat.

He nods. "It's an acronym. It stands for 'Down Under the Manhattan Bridge Overpass.' Residents coined the name in the seventies in an effort to deter gentrification. Who would spend millions of dollars to live in a place called DUMBO? Apparently a lot of people, because now it's one of the most expensive neighborhoods in Brooklyn. Which is—"

Levi stops himself midsentence, stuffing his hands in his pockets. "Sorry! I'm using my tour-guide voice again."

"So? I like Tour Guide Levi."

I don't look at him, but I do see the smallest smile in my peripheral vision as we turn onto Pearl Street. I'm not sure what I register first—the up-close view of the underside of the Manhattan Bridge or the dozens of white-canopied stalls that are packed onto the closed-off cobblestone streets. Racks of clothes. Vintage accessories. Antiques. Oh my God. Nestled under the Manhattan Bridge is an entire flea market that's so beautiful and I'm going to have to convince Levi to pause here, just for a minute, before the surprise so I can—

"Surprise!"

Wait.

"This is the surprise?"

"You're surprised!" he says, sounding so proud of himself. "Welcome to the Brooklyn Flea. I know it's not all clothes, but I still thought it could be . . . I don't know. Inspiring?"

I'm so overwhelmed in the best way. "I'm going to need three hours. At least."

Levi nods. "Okay."

"Cool."

Then I bolt for the nearest rack of clothes. It's total sensory overload. I start at a vendor who sells vintage smock dresses in an assortment of lengths and prints that are so seventies. I comb through each one, feeling the texture of the fabric between my fingers. Some have potential, but none speak to me.

"Fitz?"

I jump at the sound of Levi's voice. "Oh! You're still here."

"Where else would I be?"

"I don't know. I thought maybe you had a plantscapade in the area?"

"Are you trying to get rid of me?"

"Sorry, I just assumed . . . this is usually something I do solo."

Levi takes a step back and tries to not look disappointed. "Oh! I mean, if it's part of your process . . ."

I shake my head. "I'm just sparing you. I've been told I'm not fun to thrift with."

"No?"

I skim my fingers along the next rack. "I cannot be casual about it. My process is meticulous and most people become over it very quickly."

Levi thinks he wants to thrift with me. Most people do. At first. But two hours later, when I haven't even made it halfway through searching the racks and refuse to leave, patience tends to wear thin. Natalie will join if and only if it's a trip related to costumes for a school play. Dani? She shops with intention, buying most of her clothes on Depop because she knows she can find what she wants with the assistance of the search bar, which is the entire opposite of thrifting. I tried to show her the magic of it once, taking her to my favorite spot in Boston. It didn't go well. After just *ten minutes*, she was over it, opting instead to check out the bookstore next door.

Levi's mouth quirks. "I am not most people, Fitzgerald."

"Right."

I'm starting to get that.

We weave our way through the vintage stalls and I set the pace. Levi asks questions when I'm not in the zone, like he's actually invested in my fashion takes, but mostly he's content to let me browse and pretend I can afford these clothes. Fifty bucks for a pair of jeans? New York even makes thrifting overpriced. Still, combing through these racks in search of something to transform? Assessing the garments as they are and seeing the potential in what could be? It's true to my process—way less overwhelming than the yards and yards of recycled fabrics that could have been anything in a past life and could become anything in their next.

I'm drawn to a rack of men's button-ups that have bold and fun prints. I've been starting to experiment with incorporating menswear into my own wardrobe. Short-sleeve button-ups that I reconstruct and hem to fit because men's clothes are made for cis men. Not for bodies with short torsos that are experimenting with their gender expression.

Some time passes.

Minutes.

Hours.

I finally look up to see Levi also skimming intently through a rack of button-ups.

And my heart, like . . . flutters?

Shit.

*No.*

I know this flutter. I felt it when I watched Dani perform

a monologue in Miss Bryant's class for the first time. Before Dani, I felt it when Luna slid into my DMs the summer before sophomore year, when Drew asked to sit next to me on the bus freshman year, when Becca whispered "Wanna dance?" during the semiformal on the last night of theater camp.

I *cannot* feel it now.

Not when I'm in love with someone else.

*Dani.*

I won't let a brief flutter bloom into a full crush. No way. We're both committed to our existing relationships. Friends can spend the day together. Friends can plan the most perfect surprises for each other. It doesn't have to evolve into a heart flutter.

I part with the rack of button-ups and walk over to Levi, determined to squash it.

"Is anything speaking to you?" I ask.

"Clothes don't speak to me."

"Cargo shorts do."

Levi snorts. "I set you up for that one."

"I'm serious. Clothing is so personal. It's a choice that we make every day: How am I going to present myself? You choose cargo shorts because they speak to you. Do I have some styling suggestions for the sake of variety? Sure. But I would never suggest ditching them entirely. They are just. You."

*Cool.*

*Good job.*

*Let Levi in on how often you think about his cargo shorts.*

"Styling suggestions?"

"Yeah." I thumb through the button-ups on the bargain rack and there's so much potential. "What about these?" I pull two different shirts that complement Levi's shorts. One is navy with a bold floral pattern and the other is white with a potted-plant print. "Either one would be great if you ever decided to add a profile photo to Thyme Is on My Side."

Levi looks skeptical. "I like to take care of plants. Not wear them?"

"I respect that."

I return the floral print one to the rack, but keep the potted plant one for me, as I can't resist the tiny cacti.

He considers a burgundy windowpane print. "Maybe this one?"

"It's speaking to you?"

His nose scrunches. "Whispering?"

"That's a start."

There aren't any fitting rooms in an open-air flea market, obviously, but the vendor is cool with us trying the shirts on over our clothes for size. As he does, I search the tables for accessories to style a whole look. It'll make for a great Instagram post. Make this moment curated, like every other "date" we've gone on. Sophie will see Levi's transformation and realize that she's losing him. Dani will see me styling someone who is not her and taking fashion seriously off my platform. Perfect. As I search for a piece that goes with the burgundy shirt, I catch Levi looking at his phone, his expression as perplexed as it just was selecting a print that whispers to him.

"Berkowitz? You good?"

"Adam and El are on their way."

Oh.

"Really?"

"Adam refuses to miss an opportunity to thrift with you."

"And Elodie . . . ?"

". . . is absolutely crashing our 'date.'"

He puts air quotes around that word, just to be extra clear that this is not one.

I nod. "That checks out."

"Why? Did she say something to you at Shabbat?"

She did. But I shake my head. "It was more of a vibe."

"She's pissed at *me*, not you."

"Why?"

"Soph."

"That's bullshit. It's not like *you* asked for the break."

Levi stuffs his phone in his pocket, changing the subject back. "It's whatever. Anyway, I still have a shirt that's whispering to me."

"Right."

I keep perusing the stall and try to ignore anxiety that blooms in the pit of my stomach. I'm not prepared to perform, but this is becoming a group thing. A friend hang that dims the flutter but also the spark of creativity I finally felt. I stop at a table of hats and pick up a brown wool fedora, the first one I see. Do fedoras whisper to Levi too? Let's find out.

I circle back to Levi trying on the burgundy shirt and buttoning it all the way up.

I swear, he's going to tuck it in next if I don't stop him.

"Berkowitz!"

He winces. "That bad?"

"Let me just—"

I go into stylist mode. I see how this shirt can work on Levi. So I place the fedora on his head and then my hands are on the shirt. First, I unbutton the sleeves and roll them up to the elbow. Then my fingers are working on the front buttons, undoing them one by one. We're so close, but I don't think. Not about how the last time we stood this close, I asked him to kiss me in the Washington Square Park fountain. Or how if that one meaningless revenge kiss was so good, then . . . what would it feel like to kiss Levi Berkowitz now?

"Fitz?"

I look up at him.

The fedora is speaking to *me*.

Fuck.

"Sorry! It's just, I see this shirt as more of a layering piece. You can pair it with any neutral T-shirt. Just because a shirt has buttons doesn't mean you have to use them. You know?"

Levi swallows. "Noted."

I nod.

Undo the last button.

It's time to take a step back, to assess the look I styled for Levi. But I don't move. I adjust the shirt so that it's even. Perfect. For Instagram. Obviously! Yet even when it is, I'm unable to take my hands off it. I fiddle with the small details on the sleeves and ignore the erratic beat of my heart as Levi removes the fedora and places it on my head.

"Hey! That's part of my vision."

"You wear it better."

It would be so easy to keep holding on to this shirt, to pull him closer, to see what it feels like to kiss Levi Berkowitz when nobody is watching. And I can't help but wonder if whatever is happening to me right now . . . is happening to Levi, too.

*No.*

I can't go there. We're not endgame. I'm not going to ruin our friendship or my getting back together with Dani for a flutter. I have to get this out of my system.

Right now.

So I let go of his shirt, take a step back, and blurt, "Dani kissed me."

Levi blinks. "Oh."

"The morning after the storm."

He processes this information. "Whoa. Wait. Are you breaking up with me?"

"No. I mean. Not yet. She's avoided me ever since."

"She freaked out."

"Yeah."

"Are you okay?"

"Dani is just *so* stubborn. She doesn't want to admit it, but it's clearly working. Us doing this."

"Right."

His tone is flat.

Refusing to read into whatever is happening, I break eye contact and spot a familiar face browsing one of the racks behind Levi. *Bless.* I walk up to him because I need to put space between me and Levi *right now*.

"Trevor? Hey!"

He looks up from the rack. "Hey?"

"Fancy running into you here."

"Students of fashion running into each other at a flea market? I'm shocked."

I ignore the sarcasm in his voice, turning toward Levi. "Levi, this is Trevor. He's in Mal's class too."

"Hey," Levi says.

Trevor acknowledges him with a nod, then steps out from behind the rack. He's carrying two tote bags overflowing with clothes. Holy shit. It's an *incredible* haul. And by my guesstimation, an expensive one. My expression must say it all, because Trevor says, "There are some great deals if you know where to look."

"Clearly, I do not."

"I can show you. If you want?"

"Seriously?"

Trevor shrugs. "Sure."

I look at Levi. "Is that—?"

"Yeah. I'll go check out the garden antiques."

"Cool."

We split up and I'm so grateful for the space, even if I don't understand why Trevor offered to show me around. I've never given Trevor Anderson a single reason to want to hang with me outside of Mal's class. But he is. Thank God. Because I'm not sure what I would've said next otherwise. I love Dani. Levi loves Sophie. That's the entire point. I can love Levi Berkowitz without being *in love* with him. Romantic love is messy. Intense.

I don't want that with Levi.

So I'm not sure why it hurts when I see him remove the burgundy shirt and place it back on the rack before I can even snap a photo.

## TWENTY-FIVE

*N*ot only does Trevor know which stalls are afford-able, but he's also on a first-name basis with most of the vendors. How? I'm not sure, but his arrival is the best thing to happen to my haul, not to mention a wel-come distraction from whatever that burgundy shirt just did to Levi and me.

"Fitz is in Mal's class too," Trevor tells a designer named Vivian Leroux, as I browse their collection of upcycled denim jackets.

"Rad," Vivian says. "Mal is the best. I was in her summer cohort two years ago."

"These are so cute," I say, thumbing the jackets, each one a unique patchwork design.

Vivian smiles at me. "Thanks! What's your handle?"

I hope I'm projecting a confidence that I do not at all feel when I share my Instagram page with Vivian and try to remember to breathe while they scroll through my feed. I don't know Vivian Leroux, but they are a former student of Mal's who has their own stall at the Brooklyn Flea. So of course, I want to impress them.

"I love this," Vivian says, pausing on a photo of me in my rose-gold bomber jacket. "Is it still available?"

"Available?" It takes a moment for it to click. "Oh! No. It's not for sale."

Vivian nods. "I get it. I only just worked up the nerve to set up an online shop. I created so much inventory after my summer at FIT and then just sat on it for a year. But now these jackets are paying my tuition!"

"You are living my dream," Trevor says. Mine too, and I'm so blown away that this super-talented sustainable designer is suggesting that I'm in any way ready to sell my clothes. Nothing about my experience in Mal's class has made me feel remotely ready for that.

"Why did you sit on starting your shop?" I ask.

Vivian snorts. "Impostor syndrome is a bitch."

"Truth," Trevor says.

It really is.

Vivian follows me on Instagram and asks if it's okay to tag me in a story wearing one of their jackets. I didn't expect thrifting to become a networking opportunity, but it feels great. When we say goodbye to Vivian Leroux and are satisfied with our haul, I text Levi where to meet up and Trevor and I share a cronut the size of my face while we wait.

I rip off a piece of doughy goodness. "This was fun."

"I am fun! We're all fun. You'd know that by now, if you put literally any effort into getting to know us?"

"I deserve that."

Trevor's metallic gold eye shadow sparkles in the sun. "You do."

"So why are you being nice to me?"

"Because you are very clearly struggling and I'm not an asshole."

I'm so *thrown* by his words. How he doesn't ask a question or give me room to deflect. It's so disarming, I drop the filter. I mean. He's seen my first shit crit, then my second nonexistent crit. What's the point of bullshitting him? Plus, he agreed with Vivian's statement about impostor syndrome. So it doesn't feel like exposing myself to a follower or not meeting the expectations of my family and friends or Mal to speak the words out loud that I'm terrified to admit to myself.

"What if I'm broken?"

Trevor shakes his head. "Burnout happens."

There's that word again.

Maybe it happens, but not to me.

"It's not that. It's my ex. The breakup."

Trevor looks at me like he's not buying it, then says, "You know, I applied to Mal's program last year . . . but my acceptance letter triggered the worst creative burnout and depression. I'm only here because Mal was kind enough to let me defer a year while I got my shit together."

"What?"

It's pretty much the last thing I expect Trevor to admit. He's so talented. Every evolution of the dress he's been designing for the runway show looks more and more like something

Billy Porter would wear to the next Met Gala. Major Christian Siriano energy.

But he nods. "Yeah. I thought, like, what if applying pressure and expectations to something that used to be just for me ruins everything? Really spiraled out. Didn't touch my sewing machine for months. It was rough."

I ignore the way those words resonate, but also the way they *don't*. I love fashion and I've been spiraling, but I'm not sure I've ever designed something just for me. How many designs have I scrapped because they felt too experimental? Because I was worried about what my followers would think? It's easy to be vulnerable alone with a sketch pad. It's a million times harder to be a work in progress when people are watching . . . and not just watching, but *looking* for flaws, mistakes, aspects to critique.

I swallow. "But now you love it again?"

"I do."

"What changed?"

"I started therapy."

"Oh."

Trevor's laughter reaches his eyes. "You were expecting inspirational bullshit."

"I was."

"I do have one inspo-bullshit line."

"Give it to me."

"'It's about the journey, not the destination.'"

I crumple my napkin. "Oof."

"Cringe, right?"

Maybe.

But it's also exactly how I got into upcycling. Fashion is supposed to be experimental. Sure, I only post finished results. First for my sisters. Then for my followers. But the *fun* has always been in the sketching, the reworking, the trying, and trying, and trying. Yet that's the work that I keep hidden in the pages of my sketch pad. It's a lot to process.

"At least I have a haul to inspire me."

"For sure."

Trevor invites me to tag along to a comedy show that he's seeing with some other people from our class, but I'm not going to ditch Levi so I tell him next time, for sure. We exchange numbers. It sucks to think that I could've had this sooner had I not been so wrapped up in my own drama, but as I watch Trevor walk away, it feels like finding joy in thrifting is a small victory, admitting to someone that I'm struggling and receiving a semi-helpful cliché and a phone number is a small victory, looking forward to being alone with my haul and trying and trying and trying again is small victory. And all these small victories may have been achieved by me but they were made possible by a boy who looked way too good in burgundy who's now approaching me with a haul of his own, Adam and Elodie, and two bubble teas. I swallow the last bite of cronut and shift back into perfect fake-girlfriend mode for this performance.

*Filter on.*

"Hey!" Levi says, then hands a Thai tea to me.

"Confession, we already split a cronut," Adam admits.

"Sorry," Elodie says, with a shrug that indicates she's very much not. "We're assholes."

"It's cool. Trevor and I shared one too."

"Successful flea?" Levi asks.

Successful. Confusing. Who's to say?

I hold up the paper bag that contains my haul. "I struck gold with Trevor. You?"

"Just picked up a couple of planters."

Adam wants to make another loop, but vendors are starting to pack up so he settles for sifting through my haul before we head toward Brooklyn Bridge Park. I notice Elodie's holding a handful of retro vinyl records. Paramore. Grateful Dead. Teagan and Sara. She's so cool. But she's Sophie's cousin, so her interest in being my friend is minimal to nonexistent.

We walk two by two, Levi and me trailing behind Adam and Elodie, as it's impossible to walk these city streets as a group. It's a rare perfect-weather day with a cool waterfront breeze and not a cloud in the sky, so for once I'm not melting.

"Berkowitz?"

"Yeah?"

"Thanks. For today."

Levi scratches the back of his neck. "It's not a big deal."

"It is. Also . . . shouldn't we be walking in a more couple-y way?"

"Oh. Probably," he agrees.

So I loop my arm through his and ignore the flutter that

accompanies this action. We stroll the rest of the way in silence, each step bringing the Brooklyn Bridge more and more into focus until we arrive at a viewpoint that's so worth the hype. The bridge is the focal point in this frame, stretching across the river, the Lower Manhattan skyline serving as its backdrop. It's beautiful—its stone anchorages, their elegant Gothic arches, the cables essential to its structural integrity.

"Holy shit," I whisper.

"Right?" Adam says.

Elodie sighs. "It's enough to remind me that the trash parts of living here are worth it."

Levi doesn't say anything at all, but I feel him watching me. Photos don't do this view justice. I never knew I had feelings about *bridges*. Well, not bridges. One bridge. What it symbolizes. It is here. *I* am here. On the riverwalk crowded with tourists, there's no way I can capture a picture without strangers in the background. But that's okay. Maybe I don't need a perfect picture to remember a perfect moment.

Maybe I don't need a picture at all.

After a beat, Adam and Levi go play tourist, looking through binoculars that line the riverwalk.

Elodie hangs back with me.

We sit on a bench and she looks at me. "Can I be honest with you?"

"You hate me," I blurt out.

Her eyebrows scrunch. "No. I don't."

"Right."

"I just . . ." She trails off, like she's considering how to phrase whatever this truth bomb is. "You and Levi? It's none of my business. But I know Levi. And I know Soph. They've been Soph and Levi since we were fourteen. I know Soph wanted this break, but when she comes home? It's them. It just is."

I keep my gaze on the bridge.

*Why is she so invested in Sophie and Levi?*

But I know I would throw myself in front of anyone who tried to get in between Nat and Reid, so on a certain level, I get it. It makes me want to admit that our relationship is curated. We're not real, so there's nothing to worry about.

Obviously, I can't say that. So what would I say, if we *were* real?

The answer comes quicker than I want to admit. "You're right. It's none of your business."

"I see the way you look at him."

"Okay."

"I wouldn't want to be someone's summer fling."

"I appreciate the concern."

"You do not."

"I do not."

She laughs, surprising me. "Cool."

"Elodie?"

"Yeah?"

"I'm the overprotective friend too, with my people. But in a few weeks, I'm going back to suburbia. In the meantime, I would much rather compliment your style and discuss how *Riot!* walked so *Sour* could run."

Her eyes widen. "You know Paramore?"

I laugh. "My sisters were in middle school in the mid-2000s. I know Paramore."

A deep dive on how our older siblings influenced our taste in music dissipates the tension, but I can't stop thinking about what I acknowledged out loud for the first time. In less than three weeks, I go home with these memories and the uncertainty of whether I'll be back next year. I'm falling in love with a temporary condition. This city.

Dani stays.

Levi stays.

I don't.

I watch him look up at the skyline through binoculars and I feel a *twinge*. Because when our plan works . . . how does friendship work? I mean. Both of our people believe that we've been more than friends. So how can we ever be with them and be friends? Even with the amicable-breakup-post plan, Dani won't be happy if we keep talking. I doubt Soph will, either. To them, we will forever be *exes* to each other. I didn't think this far ahead. I didn't consider what happens after we're reunited with our people and this realization is so much worse than the flutter of a crush. It's a moment of clarity. In order to be with the people we love, our friendship will have to be as temporary as this summer.

I cannot believe I rebuilt a friendship with Levi Berkowitz just to have to break it all over again.

## TWENTY-SIX

I return to my dorm a clusterfuck of emotions and lay out my finds—a variety of printed button-ups, a silk chiffon wrap skirt, a pair of black cargo pants that cinch at the ankles, and a utilitarian taupe jumpsuit. Pieces I selected because they spoke to *me*, not a particular idea or aesthetic. I focus on these clothes. My clothes. Not the burgundy shirt, not my fingers working its buttons, not the way Levi looked at me when I told him about the kiss—

Shit.

I reach for my sketch pad. I owe three sketched designs to Mal and I'm feeling inspired by the flea, by my conversation with Trevor, by the Brooklyn Bridge, so I want to do better than deliver sketches. I want to flip this haul into something. Follow this spark and see what it feels like to design something just for me.

I keep coming back to the button-ups. Upcycling them could be as simple as tailoring them to fit my body or as complicated as ripping them apart at the seams. Some of these prints would look so cool together. Hm.

I've never made my own textiles before.

But.

What if I tried?

Headphones on, I lose myself in the project—sketching flats, then measuring, cutting, and reconstructing two of the button-ups from my haul. I choose the potted-plant print and a dark green with white pinstripes. Working with menswear is a new-to-me challenge, so I use my measurements and three online tutorials to piece them together into a new mixed-print shirt with a hem that should skim the top of my hip.

When it's ready to try on, I style it a few different ways— buttoned and tucked into high-waisted white shorts, unbuttoned with a white tank top over wide-legged cropped denim, tied at the waist over a black maxi dress. It needs to be hemmed a bit shorter and taken out a bit in the bust so that it maintains the unstructured silhouette that I'm going for. But . . .

I think I love it.

I'm so relieved, I burst into tears. I've missed my sewing machine so much, missed being in a creative zone where time is meaningless. It's been impossible since I got here for the critical part of my brain to shut up and let me try. But when it finally did? I transformed the tiniest spark into a full (presentable!) shirt in just a few hours. I can't remember the last time it felt this way.

Fun.

Easy.

Free.

I snap a photo and text it to Levi without overthinking it. If I pretend that the burgundy shirt didn't happen, maybe he will too. Because getting back together with Dani is still a priority. I love her. And today reminded me that there's a countdown clock on my friendship with Levi and I don't want a single moment of what's left of it to be awkward. Like. We're friends. His surprise was nice. Someone doing something nice for me should not make my heart feel like it's going to lowkey explode. Fuck this flutter. I literally don't have time for it.

Levi likes it. Not in words, just with a tap of the photo.

Cool.

I turn my phone off and refocus on the clothes, on making this shirt as perfect as it can be for tomorrow, not forever. When I slip it back on after a few more tweaks and minor adjustments, I check myself out in the mirror.

It fits.

And it feels like *me*.

As I'm me, I'm back to second-guessing everything when Mal calls my name to present the next day. But I stand, swallow the self-doubt, and remind myself that the bar I've set for myself is already on the floor. I can't disappoint her more than I already have. Sunday night, I felt incredible about this shirt. I channel that energy as I drape it over the display mannequin and button it up even though the proportions of the shirt look off on the mannequin's silhouette. It's fine. I'll explain.

"Button-ups are a universal staple that will never go out of style. Using a classic silhouette allowed me to experiment with designing my own textiles for the first time. At ScrapFAB, none of the fabrics spoke to me. I think that's because my favorite part of upcycling is being inspired by clothes with history and reimagining what they could be. I love that making my own print gives me a new way to do that, by offering greater creative freedom to make a unique piece, but still honors that history."

I continue my presentation with a more technical break-down of the construction and the materials used.

Then Mal opens the floor to student feedback.

"Your ability to mix prints is aspirational," Trevor says.

Lila nods. "It is . . . but it's still just a custom shirt from a thrift flip. Isn't the whole idea to present a design that Revived by Mal can scale?"

". . . cool, but I'm confused. Are you a textile designer now . . . ?"

". . . one-of-a-kind *is* a selling point . . ."

". . . but could also be a logistical nightmare . . ."

I process the critiques and they don't make me want to melt into the floor and disappear. It's valid, their feedback. Honestly, scalability was the *last* thing on my mind when I made this. I just needed something to not be disqualified from the final runway show.

So I made something.

Now that it exists, I still have time to perfect it.

Mal always has the last word. And her expression has been neutral this entire time.

I brace myself.

"It's a start," she says.

*A start.*

She smiles.

And I float back to my seat.

## TWENTY-SEVEN

*I* am restless energy after my first crit that isn't a flop. I could run a marathon. I don't, but I do maintain a brisk city-walk pace down Broadway, Cardi B blasting in my ears. After weeks of suffering and being convinced that I had lost my last remaining brain cell . . . I made something I love. Something Mal didn't hate. I'm not broken. I just needed a flea, a bridge, and a button-up.

As soon as I enter my dorm, I FaceTime Levi because one cannot simply text a creative breakthrough. He answers on the first ring and, seeing him on a screen? I don't understand why Levi Berkowitz is camera-shy. Not at all.

"Fitz?"

"I wasn't a flop!"

His eyebrows scrunch. "What?"

"My flea flip? It didn't flop. Mal said, quote, 'It's a start'!"

"That's good?"

"It's the nicest thing she's said to me all summer."

Levi laughs, and it's the first time since the burgundy

button-up that he sounds like himself. "That's amazing."

"Are you free? I owe you lunch. At least."

"I have a plantscapade."

"Cool. When and where?"

"It's actually a larger pickup in Coney Island. R and R rented a car and a few of us are driving down."

"Oh."

"Sorry! Also, you don't owe me anything, okay?"

I shake my head. "You inspired me."

The best and worst thing about FaceTime? Even the tiniest shifts in expression seem huge. Levi's cheeks tint pink and then so do mine. And there's a very real chance that if I can hear my heartbeat, he can, too.

We ignore it.

Levi snorts. "Because my style is so iconic."

"I thrifted a pair of cargo pants. So."

"Seriously?"

"I'm going to elevate them."

Levi's laughter is becoming my favorite sound. "What's next? Birkenstocks?"

"You do not wear Birkenstocks."

"I just haven't broken them out yet."

"Shut the fuck up."

"I'm serious."

"I hate you."

We're both laughing and there it is again. A flutter,

accompanied by a *twinge* because I don't know what I'm going to do without that sound, without this easy back-and-forth, without Levi's friendship.

"Come over for dinner tomorrow night instead," Levi says. "You don't owe me, but you do owe my mom."

"I absolutely do."

"Six o'clock?"

"I'll be there."

"Cool. I—"

A knock on my door makes me miss whatever Levi was about to say.

"Fitz?"

Dani.

We haven't spoken since she freaked out about the kiss.

"One sec!" I say to the door.

Levi's eyebrows rise.

*Dani*, I mouth to him.

He nods, then disconnects our call without saying good-bye, probably because he thinks that's what I want. Is that what I want?

I blink. What? Of course that's what I want.

Dani is who I want.

I check my hair in my selfie mirror, then say, "Come in."

The door swings open and it's a sort of déjà vu because once again Dani is in my room, my flannel in her hand. Sort of. This time she's makeup free—puffy eyes and red cheeks exposed. If clothes are my armor, makeup is Dani's, and without it she looks so sad and exhausted. Even though, in theory, I *wanted* her to be miserable without me, seeing it . . . I actually hate this so much.

"Dani?"

She holds out the flannel. "You need to take this."

"It's yours."

"Please."

Her voice is soft, a whispered plea that breaks me, and I take the flannel, my fingers brushing against her hand.

And she bursts into tears.

"I'm sorry. I'm *so* sorry," she cries, wiping her eyes. "First, I thought Levi was bullshit. Like Em! But—"

"Wait. What do you mean, like Em?"

"Fuck," Dani whispers.

"What do you mean *like Em*?" I repeat.

"Um. I saw you in the park at Pride and I sort of asked Em to pretend to be into me. But we're just friends. Actually."

I—

What?

"Seriously?"

"It wasn't my best moment, okay? I just saw you walking toward us and you looked so cute that I panicked and took a cue from a basic romantic comedy."

I don't have words.

Em isn't real. Dani and I both had a similar scheme. Except, mine was to make her jealous, to *win her back*, while her fake-dating plan sounds like it was meant to keep me away.

"I'm sorry," she repeats. "And then after the storm? I saw how cool Levi is and how you're different with him and I hated that. So I reacted in the most jealous-ex way. It's so embarrassing."

Oh my God.

It *did* work.

Sure, it sucks that Dani pretended to be into Em. But she clearly realized she was wrong and I haven't exactly gotten here by being one hundred percent honest either. "Levi and I . . ." I let my voice trail off, not sure what to say. I settle on what I wanted to say the night we broke up. No interruptions, no over-thinking. "It doesn't matter. I love you."

Dani shakes her head. "You have to stop saying that."

"What do you mean? It's true."

"Clearly, it's too soon to be friends," Dani says, almost to herself.

"Friends?"

I thought she was here to get me back.

Dani nods. "The kiss should never have happened, okay? It was just a moment."

No. Not okay. She doesn't get to reduce what she said, what she did, how it *felt* . . . to a moment. "You miss me."

"That doesn't change anything."

"But *I* changed—"

"Because of Levi."

I shake my head, so frustrated. "*No*. Because of *you*. I don't want to fixate on perfect pictures anymore. I'm on hiatus—and it's really made me think about, like, balance. I can turn that part of me off sometimes. I can be who you want me to be."

Dani frowns. "Who *I* want you to be?"

"As in, like, the best version of myself. I can do that now."

"I can't."

"What?"

"I can't be the best version of myself with you."

My eyes sting like I've been slapped.

"So you . . . don't love me?"

She squeezes her eyes shut. "*You* don't."

"Danica."

"Come on. We had fun together . . . but we never exactly went deep, you know? Every time I tried to open up or to get you to open up you would just deflect. I mean. Beyond the physical chemistry what even *was* our relationship? When did we talk about anything real?"

Her words cut deep but they don't make sense. I opened up to Dani more than I ever opened up to anyone in my past relationships. Like, back when I applied to FIT? She knocked on my door as I was mid–panic attack with portfolio-related impostor syndrome and I still let her in. Sure, I then promptly freaked out afterward, but that's because she *literally told me* she wanted fun, low-maintenance, casual when we got together.

She's not done. "You have a sister! Here! In the city! And I only know this because Em told me that's where you go every weekend."

I'm sure I told Dani that Tessa lives here.

Didn't I?

"I'm sorry," Dani says again. "After you got into FIT, when it became real, I started questioning what I wanted . . . but I didn't know how to talk to you about it. And I didn't want to be the reason you rejected that spot. I wouldn't have been able to live with myself if you had said no because of me."

"Because being fresh off a breakup is the best way to start an intense summer program? Cut the faux sacrificial bullshit. That was *my* choice to make."

Dani blinks back tears, surprised. "Oh my God. It wasn't *that* calculated. I'm not a sociopath. I thought being here would change things, but our first week together just, like, clarified what I wanted."

"Yeah?"

Dani nods. "I want to be single."

"Okay. Cool. So then why did you pretend to make our issues about my social media if it wasn't really about that at all? I've been on hiatus for you. I've lost an entire month of posting and engagement for you. You know how important If the Shoe Fitz is to me and you made me feel like trash for caring about it because . . . what? You wanted an out?"

"No, I mean it wasn't the whole story. But you *are* kind of obsessed with it."

"Come on, like you're *not* obsessed when you're cast in a show?"

"That's different."

"How so?"

"Acting is my art."

"And fashion is mine!"

"Sure . . . at your sewing machine. Social media isn't an art."

Wow.

I always sort of knew that Dani didn't understand how much work went into my platform or why I obsessed over the little things—but I thought she at least got the art of it. She has a stage to showcase her craft. I have social media. *All* summer I've been questioning myself, how I share my art and what it says about me as, like, a *person*. Why I want a photographer, not a partner. Or why I fixate on perfect photos.

When maybe I should have been questioning Dani, too.

"We don't work," Dani continues.

"We don't," I repeat, a sentence that would've been unthinkable just an hour ago.

Dani takes a step backward and reiterates, "It's different with Levi. I'm so sorry if the kiss complicated that."

I wait for it. The nose scratch that will confirm that she doesn't mean this, that she's just saying words to hurt me.

She doesn't do it.

Dani exits the scene, leaving me alone with a flannel, another heartbreak, and the remnants of an entire summer-long plan that was never going to work no matter how perfect a girlfriend I tried to be. It wasn't enough for her.

It doesn't matter what I do.

I am never enough.

*'m taller than Esther Berkowitz.*

It's my first thought as her paint-stained fingers reach out to me and I'm wrapped in a hug, because it seems so illogical that this woman who once covered my scraped knees with Band-Aids, who taught me how to hold a paintbrush, is not even five feet tall. In every childhood memory, I'm looking up at her. Now she looks up at me.

"Ava Fitzgerald! Finally."

*Finally.* As if she's been waiting for me.

I lean into her embrace, so grateful now that I didn't cancel. I almost did for a second time, to spend tonight curled up in bed with chocolate ice cream and movies that make me ugly-cry. But being wrapped in her embrace is a much more comforting distraction. She still gives the best hugs.

"Hey," Levi says.

I make eye contact with him. He's swapped cargo shorts and a polo for faded jeans and a basic black T-shirt. I note how perfectly they fit. The jeans. Wait. I am *not* checking out

Levi Berkowitz . . . while I'm hugging his mother? And heart-broken? What is *wrong* with me?

*Sorry*, he mouths.

I just smile at him as Esther releases me saying, "Dinner just came out of the oven."

Levi and Esther live in a cramped two-bedroom fifth-floor walk-up with floorboards that creak under our feet, so much exposed brick, and so many plants. They're everywhere. Ivy hangs from the ceiling. A massive snake plant chills in a corner away from direct light. Prayer plants even line the shelf above Esther's easel.

Huh. I can name varieties of plants now.

Processing this, I slip out of my platform sneakers at the door and step farther into the space.

"You own denim," I say to Levi.

"I contain multitudes."

"Clearly."

Dinner is kugel. Grandma Jo's recipe. It smells delicious as we sit around a small birch table truly only meant to seat two people. Esther's painter's stool is a makeshift third chair. It's a tangible reminder that it's just the two of them now. Levi and Esther.

She asks how my family is and I share the highlight reel of dream jobs, dream schools, dream homes, the way I always depict them now, leaving out all the messy emotional parts that I once would've told her. While I talk, Levi's knee keeps bumping into mine and it's, like, an actual electric shock every time it does. But I'm in no place emotionally to acknowledge it or anything that Dani said about Levi and me. Nope. She's wrong. We're just friends. Also? Just because our plan didn't work for me doesn't mean it won't work for Levi and Sophie. So I focus on the food, on conversations about life and art, on Esther's tattoo origin stories. I don't remember her arms being covered in so many tattoos.

She points to the tiny potted succulent on her right bicep. "This is Spike. Levi's first plant."

Levi sighs. "I murdered him."

Esther picks up her wineglass. "Cause of death, a Mickey Mouse watering can. Succulents are near impossible to kill. But, alas, Spike fell victim to an overeager eleven-year-old."

"That's a misconception about succulents."

"Poor Spike," I say.

"We took Spike to a plant doctor, but it was too late," Esther continues. "Levi cried for *weeks*. He hadn't been so inconsolable . . . well, since after we said goodbye to you."

Esther throws this in so casually.

But no, *I* was the inconsolable one.

*He* left *me*.

Levi shakes his head. "Spike didn't deserve to be my lesson in the perils of overwatering."

So we're not acknowledging that?

Cool.

I can do that.

Esther continues telling us about her tattoos, and I learn that they're her story. In addition to Spike the succulent, *Bluebird Lane* is written on the inside of her forearm in Grandma Jo's elegant cursive. A monarch butterfly on her wrist is the mascot of the elementary school where she taught in Austin. Wildflowers on her tricep grew outside the loft she rented as an artist-in-residence in middle-of-nowhere Pennsylvania. And a Dolly Parton quote she got when Levi's dad left for Nashville runs from the crease of her elbow to her wrist: *Storms make trees take deeper roots.*

It's a lot to take in. Esther Berkowitz has lived so many lives since I saw her last.

Levi, too.

"It was hard after David left," Esther admits, looking at Levi. "I deserved way more shit for uprooting you than you gave me."

Levi shrugs. "I'm just happy we landed here."

Esther smiles. "Me too."

Wow. Esther is so cool and self-aware in a way that I've never seen my parents be. I can't imagine them admitting that they're imperfect, flawed, *human*. At least not to me. Esther's statement feels radical. I almost tell her this, but then the subject changes and the moment is over. Dinner is over. Esther and Levi stand and take empty plates to the sink.

As they do, Esther says, "Levi showed me your Instagram."

"Oh."

Eloquent.

I just . . . it's weird enough to imagine Levi scrolling through my Instagram. But Esther, too?

"Who taught you how to sew?"

"YouTube."

She nods. "You're so talented. You have an artist's soul, Ava Fitzgerald. You always have."

I bite down on the inside of my cheek to stop my eyes from welling up because it means *so* much. My parents don't see me that way. They only support my social media because I'm somewhat good at it and they think it'll look good for college admissions. Never do they ask about my designs or comment on the actual posts. I thought maybe getting into FIT would change that. But so far it hasn't. I still have no idea if they're even coming to the final runway show.

"Most people don't get it," I say, my voice soft.

"I know."

Esther just *looks* at me, and that wordless language Levi and I have?

I still have it with her, too.

Before I start crying, I stand and walk over to Levi to help with the dishes. As I dry the plates that he passes to me, I think about Esther's tattoos and how many places they've both been before we reunited on a downtown 1 train. *Cosmic shit.* That's what I said just a few weeks ago. That's how it still feels. Like the universe had a hand in this.

The *universe?*

I need to calm down.

After the last plate is dry, Levi looks at me. "So. Want to see how Millie is doing?"

Millie.

My first plantscapade.

I nod. "She better be thriving."

Levi leads me down a narrow hallway to his room.

His *room*.

Esther calls, "Door open!"

*"Mom."*

Levi sounds mortified at any insinuation that a door needs to be open, but I note his tinted pink cheeks as we enter his room. It's minimalist in everything but plants. Between here and the living room, there have to be over a hundred in this apartment. Planters line the windowsill and cover the floor but for a narrow walking path. On his desk is a miniature greenhouse made of bamboo. Millie's inside it, in a new pot but with fewer leaves than when I saw her last.

"Is she okay?"

Levi nods, then points out new growth. "Millie is resilient."

"Are these all rescues?"

He shakes his head. "We rehome them pretty quickly. Most of these are mine."

"Whoa."

"Yeah. I'm on a self-imposed ban. I kind of stress-purchase plants? It got pretty out of hand last year. I forgot to add a few to the watering calendar and Calliope's leaves started to brown. She's a temperamental calathea. Forgetting about her was pretty much rock bottom for me. So I just rehab the rescues now, because mine need room to grow. And I need a place to sleep."

My eyebrows rise. "Sophie?"

"My dad."

Elodie's words on Shabbat come back to me.

*He's had a rough year, between his dad and Soph, you know?*

I didn't know. Not the whole story, at least. I still don't. Levi hasn't said a word about his dad since bubble tea in Tompkins Square Park, when the word "divorce" shattered the perfect pictures that are my memories of his parents. Even after Elodie's statement, I didn't ask because whatever it was, I just assumed I'd find out when Levi was ready to tell me.

"You miss him?"

He sits on the edge of his bed and shakes his head. "He's a biphobic asshole."

*Oh.*

I process, as I sit next to him and whisper, "Shit."

"I came out to him last summer and his first question was if Sophie knew. As if it's a reason to, um, not be with me."

I am rage.

"That's beyond fucked up."

"It messed me up for a second. He's never been, like, blatantly queerphobic. He has a Pride flag in his classroom. So I didn't see his reaction coming at all. But it's performative bullshit. Clearly. We haven't spoken since."

It's so much, Levi trusting me with his wound.

His hand rests on the bed and I cover it with mine.

"I'm so sorry."

"Mom filed for divorce after that. You know they were high school sweethearts. So I think she held onto this idea that their separation was just a break and that Nashville was, like, some kind of midlife crisis? I did too. But his reaction and the doubling down that followed was, like, bi-erasure bingo. It was the first time I was glad he left us. Who knows what shit I would've internalized if he didn't?"

Parents can be the worst.

"You deserve so much better, Berkowitz."

"Thanks."

"Seriously. His claim to fame is a shitty cat jingle."

Levi's mouth quirks ever so slightly. "It's so embarrassing."

"Humiliating."

We sit in silence and I think about how deceptive a perfect picture can be. It's what Levi's family always was to me—an image that I held on to and wished for every time my parents disappointed me. I should've known better. We all have filters on. All the time.

I keep my hand over his and let Levi be the one who decides when to let go. When he does pull away, I stand and cross his room to look at the corkboard above his desk and the photos and mementos tacked onto it. Plants. His friends. Soph. Concert tickets. Postcards. Me.

*Me?*

I untack the photo. I know this photo. I *have* this photo somewhere in the box under my bed. It was taken at the tire swing—the best part of Levi's backyard. We're six. I know this because that's when I lived in the *Tangled* shirt I'm wearing. (I can trace the genesis of my queer awakening back to that movie. Did I want to *be* Rapunzel or did I want to live happily ever after *with* Rapunzel? Who's to say?) In the photo, I'm hanging upside down from the swing and cheesing hard at the camera. My hair skims the grass. And Levi? He's hiding behind the tree. All that's visible of him is one light-up sneaker, and it makes me laugh because it's totally us. It's *still* us. If a perfect picture does exist, I think it's this one.

"My mom found that one in an old album."

"I have it too."

"Seriously?"

I nod. "Look at us! Two bi babies."

Levi laughs. "Generous of you to include me in this."

"I see a sneaker! I see you!"

"You still do."

"What?"

"See me."

I look up at him . . . and this moment? His words? His expression?

Totally unfiltered.

*Too* unfiltered.

I turn and tack the photo back to the corkboard in an awkward attempt to defuse the energy. Levi does his part, introducing me to each of the plants by name. Including Delilah and Petunia, Sophie's plants. Both are perched on a windowsill in a prime sunlight spot.

Seeing Sophie's plants thrive? I'm so dumb. There's no *energy*. He's taking care of his maybe-girlfriend's plants and waiting for her to come home. When she does, it won't matter that I see him. This? Us? Being best friends?

It's over.

Levi and Sophie will *un*break, I will go back to Massachusetts alone, and we'll become a collage of memories once more.

Esther knocks on the doorframe, interrupting the thought spiral that is me feeling sorry for myself. "It's going to be dark soon. If you're going to show Fitz the roof, better do it now."

Levi stands. "Right."

"The roof?" I ask.

"I have a garden up there."

"What?"

Esther crosses her tattooed arms. "Is it legal? Questionable."

"Does Patsy get first dibs on the harvest to look the other way? She sure does," Levi says.

"The landlady," Esther explains to me.

Oh my God. Levi and Esther are running an illegal vegetable ring?

"I've been here for"—I check my phone—"two hours. Why am I just learning about this now?"

Levi laughs. "Let's go."

He goes to his closet to grab two sweatshirts because apparently it'll be windy up on the roof. As soon as the closet door slides open, I see it. Burgundy. The shirt from the Brooklyn Flea. It sticks out among his greens and neutrals.

It's so overwhelming. Seeing it in his closet.

I cannot contain the flutter.

It slams against my diaphragm.

Levi hands me a sweatshirt, entirely oblivious to the medical emergency that's currently happening, and all I can do is take it before following him from his room to his rooftop garden, my heart hammering in my chest because he went back for the burgundy button-up and I am more confused than ever.

## TWENTY-NINE

**L**evi tends to an entire garden that's thriving on the rooftop of a residential building on Avenue C. It's so cool. He points out each vegetable at their various stages of growth in their self-watering planters. Tomatoes. Lettuce. Cucumbers. Herbs. Then he details the environmental benefits of green roofs. New builds in the city are actually required to have them, thanks to a local bill that passed a few years ago. When he cites Local Law 97? Environmental legislation is hot.

*Levi* is hot.

After his tour, we sit on a blanket and sip on fancy root beer in glass bottles as the sun sets over Levi's garden in the sky. It's our third sunset, but it's the first one that's not a tourist spot or a staged moment. Not everyone gets this sunset view. But I do.

And I can't even enjoy it. I'm too fixated on the burgundy shirt and the fact that I'm wearing his sweatshirt that smells like fresh-cut herbs. I need a distraction. I need to remember that this flutter is the result of one too many fake dates. It isn't real, even if everyone thinks it is. Also? I'm not thinking straight. Dani *just* closed the door. She wants to be single and my heart is broken and confused. Just because our plan backfired on me doesn't mean Levi wouldn't still want it to work. I can curate a few more moments for him to make sure Sophie regrets the break.

So I reach for my phone and open the camera.

"It's been a minute since our last post," I say.

Levi wraps his hand around my phone. "Can we not?"

"But—"

"Fitz."

My name is a soft plea on his lips.

So I let go. "Okay."

He places my phone facedown on the blanket and looks at me. "I mean. We're breaking up soon anyway, right?"

Two weeks.

It's the first time either of us acknowledges *the end* out loud.

"Right. My hiatus ends *so* soon."

"Do you miss it? Social media?"

I shrug and sip on my root beer, considering.

Do I?

"It's complicated. At the beginning of the summer, it felt like such a grand, almost impossible gesture, temporarily letting go of social media. Dani said that was our issue and I believed her. I don't think I do anymore. But six weeks ago, I never would've experimented with designing my own textiles. Because it's not a part of my brand, and what's the point of making something if I'm not going to post it? Like, a shirt I'm so proud of wouldn't exist if I hadn't stepped away from social media. I told myself that I was struggling so much because of the breakup, because it was easier to blame my creative block on Dani than to admit that the more popular I become on social media, the more pressure I put on my designs . . . and creating isn't fun when there are thousands of voices in my head. I guess I'm not sure how to reconcile that I went on hiatus for the wrong reason, but I'm still grateful for the break."

Levi nods. "That does sound impossible."

"Not anymore. I had a breakthrough. Because of you, I designed something for just *me* for the first time . . . maybe ever?"

"I don't need credit."

"You willingly spent an entire day at a flea market with me."

"It was fun for me, too."

I look away because this is all too much. His delivery is so earnest and it's so rude because I'm trying to contain this unmanageable flutter that cannot differentiate between a platonic friendship statement and something more. Not when he's wearing a fantastic pair of jeans. Not when I know that a burgundy button-up is hanging in his closet. Not when he's looking at me like I made his summer.

"So why still do it?" Levi asks.

"What?"

"If the Shoe Fitz."

I wrap my arms around my knees and attempt to let words overtake the flutter. "I don't know. I only started it as a way to keep in touch with my sisters. I didn't expect other people to pay attention. But when they did, I *liked* it. Suddenly, I started getting way more attention and validation from *strangers* than I was from my sisters. At some point, my posts became armor. During a crit, someone told me I chase trends, but the hiatus made me realize that isn't true. I use trends to chase the community, the follows, the likes. Because if enough people like me, maybe I won't be so fucking lonely."

I cannot believe I just said that out loud.

Or that my unfiltered truth is a sad, lonely monologue.

"I mean—"

Levi stops me from walking it back. "I get it. I created a whole plant family for myself in the years between Allen and here for the same reason."

We sit close enough for me to lean toward him.

I do.

Then I nudge his shoulder and finally just say the words I've been keeping in all summer.

"You could've called me."

He looks at me. "I know."

"Or at the very least, responded to my emails. RSVP'd to my bat mitzvah. *Something*."

Levi's eyebrows rise. "You invited me to your bat mitzvah?"

"Of course."

"We probably weren't in Austin anymore then, Fitz. I never got the invitation."

Well. That's one question answered.

"Okay. But that still doesn't explain why moving away had to also mean leaving me."

"I don't know. Staying in touch would've meant hearing about your life without being able to be a part of it. And that would've sucked. You were always right down the street and then you weren't . . . and I guess a clean break felt like it would hurt less?"

I thought I lost Levi because *I* did something wrong, because *I* was too much.

But it wasn't about me at all.

"You're an idiot."

"I cannot explain my ten-year-old logic."

"If you'd called, at least we could've been lonely together."

"Or not lonely at all."

"I used to make up these, like, ridiculous stories about you. Ask myself, 'Where in the world is Levi Berkowitz?' You were always doing cool shit. Hanging out with kangaroos in Australia. Exploring the Galapagos Islands. In one story, you learn that you're the descendant of royalty and are whisked away to learn how to be a prince. Okay. So that's just the plot of *The Princess Diaries*—" I attempt to defuse another earnest confession with an awkward laugh. "I don't know why I'm telling you this. Long story short, I missed you an embarrassing amount, Berkowitz."

I finish my root beer in silence and wonder how life would've been different if he'd called. Could we have been a fixture in each other's lives, no matter where in the world we were? I don't know. Then maybe we wouldn't be here. Maybe we were meant to grow apart and cosmic shit caused our universes to collide at the precise moment when we needed each other.

And the way Levi is looking at me right now?

I think he might think the same thing.

"I wondered about you, too," Levi admits.

My heart rate triples.

"You did?"

"I actually . . ." Levi pauses. Scratches the back of his neck. "I follow you on Instagram."

Um. I assumed so.

"Cool. I mean. I will too, when I get mine back."

Levi shakes his head. "No. I mean. I've been following you. Since before this summer. That's how I recognized you on the subway."

What?

Levi didn't just *miss* me? He *found* me? I have over twelve thousand followers and Levi Berkowitz is one of them. Has been for—

"How long?" I ask.

Levi swallows. "Two years."

"Seriously?"

Levi nods, wordless.

I gape at him. "Berkowitz! Why didn't you DM me?"

"I drafted a few, but I always convinced myself that you

wouldn't remember me and I'd have no one to blame but myself. I thought I'd let too much time pass, that we could be too different now. I mean. You became this confident, incredible fashion designer and it's a good day for me if my socks match."

*Confident.*

*Incredible.*

"It's just a filter."

Levi shakes his head. "You're not as filtered as you think you are, Fitzgerald."

Maybe not, but only with him.

In the silence that follows, I shift to face him. "Levi."

Our eye contact right now is next level.

"You were my best friend. I never stopped wondering where in the world you were. Never."

I'm not sure who leans in first.

Him.

Me.

Or if we meet in the middle.

But I surrender myself to the flutter the moment Levi Berkowitz's lips brush against mine. He lifts my chin with his thumb, his teeth grazing my bottom lip in a soft kiss that silences every logical brain cell.

"Damn, Berkowitz," I whisper against his mouth.

He breaks the kiss to laugh and I look at him, searching for any sign that this is a mistake.

But Levi just looks at me as if he's surrendering to the flutter too.

"You got the burgundy shirt," I say, almost breathless.

Levi nods. "It spoke to me."

I pull him back in. Savoring this fleeting moment, I wrap my arms around his neck and deepen the kiss because I don't want soft. I don't want tentative. I want my fingers in his hair. I want his mouth on my neck. I want him, this boy who sees through my filters, who went back for the burgundy shirt, who makes me feel confident and incredible and safe.

And I let myself get lost in kissing Levi until the moon replaces the sun in the Manhattan sky.

## THIRTY

**M**y lips still raw from a reckless perfect kiss, I float back to my sewing machine later that night with an epiphany. I've stressed so much over making sure If the Shoe Fitz appeals to other people. First, my sisters. Then, my followers. But as Levi walked me back to my dorm after the hottest and most emotionally connected make-out session of my *life*, I had a breakthrough.

The button-up is more than a button-up.

Like Esther's tattoos, it's *me*.

Part of my story.

I got into upcycling because it kept me connected to my sisters and I felt them in their old clothes. And that history matters to me. When I'm thrifting, I don't know those clothes' stories as well, but I can still feel the history in a vintage fabric and that inspires me in a way that rolls of fabric just don't. But . . . I still need to tell my own in them too. I want my presentation to lean into this revelation instead of overcoming it. Creating my own textiles can be my way of honoring the history of the fabrics I'm deconstructing, while still giving myself the creative freedom to design clothes that feel like *me*.

Because everyone deserves clothes that empower them to feel like the best, most authentic versions of themselves.

*That's* my brand.

It's always been my brand.

I just used to care more about my followers seeing themselves in what I made than letting them see me.

I reach for the bin of fabrics under my bed and thumb through my thrift haul, ultimately choosing a satin shirt and ripping out the seams. One of my favorite parts about upcycling is how it begins with deconstruction—how it demands to be ripped apart just to be pieced back together.

Satin can be a bitch to work with, so I finish the edges first to prevent fraying. It's a simple stitch on a delicate fabric. A perfect, soothing, repetitive motion for when I don't want to think, just *be*. And right now, I just want to live for as long as possible in this breakthrough and the sense of surrender that I felt while kissing Levi.

So I sew. Lose myself in a project until I hear the sound of Dani's cackle-snort on the other side of the door.

I loved that sound.

And I don't know how I can listen to her laugh and feel okay. Because of a burgundy shirt? Because I learned that he's been following me for years? Because we kissed? Is Levi just an antidote for the pain of losing her? It doesn't feel that way, but it's too soon to like someone this much, so I'm not sure. I *am* sure that I'm so confused.

No. I should be focusing on the satin in my hands.

Satin I found at the Brooklyn Flea.

Because of Levi.

*Shit.*

The material jams under the presser foot and snags.

I freeze, then stand and step away from the machine because one more wrong move and this fabric is ruined. I don't trust myself to coax out the jam right now, so I abandon this mess and lie on my bed with my phone. But now nothing distracts me from the other mess I'm currently making. I have a new message from Levi, but as much as I want to lose myself in talking to him again, I don't open it. I need a beat. After a summer spent staging moments and chasing unrequited love, it felt so good to want and feel wanted tonight. But Levi isn't a rebound. He can't be. He's my best friend.

I shouldn't want to kiss him again.

I shouldn't have kissed him at all.

But then it hits me.

In two weeks, there is no *us* to ruin.

I open Instagram, where I'm still logged into Levi's account that has been documenting our summer. I need a reminder of what's real. I type @sophhsweeneyy into search and scroll through her feed. Levi is all over it without even showing his face—his hand in a photo with Delilah and Petunia; his black shiny dress shoes and her red block heels at prom; a from-behind shot of him on a hike in the Catskills.

Sophie is a person. *Levi's* person. And when she returns he'll remember that.

Right.

Sophie is his present. I'm childhood nostalgia. She's three years. I'm one summer. She's coming back. I'm leaving. Their break will end and our friendship will dissolve into a memory. Maybe that's why I leaned into the reckless moment . . . because either way, I'll lose him.

Unless.

Maybe there's a way to not.

I log out of Levi's Instagram and create a burner account to slide into Sophie's DMs before I can overthink it.

> hey sophie!
> 12:03AM

> this is objectively weird
> 12:03AM

> but
> 12:03AM

> we're friends in my head so
> 12:03AM

> holy shit that sounds deranged
> 12:04AM

i am so sorry. what i meant is that your
friends miss you. they've been talking
about you a lot. so i just FEEL like
i know you
12:04AM

especially levi
12:04AM

also hi i am fitz!
12:05AM

I drop my phone.

Oh my God.

I am messaging Sophie from a photo-less burner account.

But I have to.

I need to blow up the image that Levi and I have been curating and declare that we never have and never will be more than friends. Because that's how I keep any piece of him.

I let him go.

My phone vibrates.

hi
12:10AM

lol i know who u are
12:10AM

adam & i LOVE your insta
12:10AM

Cool. Sophie has great style and quality taste.
Maybe we can all be friends.

oh! thanks
12:11AM

sorry, i know this is so random
12:11AM

but i guess i wanted to let you know that
levi and i are 1000% just friends
12:11AM

1000%?
I sound so sus.

cool
12:12AM

noted
12:12AM

el scared the shit out of u, didn't she?
12:14AM

. . . maybe
12:15AM

I don't even know what else to say. Sophie is way too chill.
I am way too . . . not.

listen. it is sweet, i guess, of you to reach out
12:16AM

and weird ngl
12:16AM

but tbh i already know everything
12:17AM

levi spilled and all it took was a "how are you?"
message lol
12:18AM

ik that he's just helping you make your ex jealous
12:18AM

I—
I thought Levi and Sophie have been no-contact.

OH
12:18AM

cool
12:18AM

noted
12:19AM

cute of you to think that levi is capable of
scheming
12:20AM

he can't even keep a SURPRISE secret
12:20AM

*Cute of you to think.*

Cute of *her* to think, because he did keep one surprise. And it was the best day of the entire summer.

Actually, make it two surprises.

So there, Sophie.

right
12:21AM

well
12:21AM

sorry for barging into ur DMs lol
12:22AM

it's chill. bummed we won't get to meet!
12:23AM

maybe one day
12:23AM

I double-tap to heart the last message, then close Instagram as fast as I can, mortified and even more confused than I was before. Levi and Sophie have been talking? Since when? For how long? I have no clue, but it's not like I'm in a position to ask clarifying questions to the person whose somewhat-maybe-boyfriend just kissed me like it was a revelation.

Oh my God.

I kissed someone who's in contact with their somewhat-maybe-girlfriend. I can't believe he's been omitting this crucial detail. Levi was supposed to be faking it for Sophie. Not for *me*. But Sophie never believed those photos were anything more than two friends reconnecting.

I turn my phone off, then attempt to coax out the jam because it's one broken thing I can fix. I gently disassemble the pieces of my sewing machine in hopes of salvaging the satin. I cut the tangled threads and remove the bobbin and don't even realize I'm crying until a tear stains the fabric. Even if Levi has an explanation, I don't want it. I trusted him with my whole unfiltered self in a way that I've never trusted anybody. I believed we were in on this together. Clearly, Levi didn't believe in it *at all* if he was so concerned with protecting

Sophie's feelings that he told her the truth. But if Sophie knows we're bullshit, then what have we even been doing? And why did he kiss me?

Fuck.

It's all so *embarrassing*.

Elodie was right.

Cute of me to think I was more than a summer fling.

## THIRTY-ONE

*I* don't have the energy to confront Levi this week, so I don't. I focus on what I should've been focusing on the whole time: the fashion. A guest lecture on Wednesday with the CEO of a sustainable sneaker company. A networking event on Thursday that I attend with Trevor and Lila, who are cool enough to make me regret not having immersed myself in the social scene at FIT at all.

Plus, the final runway show is in ten days and I have clothes to sew and a business plan to write.

So.

I'm not avoiding Levi.

I just don't have time for him or these feelings. Or that's what I tell myself when I blow off our Battery Park date plan that's on the content calendar in favor of my sewing machine, cold brew lattes, and motivational Tim Gunn compilation videos on a loop. I don't ghost. I assure Levi that I'm fine. Just busy. Stressed about my collection. Over text, we pretend like it didn't happen. The kiss. And I act like I'm not furious that Sophie knows everything.

So of course, Levi texts me just as I finally open a blank Word document to begin my proposal.

**Levi Berkowitz**
Hey! I'm outside with Dos Toros
1:01PM

For you
1:01PM

Just a drop-off, I swear! I know you're busy
1:02PM

I was in the neighborhood
1:02PM

Shit.

He'll know that something is wrong if I refuse Dos Toros, so I toss my hair into a messy bun, step into pink slides, and exit my room. I look at my reflection in the elevator. Gray flare sweatpants and a pink tank top with a coffee stain. Messy hair. Tired eyes. Whatever. I didn't plan to put on real clothes today and I'm not about to just because Levi Berkowitz showed up with oops-we-kissed-and-now-it's-awkward Dos Toros!

Outside, Levi is looking at his phone under the awning. Texting Sophie, probably.

Filter *on*.

"Hey."

His head snaps up from his screen. "Hey!"

He holds out the Dos Toros bag.

I take it. "Cute move, Boyfriend! Sorry I'm not dressed for a photo."

His eyebrows crinkle. "You think that's what this is?"

I know it's not, but he doesn't know that. "I think—"

"Fitz!"

The voice that cuts me off isn't his.

"Natalie?"

It's so unexpected, I don't fully process her presence, not even when her arms wrap around me in a way that I've missed so much. I nearly drop my lunch from the frenetic momentum in this dramatic hug. Natalie is here? In New York?

"Surprise!" she says, then lets go to assess the mess that is me. "You're busy."

Natalie knows the worse I look, the better a project is going.

I shrug. "Whatever. You're here! Why didn't you text me?"

"My dad is attending a band-teacher convention and I convinced—well, begged—him to take us."

"Us?"

"Fitzgerald!"

It's Henry's voice. I look past Natalie and see him and Natalie's dad approaching us. I swear, I've had more intentional surprises thrown at me in one summer than I've had in my entire life.

"Hey, Chao," I say as both of my friends register Levi and me at the same time.

"You must be Levi," Natalie says, going in for a hug. "I'm Natalie! It's *so* nice to meet you. Fitz has—"

"I'm Henry."

Henry interjects with a bro handshake, saving Levi, who's clearly so unprepared for Nat's energy to be directed at him. I mouth *Thank you* to Henry, grateful that he intercepted whatever embarrassing no-chill thing she was about to say.

I'm not sure that I ever imagined this moment. My people meeting Levi. But if I had? It would not be like this, introducing him to one friend who knows about the fauxmance and the other who does not, while in my pajamas and confused about where we even stand. But alas, this is my life. It's happening. So I go back to doing what I do best.

Act like everything's fine.

"How long are you here?"

"Just the weekend," Natalie's dad says, entering the scene. "Hi, Fitz."

"Hey, Mr. J. Exciting for you to have a band thing here."

"Yeah. Don't you have an opening keynote to get to?" Natalie asks.

Mr. J laughs. "Getting rid of me so fast?"

"I'll text you every hour and drop location pins. We'll be *fine.*"

After a back-and-forth exchange in which Mr. J goes full

Dad Mode and lists the terms and conditions for letting Natalie and Henry live their own life today, he says goodbye and is off to live his best band teacher one.

"Sorry! He's so extra," Natalie says.

Levi takes a step back, awkward. "Well. It was nice to meet—"

"Don't leave!" Natalie interjects. "I mean. You don't have to."

Henry elbows Natalie in the rib cage, like, *chill*, while Levi defers to me. I genuinely have so much work to do and I'd much rather talk to Natalie about Levi than have to perform with him for this whole visit with the friends I've missed so much. But Filtered Fitz would not send Levi away.

So I say, "Stay."

Levi nods. "Okay."

I sign everyone in with security and we take the elevator up to my room.

"Our plan is that we have no plan," Henry admits.

"Not true. We're meeting Reid at Grand Central," Natalie says.

"Sure. But after that?" Henry asks.

"No plot. All vibes," Natalie confirms.

"That's new for you," I note.

Natalie flips me off and I laugh as I push open the door to find Dani chilling with Em in the common area as if she's, like, waiting for us. Never date someone within a friend group. It's so messy. I don't want to share Natalie and Henry today. But I have to.

And because Levi is a quiet observer in new social situations, he picks up on that vibe. I see so many questions on his face as he takes in the dynamics while I sit at the table and eat my burrito bowl, listening to Dani go on and on about her incredible summer to our friends.

My phone lights up.

**Levi Berkowitz**
If this is too awkward, I can fake appendicitis right now
1:16PM

You can offer to walk me to the closest urgent care
1:16PM

Despite everything, I laugh.
Loud.
Everyone looks at me.
"Cat meme," I say.

i'm okay
1:17PM

but thanks
1:17PM

"Fitz! Can I see what you're working on?" Natalie says.
She's a hero.

I stand and leave Levi with Henry, Dani, and Em.

In my room, Natalie says, "I'm totally going to facilitate a group hang that includes Dani and Levi today. You're welcome."

I snort. "So there *is* a plan."

She flips me off a second time, then smiles. "Always."

"I missed you, Nat."

"I missed you too. How's the *fauxmance* going?"

She whispers the word "fauxmance" as if she's a coconspirator, which I guess she has been since I've been keeping her in the loop until everything went to shit. She doesn't know that Dani closed the door on us and it cracked open all these stupid feelings for a boy who kissed me but is still so in love with his somewhat-maybe-girlfriend that he didn't even try to go along with the plan. I don't want to admit to Natalie that I've failed in a massive way.

At least not today.

"It's going!" I say, then change the subject before she can press. "What time does Reid get in?"

"Three."

"Cool."

"It's the longest I've gone without seeing him my entire life."

I snort because just a year ago, a monthlong break from Reid Callahan would've been grounds for Natalie to throw a party. Also? One month? Try being separated from your person for *seven years*.

No.

Levi isn't my person.

"Anyway. I'm dying for intel. What's the vibe with Dani?"

I should've known Natalie wouldn't be deterred.

"I mean, we're not back together. So we don't have to make today about that."

"All the more reason for a group hang."

I consider it as if I even have a choice. "We can do the group hang."

"Interesting."

"What?"

"Dani said that too."

Natalie leaves me with that information so I can change into actual clothes, but what do I do with that? Is the door with Dani not as closed as I believed? Does that even matter? I don't know. I focus on styling an outfit instead, choosing something casual that complements Natalie and Henry's no-frills vibe. I settle on high-waisted shorts and a faded rose-pattern button-up tucked in with the sleeves rolled up to my elbows. Makeup is quick and basic—a tinted moisturizer with SPF, mascara, and a rose-gold lip gloss. My hair isn't cooperating, so up in a messy topknot it stays. I complete the outfit with excessively large gold hoops.

Then I assess myself in the mirror.

Inhale.

Exhale.

I need to calm my racing pulse and center myself before I

rejoin a group hang that will involve lying to so many people and pretending in so many different ways. Pretending that the plan is still on for Natalie. Pretending that Levi and I are together because Dani and Henry believe we are. Pretending that I'm not furious with Levi for admitting the truth to Sophie and not telling me.

And the worst of it all?

Pretending that I'm not so incredibly into Levi Berkowitz.

## THIRTY-TWO

*L*evi and I are cornered with our backs up against a wall as a harrowing number of prepubescent children surround us. We are outnumbered and our options are limited. It's either give up a hundred points per boob shot; turn around and expose our back sensors, which will probably give these little assholes even more points; or get thrown out for yelling at actual children.

It's what I deserve, for rolling with the military industrial propaganda that is laser tag.

"Now can I fake appendicitis?" Levi asks, his voice low.

"You think these monsters will give a shit?"

Levi laughs. "Valid."

*No.* I don't want to make him laugh right now.

But then he looks at me seriously and says, "I have another idea."

My heart rate triples. It's so confusing. If he's in contact with Sophie, why is he looking at me like his idea is dropping his laser and scandalizing these children?

Levi does drop it.

But only to cover his chest sensors with his hands.

I should not be so disappointed.

We are heckled by fourth graders who play way too much Fortnite.

"Losers!"

"So dumb!"

"Stupids!"

But then, almost like magic, they lose interest and run off to torture someone else and for a moment Levi and I are alone in our own dark corner of this maze. It's dangerous, being alone with him. Acting like nothing has changed but feeling like everything has. Because I swear, no one has ever looked at me the way he does. Ever. I didn't know what to do with that even before Sophie's revelation.

"Fitz."

He drops his hands and it reminds me that although we were working in solidarity against the little monsters in their green vests, his vest is blue. Mine is red.

We aren't on the same team.

So instead of listening to what he's going to say next, I take a step back and aim, scoring a few points while his defenses are down. Then I run away before I can catch his reaction, back to the base that Natalie is attempting to defend from the children who've now swarmed toward her. I watch her deactivate three back-to-back-to-back as she dodges hits and maneuvers with an intensity that makes me laugh. Natalie cannot *not* be competitive—even when the prize is bragging rights and the competition is literal ten-year-olds.

"Where have you been?" Natalie asks.

"With Levi."

"Consorting with the enemy? When I specifically made sure that you and Dani are on the same team?"

Our team divisions within our six-person group are Levi, Reid, and Henry vs. Dani, Natalie, and me because though gender is a construct, we are basic bitches. We could've all been on the same team. At the very least, we could form a temporary alliance against these little shits. But no.

"We got cornered! These kids are brutal."

As if to prove the point, Natalie is deactivated.

A kid yells, "Stupid girl!"

"Hey! Unsportsmanlike conduct!" Natalie shouts back.

Honestly, I wouldn't put it past Natalie to march over to the game master and attempt to get this kid ejected from the game. She's ruthless. But instead she looks at me, her brow furrowed, and delivers instructions for our next move.

"Dani needs backup over at the boys' base."

"I'm pretty sure we're losing, Nat."

"We can still beat the boys."

She's deactivated again.

"Doubt it," Reid says.

Natalie turns around and mock-clutches her heart at his betrayal.

"Get a room," I mutter, making my move toward the boys' base. Natalie and Reid haven't seen each other in a whole month and of course their Plan A activity is an arbitrary competition. But it's better than Natalie's earlier ideas. We spent the afternoon being tourists and weaving through the crowds in the most congested and objectively worst Manhattan blocks on a walking tour of iconic landmarks after Reid's arrival. Grand Central Station. Bryant Park. Times Square. Macy's.

Before I make it to the base, someone grabs my arm and pulls me into a hidden nook, catching me so off guard with the pressure of their nails against my skin that the momentum slams me into them.

Her.

Dani.

She puts one finger over her lips.

"Shh."

Then she nods toward the boys' base, where Henry and Levi are working together to fend off an attack from the children. How are there so many of them and so few of us? I don't know. But right now it's a good thing because time is limited and most of the points come from deactivating the opposition's base. We have to move.

"Let's work together," Dani whispers.

I nod.

We are so close, I can smell her bubblegum lip gloss.

And I'm okay.

The first time I felt *this* okay was after hearing her adorable snort-cackle while I was still floating from a garden rooftop make-out session. But the adrenaline from that night has worn off and still, I'm okay.

Is this what acceptance feels like?

"Distract Levi," she instructs, her voice low in my ear. "Henry will be focused on the kids. Neither of them will suspect that we're together, and we can use that to our advantage. I can loop around and sneak up from behind to deactivate the base. Dudes won't even see it coming!"

It's a good plan.

But distracting Levi? It feels dangerous in a way that I can't articulate to Dani. So when we separate I attempt to lean into the game of it all. I make my move, stepping into the base and aiming for one of the three sensors that we have to hit in order to deactivate it. The bases are designed to look like the interiors of a spaceship, with two sensors located on the motherboard and the third on the ceiling. I take out one of the motherboard sensors before Levi strikes my vest and temporarily deactivates me.

I laugh. "Nice shot, Berkowitz."

Levi winces and lowers his laser, then says, "I think I hate this."

"And yet you're here."

Levi scratches the back of his neck. "Well. Yeah."

"Why?"

He shrugs. "You asked me to stay."

In an alternate timeline where there's no Dani or Sophie, I grab Levi's hand, pull him toward the secret nook, and kiss him until we get kicked out. But that's not the timeline we live in. Here, Sophie and Levi are on the precipice of an inevitable reconciliation. Dani and I have a base to deactivate.

I am only a distraction.

So I distract.

"What are we doing, Berkowitz?"

Levi swallows, his Adam's apple bobbing. "I don't know."

I'm not sure what I expect, but it's not him sounding just as confused as I am. It takes me out of the game. Just for a moment, we're the only two people in this overrun base.

Until his vest deactivates.

A direct hit in the back, by Dani. Followed by an AI voice announcing that the blue base has been deactivated. Moments later, the lights go up.

Game over.

We remove our vests and wait for the scores to appear on a large screen above the arcade prize counter, engaging in trash talk as if there are actual stakes. The teams of children come in first, second, and third place.

But Natalie, Dani, and I are fourth.

"Yes!" Natalie cheers.

Dani throws her arms around me like it's no big deal.

And Levi watches us.

"We destroyed that base!" Dani says before letting go.

"Losers!" Natalie teases the boys.

Reid snorts. "You are worse than the children."

After we celebrate our not-last placement, we exit the

Bowlero at Chelsea Piers and walk east on 17th Street to Odd-fellows Ice Cream to ease our collective trauma with ice cream. We walk in pairs. Natalie and Reid. Dani and Henry. Levi and me. But outside of the structured chaos that is laser tag, I don't know what to say to Levi and he doesn't say anything, either. When we arrive, I order a scoop of S'mores Brownie to distract myself from the awkwardness. But then we have to squeeze six of us into a four-person booth.

Dani sits across from me.

Levi is next to me.

And I have no idea how to act around either of them.

So I pivot to a neutral third party. "Reid! How's Albany?"

"Intimidating. But I'm learning so much for the *Boiled* score."

Natalie swats his arm. "*Scorched* is the working title."

"*Scorched*?"

"It's a companion musical to *Melted* that we've been working on. New characters, same universe."

Dani points to herself. "Because there's only one Emma."

"Another musical?" I ask.

"Yeah," Natalie says.

"It's our *High School Musical Two* moment," Reid adds.

Natalie shrugs. "If we pull it off."

*We* being Nat and Reid. Because I cannot sing. Or dance. At all. But of course she wants to write another musical to direct with her boyfriend instead of a play I could actually be in.

This is the preview of senior year.

Natalie and Reid . . . plus me in the audience.

The news about *Scorched* is just another thing that has me itching for this night to be over, to reunite with my sewing machine and focus this restless energy on stitching together the finishing touches on my runway project. I missed my friends, but I'll be back in Massachusetts in ten days and this program is a big deal.

"We have a personality outside of theater, I swear," Reid says to Levi.

Henry shakes his head. "We're insufferable. Own it."

"It's okay," I say. "He's one of us."

"Just set design," Levi says.

"There's nothing *just* about that," Natalie says.

Levi shows some photos of the sets he's worked on for *Newsies*, *In the Heights*, and *Carousel*, but as he does a notification from Sophie pops up on the screen. Levi swipes it away quickly, but I see it. A necessary reminder that I'm still quite mad at him.

Reid nods. "Your director has range."

"And a budget," Natalie says.

But Levi doesn't respond. He's fixated on his phone, his eyebrows rising.

I nudge him. "Berkowitz?"

His eyes snap up. "I have to go."

"Is everything okay?"

Levi nods, then turns to my friends and says, "Sorry to run off, but it was really great to meet y'all."

I frown. *Y'all?*

He then slides out of the booth and exits without another word.

"Abrupt," Dani comments.

I stand, because at this moment I'm more worried than pissed. Something is wrong.

"I'm just going to . . ."

I exit the creamery without finishing the sentence. Is it Esther? It's something serious. I run across the street just as the light changes and I think my life is going to flash before my eyes, but I'm just cussed out by a disgruntled taxi driver.

"Berkowitz!"

He just keeps walking.

"Appendicitis?"

He stops.

Pivots.

But doesn't smile.

"Did you talk to Soph?"

Shit.

Of course she told him.

I nod.

"She sent screenshots. 'One thousand percent just friends'?"

Fuck.

Me.

"So that was not my best look! I just needed Sophie to know that I'm not—*we're not*—anything more than friends, so I could salvage our friendship once I leave and you two are back together. How was I supposed to know that you already did that? Why have I been curating an adorable Instagram account for absolutely no reason? Sophie told me she knows everything. That you're just, like, helping me make Dani jealous? Seriously? You couldn't take letting Sophie think that there's a chance she lost you . . . but then you kissed me? I'm so confused."

Levi frowns. "*You're* confused? *I'm* confused. Salvage our friendship? Where exactly in that kiss did you get that I wanted to be just friends?'

"What about Sophie?"

"Soph isn't here!"

I step backward. "And I am."

Until I'm not, and he ghosts me again.

His eyes widen. "That's *not* what I meant. Soph and I—"

I cut him off because if I hear him say *Soph* one more time. "You messed up, Berkowitz."

"I know. I should've told you as soon as we—"

"Levi."

I say his name the way someone says *stop*.

He does.

So I continue, "It doesn't matter. I meant it. The DMs. One thousand percent."

It's the first time I lie to Levi Berkowitz.

"Dani?"

I nod.

He swallows. "I noticed."

I step backward into a pile of trash.

"Shit."

"Fitz."

I shake my head. "We're fine, Berkowitz! Do I wish I knew sooner? Yes! Should I not have messaged Sophie? Probably. But I'm back on flirty speaking terms with Dani. You will fix things with Sophie when she gets home. So it seems like we both got what we needed out of this. Right?"

"Right."

"Then we can stop. Go back to being friends."

Levi's eyes meet mine and I hate that I want him to push back, to tell me I'm wrong, to call me out on my bullshit.

But he just nods once, then says, "One thousand percent."

And before I can say anything else, he leaves me on this semi-crowded block to absorb the aftershocks of a fake breakup that feels way too fucking real.

## THIRTY-THREE

*I* run to Tessa. As soon as Levi walks off I text Natalie and Henry the reverse excuse for my impromptu departure, *Tessa needs me*, then book it to the nearest station. Due to my deadline and the inability to haul my sewing machine onto the subway, I haven't seen her since our movie night. But we've texted daily, like actual sisters. She sends me Tim Gunn memes. I remind her to water Harriet (but not too much!). We're good. So now I take the 1 to her because I want to repress whatever the hell just happened with rom-coms and M&M's popcorn and laughter.

But when I unlock her apartment door and spot a pair of navy Sperrys on the shoe rack?

I am absolutely *not* laughing.

"You've got to be kidding me."

Bennett Covington III's eyes shift from a worn paperback copy of *The Sound and the Fury* to meet mine.

"Nice to see you too, Fitz."

"What the fuck are you doing here, Bennett?"

It better be to pick up the rest of his shit. But he's just, like, chilling here, in Tessa's apartment. Sitting on Gertie—*my* Gertie—and reading Faulkner like the literary douchebro he is.

Before Bennett has a chance to respond, Tessa comes out of the bathroom. She's in an oversize T-shirt and scrunching her hair with a microfiber towel. It's then that I spot the overnight bag on the floor next to Gertie.

Tessa's eyes widen. "I wasn't expecting—"

"Seriously, Tess?"

Bennett stands, raking a hand through his blonde undercut, and picks up his bag. "I should go."

I nod. "Get the fuck out."

"*Ava*," Tessa snaps.

Bennett crosses the apartment and kisses her on the forehead.

And she *lets* him.

I've never wanted to dismember a person more in my life.

When he exits, closing the door behind him, I start, "Tess—"

"Don't."

I'm so pissed. But the way Tessa looks at me? I see it. She's still so in love with him. Tessa, the smartest person I know, is in love with a man-child with a chiseled jawline and an unfinished manifesto. It makes no sense. Love makes no sense. Not at seventeen. Not at twenty-five.

My eyes sting with fresh tears. "Tess—"

"Maya and Clara are already giving me enough shit."

"Good."

Tears do not stop streaming down my face, but now they're not about Bennett. Not really. Once again, I'm the last sister to know vital information.

And I'm over it.

"You FaceTime Maya and Clara without me."

"What?"

"That fucking *sucks*."

Tessa swallows. "Those calls? It's just us bitching about adult shit."

I wipe my eyes. "You'll need a new excuse soon."

"Fitz—"

"Also? Roasting Bennett isn't even *adult shit*. It's actually my third-favorite pastime."

*"Ava."*

"He hates puppies! Only sociopaths hate puppies!"

"He's allergic."

"Is he also allergic to monogamous relationships?"

Tessa recoils. "Fuck off."

Whatever. This isn't even about Bennett. Why am I making this about him again?

"You don't get to judge me," Tessa continues. "I know Bennett fucked up, but I'm holding him accountable. We're in therapy. Because *real* relationships are messy. People are messy. Even *you* are messy! Rebounding with Levi? *That is so messy.*"

"Levi is *not* a rebound. He's just the only person I can talk to about anything real."

Not *can*.

Could.

Tessa's eyebrows rise. "Seriously?"

I wrap my arms around my knees, folding into myself. "People are messy? I'm not allowed to be. Not around Mom and Dad. Not around my sisters. Or else I'm just the baby. I wanted things to be different this summer. I wanted *us* to be different. I came up every weekend—"

"—to escape your awkward living situation. Not to actually spend time with me."

"That's not true."

"How did this even *happen*? How are you even here? Mom and Dad never would've let any of us follow someone to New York when we were seventeen."

"I didn't *follow her*. I'm at FIT."

Tessa's laugh is sharp. "Right. Because you're going to be a fashion designer when you grow up."

My mouth hangs open.

Tears slide down my cheeks.

"Fuck you."

"Fitz. I—"

"I'm here because I worked my ass off on my craft and built a platform that now has thousands of followers who see me . . . and all I ever wanted was for *you* to see me, to include me, to not leave me on the other side of the door."

"Youngest siblings often—"

"Here comes the psych PhD bullshit."

"It's behavioral neuroscience."

"Same fucking difference."

"It's really not."

I wipe snot with the back of my hand. "It used to be *big-kid stuff*. Now it's *adult shit*. I will never catch up to the three of you, but that doesn't mean—" I hiccup. Swallow. "I'm your sister too."

Tessa's expressions softens. "I'm aware. I don't just hand out keys to my apartment."

"You may as well have."

"What?"

"We are strangers, Tess. I hate that."

"And that's my fault?"

"Yes! Because every time I try to talk to you—*really talk*—this is what happens. You're so willing to let all of Bennett's mess in, but you want nothing to do with mine."

Silence.

I don't do this with my sisters. For so long, I've filtered these feelings. But where has that gotten me? Nowhere.

It still gets me nowhere.

"I'm done." Tessa stands and storms toward her room.

"Sure, walk away! Real mature!"

She doesn't pivot.

Instead my sister, the stranger, closes the door between us once more.

I pinch the bridge of my nose so hard it hurts. Nothing matters. Not filtering my words, not being honest about how shitty Tessa, Clara, and Maya's relationship makes me feel. I'm not enough. I'm too much.

I unlock my phone. It's a new muscle memory, to open my messages, not Instagram, to tap "Levi Berkowitz" and start typing. But I stop myself, remembering. Instead I scroll back in time, reading every word. Then I go to the camera roll and examine each unnecessary photo of him. Every candid I snapped when he wasn't looking, featuring his stupid, perfect mouth-quirk and those cargo shorts. Photos for Instagram. Photos just for me.

*1000% just friends.*

I'm so full of shit.

My finger hovers over Instagram and my vision blurs. I want it back. All of it—my content calendar, my engagement metrics, every comment, like, and piece of data that supports what I know to be true: Filtered Fitz? The person I was before I gave it up? That's who people follow. When I'm just me . . . people leave.

Dani.

Levi.

Tessa.

So if I'm alone either way, give me filters. At least they're a protective barrier when I take a door to the face.

Because I will.

Every. Time.

## THIRTY-FOUR

*H*mm."

That's the sound of Mal processing the new direction my final presentation has taken. It's the week before the runway show, so in lieu of lectures and workshops, we each get a thirty-minute private critique with Mal. Precious time to preview our presentation, to ask specific and technical questions, to have her undivided attention.

So naturally, I woke up with a stomachache, doubt stabbing my abdomen as it has ever since I returned to my sewing machine after slamming the door to Tessa's apartment shut without saying goodbye. If I shift from thrift-flip content to focusing on textile design, will I lose followers instead of growing? What if people don't like my aesthetic? What if I put out something I believe in and it flops? I cannot handle another flop moment right now.

So I've retreated back to the trendy thrift flips that have defined If the Shoe Fitz thanks to Saturday night's epiphany.

Fuck risks.

I'm showing Mal the rose-gold bomber jacket that Vivian

Leroux wanted to buy and a proposal about selling DIY patterns for people who want to make their own flips. I think about Gina, the girl who recognized me at the beginning of my summer. *She* is my audience. Crafters are my audience. So why branch out and create a whole fashion brand that might not appeal to my core audience, when I can just monetize helping them do what I do?

"It's a return to form," I say to fill the silence. "I realized I needed to step away from If the Shoe Fitz to remind myself why I love it, why it *is* me. It's not about chasing trends, it's about being an accessible point of entry to anyone who wants to thrift flip and engage with fashion in a more ethical way."

"I see." Mal's lips press together before releasing a soft, disappointed sigh. "What happened to your textile designs?"

I shrug. "It wasn't coming together."

"Bullshit."

Mal's words reverberate in my ears, but I'm ready for them. We're eight days away from a runway show, and even if it's obvious that I won't be collaborating with Mal or attending Fashion Week or whatever, she's just one person. The runway show will still be filled with industry people who could change my life. This isn't some amateur paint night. If there's any moment to not present less than my best, to *be* the persona that has thousands of followers, it's right now. So I'm not going to let Mal make me second-guess my choice.

"You're a perfectionist."

I shrug again. So?

"Has anyone ever told you that perfectionism is a trap?"

Nope.

Not once.

I shake my head.

"No one told me either," Mal continues, softer now. "Everyone in my life conflated it with talent, with achievement. It's a mindfuck. Because they don't live with the unrelenting pressure that we put on ourselves, they just praise the pretty end result. When I got into FIT, that was right as my videos started gaining popularity. I didn't even make it through my first semester. It was way too much—hitting deadlines on assignments, trying to please my professors, my peers, the people who watch my videos. I had to take a year off to relearn how to trust myself and really figure out who *I* was as a designer without all the external pressure."

I chew on the inside of my cheek, hating how much Mal's words resonate, even as I push them aside. "I'm just trying to stay true to the brand I've built."

"Fitz."

"I get it. You hate my clothes."

"No."

"You hate me."

Mal's eyebrows crinkle. "I *was* you."

I take a step backward, because I don't want Mal to call me out like this. I don't want to know that she sees the part of me that overthinks every decision, that would take down a post if it failed to meet my minimum engagement threshold, that will spend an entire day filming a thirty-second video. My filter? It doesn't work on her. It never has. But that doesn't mean I have to listen. I'm here for feedback on my clothes, not, like, my personality.

"Do you have any notes on my jacket?"

"If you're happy being an influencer and selling DIY patterns for your niche audience, that's fine. But if you want to be a designer you have to be able to accept the possibility of failure. You're not going to grow if you're too scared to take risks."

I nod and plaster a fake smile on my face. "Noted. Thanks!"

Then I turn and exit the classroom. I'm not oblivious. I expected Mal to be surprised by my pivot. I didn't expect her to wake up this morning and choose violence. I deserved thoughtful notes on the construction and execution of my designs. What I got was a critique of *me*. Yes, I work so hard. I try *so* hard. But I don't understand why that's a flaw. If perfectionism is such a trap, why does my follower count increase with every new post? Why did she accept me into this class if not because I set high standards for myself? Because I pay attention to the comments? I learn what people like, churn out quality content for them, and make it look easy.

It's not. It's exhausting.

But it works.

You know what doesn't work?

Being myself.

So it's time.

When I get back to my room, I FaceTime Henry.

He answers on the second ring. "Are you okay?"

I ignore the question that my blotchy face answers. "Can I have my passwords back?"

Silence.

I'm prepared for a fight, but then Henry blinks and recites my new passwords to me.

And just like that, If the Shoe Fitz is mine again.

"I miss you," Henry says.

I wipe my eyes. "You just saw me."

"Barely," he says. "What happened the other night? Are you okay?"

"Yeah," I lie. "I just want to be back online to hype up the runway show. Summer is pretty much over, so my hiatus can be, too."

It was over before it started.

Dani and I were over before it started.

My brilliant plan never had a chance.

So I'm done sacrificing the people who want me for someone who doesn't.

I wipe my cheeks. "Anyway! I have to run."

"Fitz—"

"Thanks for my passwords! Sorry I wept."

I tap end call and Henry's face, complete with the wrinkle between his eyebrows, disappears. My passwords reclaimed, I log into If the Shoe Fitz and it's a rush of adrenaline. My notifications are broken.

A text interrupts this reunion.

I expect Henry.

It's Levi.

**Levi Berkowitz**

Can I ask you something?

4:01PM

Yes.

No.

I don't know.

Cue the typing bubble. My knuckles turn white. Ask me what? It's been three days since we "broke up" and despite insisting that we're 1000% just friends, this is the first text Levi has sent. It could be anything. Or nothing. The bubble disappears, then reappears. I can't take the anticipation anymore so I type.

what's up?

4:01PM

Instead of words, I get photos. Levi sends two shots of Millie, repotted in a terra cotta planter. In one photo, Millie sits perched on the windowsill at sunset. In the other, she's surrounded by dozens of Levi's plants, but she's the only one in focus.

Our first plantscapade is thriving and ready to be rehomed. It's so overwhelming.

Help!
4:03PM

I can't decide which one is more Millie
4:03PM

I blink.
Levi is asking for plantstagram help?
Is this an actual effort at friendship?
Okay.
I can do that.

#2
4:04PM

mil looks lonely in #1
4:05PM

Levi types.
The bubble appears.
Disappears.
Again.
And again.
Until—

Thanks
4:05PM

ofc!

4:06PM

It's so awkward.

But whatever. I'm leaving. Levi is staying. Distance will make this weird electric fake chemistry fizzle. It's already happening. Our first communication in three days is about a plantstagram. Soon it'll just be an occasional like on social media. If our history is any indication, once I'm gone—once Sophie is *back*—he'll ghost again.

Maybe it's for the best. Because if this is what "just friends" is? I hate it here.

I hate feeling this way.

So I open Instagram and scroll until I don't feel anything at all.

## THIRTY-FIVE

*E*very day that passes is a countdown to the runway show, to the end of this summer, to goodbye. I haven't left my dorm in forty-eight hours because as it turns out, I should not have waited until the last week to finish a whole business proposal. Who knew. But currently, I'm at my sewing machine working on a demo I'm going to give to show the accessibility and versatility of my patterns using a partially constructed bomber jacket. It's all coming together, miraculously. All I had to do was stop trying to be more than who I am online.

Someone knocks and I stab myself with a pin.

Shit.

"Fitz?"

"Dani?"

She pushes the door open to find me in ratty cut-off sweats, a tape measure around my neck. I stretch my cramped fingers and see concern wrinkling her forehead. I don't have time for this. Her. I have a proposal to finish.

"You're bleeding."

I look at my hand and sure enough, blood drips from my index finger.

I also don't have time to bleed on this proposal, so I exit my room and walk past Dani to the bathroom, where I run my finger under cold water and open a vanity drawer over-stuffed with creams and makeup pads and tweezers in search of a Band-Aid.

"Henry called. He's worried about you."

"Okay."

Where the fuck are the Band-Aids?

"*I'm* worried about you."

"I'm fine."

The Band-Aids are under some tampons. I wrap a purple one around my finger. It's just a cut. Dani takes a step closer, forcing me to look at her and at least her proximity doesn't cause my heart rate to spike. Her concern doesn't instill, like, false hope.

"Are you hungry?"

I shrug, but my stomach growls.

Dani laughs. "Come on, I'm making gnocchi."

I follow her to the kitchen, where she pulls a bag of gnocchi from Trader Joe's out of the freezer. She rips it open, dumps its contents into a pan, and turns on the gas range. Above it, the digital clock reads . . . four o'clock? It was just noon. I'm running on Red Bull, powdered doughnuts, and a bag of Cheez-Its because I'm great at taking care of myself on a deadline.

It should be weird, Dani cooking gnocchi for me. But it's nice. She sighs. "We're so messy."

"Yup."

"I should've been honest," she says, her eyes focused on the defrosting meal. "At home."

"I still would've followed you here."

I open a cabinet and reach for two ceramic bowls. When the food is done, we sit. I crisscross my legs on the stiff wooden chair and stab my gnocchi with a fork. Our New York summer started with overpriced Italian food in an Instagram filter and is ending with a three-dollar bag of frozen gnocchi in an ugly dorm. It feels like a lifetime ago. Serra by Birreria. Us together. I didn't see any of what happened after coming.

The breakup.

Levi.

Everything.

"I didn't mean to hurt you," Dani says, her eyes focused on the Band-Aid, but I don't think that she's referring to the pinprick. "It was messed up, blaming our issues on social media when we were together. I'm sorry. After some soul searching and talking to my therapist I realized that it was easier to act above it all than to admit that I am incredibly jealous of it. Your platform. Your followers. All of it."

"Shut up."

"I'm serious! You're so cool and effortless and comfortable with yourself, your style, your identity. It's intimidating. I mean. Thousands of people follow you. And yeah, sometimes I felt like I was competing for attention with a follow count . . . but a lot of the time I was simultaneously wishing that even a *fraction* of those people would follow me on TikTok. It was confusing and hypocritical and I didn't like the person I was becoming. So when that girl recognized you? It *was* a moment of clarity, and I was grasping for an excuse. Social media was *right there*. I'm sorry the timing and execution sucked."

I blink.

Dani?

Intimidated by *me*, the person who never feels enough in any space?

"You intimidated me, too," I confess. "I had a crush on you for, like, an entire year before you even knew I existed—before *I* even knew if you were queer too. But then when you did like me back, I was so terrified of ruining it. And I wanted to be the perfect girlfriend. Especially since I was your first girlfriend."

"I didn't want perfect."

I nod. I get that now.

I've always thought of filters as armor. Protection. But there's another side. Filters hurt, too. They kept us apart. Dani and I were six months of lust and laughter and picture-perfect moments. But behind the scenes, we were both playing parts, scraping at each other's insecurities and not letting each other in. And instead of having this conversation, we hurt each other so much more than we needed to. It still hurts, but more like a bruise and less like the gashing open wound that I spent the entire summer trying to heal.

Danica Martinez was an all-consuming crush, a mesmerizing scene partner, and my first, disastrous *I love you*.

But she's not my person. I'm not hers.

And that's not either of our faults.

Behind me the door unlocks, announcing Em's return home from their creative writing workshop.

I watch Dani's eyes shift past me. "Oh! Hey, Levi."

Levi?

"Hi."

I twist in my chair to see him walking in with Em holding a lucky bamboo in one hand and a plastic Strand bag in the other. I'm so thrown by his impromptu appearance, by how good it is to see him, but especially by the burgundy shirt he's wearing, which makes me feel all the things I've spent the last few days trying to push aside.

"Hi!"

I cringe at the exclamation point in my voice.

"We ran into each other at the Strand," Em says.

"I texted," Levi adds.

"Oh."

If Dani and Em can feel the awkward energy between us, they sure do a great job ignoring it. Dani takes her empty bowl to the sink and asks Em how the workshop went. Em takes a clean fork off the drying mat and eats extra gnocchi from the pan. I stay in my seat, finishing my food while Levi slips out of his shoes—his *Birkenstocks*—at the door.

"So. How goes the clothes?" Levi asks, then wrinkles his nose. "Smooth. I am."

I hold up my bandaged finger. "I maimed myself."

"Ouch," Levi says, placing the bamboo on the table in front of me. "You need this more than I thought."

I shake my head. "I'm going to kill it."

Hs mouth quirks. "You won't."

"I will."

"Bamboo are low-maintenance. Pretty much impossible to mess up."

"I'll find a way."

I always find a way.

"No, because I won't let you. You will call me if the situation is dire. Or even if it isn't."

*Oh.*

The bamboo is not just bamboo—it's a promise. When I'm home I can call him and he'll answer.

"Okay." I reach a not-maimed finger to touch one of the leaves. "Thank you."

Levi runs a hand through his hair. "I didn't mean to interrupt, um, whatever this is."

Dani sits on the adjacent couch with a pint of ice cream, her eyes amused. "Exes sharing a mediocre meal?"

"Is this friendship?" Em teases.

Shit.

Dani laughs. "Too soon to say."

Understanding flickers on Levi's face in the tiniest twitch of an eyebrow. *Exes. Friendship.* With this new information, he's retreating to the door.

"I can't stay anyway," Levi says, then coughs. "I have an R and R pickup in Tribeca."

Levi doesn't say "plantscapade" and that has no right to hurt as much as it does. He steps back into his Birkenstocks and says goodbye to Dani and Em, and it's a decent performance but I see through it.

"Berkowitz."

"Good luck, Fitz."

Levi leaves me with a bamboo and my heart in my throat. There's something final about this goodbye, like the promise is already broken, and watching him walk away feels like the first time he left all over again. So I stand and step into my slides. I don't know what to say. I don't have time to think or plan or remember all the reasons I've been mad at him, too.

I just follow him out the door.

## THIRTY-SIX

**I**miss the elevator, so I take the stairs and book it down all fourteen flights. It's a miracle I don't trip over my own two feet and that Levi is still in the process of retrieving his ID and switching out his glasses for those goddamn Wayfarers when I emerge from the staircase, breathless and unreasonably sweaty. I wipe my forehead with the back of my hand before I say his name. When I do, Levi looks up, but I can't see his eyes, just the wrinkle between his eyebrows.

"Can we plantscapade?"

He hesitates.

Then says, "Okay."

So I follow him to the 1, my train, our train, ignoring the hesitation in his voice. The platform smells like stale urine so when we board a half-empty car, I exhale the breath I was very much holding. I shiver when the back of my arms brush the cool metal and notice my soft pink tape measure is still around my neck. I remove it and roll it up as I ask who we're rescuing and learn about a fiddle leaf fig named Sid. Levi shows me a photo. Sid has lost most of their leaves. But Levi is on his way and he will make Sid better. He makes everything better.

"We're on the same train," Levi says.

"Yeah. Downtown 1."

"No. Literally. You were sitting there." Levi points to the empty seats across from us. FUCK IT is written in thick block print across the top of one of them. "I hid behind Eloise and debated what to say, if I should say anything at all. I almost didn't. But then the person next to you stood and left and you started rubbing that peach hand sanitizer all over yourself. And just like that, I was seven years old, and you were chasing me around the Dallas Zoo with it anytime we touched anything."

I remember that.

"Salmonella was and continues to be one of my greatest fears."

Levi laughs. "That and a literal 'Fuck it' sign felt like, I don't know . . ."

"Cosmic shit," I finish.

I picture the image of myself that Levi first saw all those weeks ago, the girl who smelled like antiseptic peaches and muttered "No photos" to a boy she should've recognized, even behind a ficus. But Levi saw me. On crowded rush hour trains, in a fountain, at synagogue, during paint night. All my not-finest moments.

At seven.

At seventeen.

He has always seen me.

An abrupt jam on the brakes sends me sliding into him,

my shoulder slamming into his before the train stops between stations. Minutes pass with nothing said but *Fuck the MTA* by a grandma with a thick Long Island accent and a knockoff Birkin bag. A static announcement that follows says nothing at all. *Sorry for the inconvenience. We should be moving shortly.* But the engine cuts off, the lights flicker, and we're not moving shortly. Levi and I sit together in this darkness and I want it to make me brave again, like the night of the storm.

But Levi beats me to it.

"Soph and I broke up."

"What?"

"Yeah."

"You told her about the kiss."

"No. We broke up after the storm."

Wait.

"But that was weeks ago."

"I know."

"Why?"

"You're seriously asking me that?"

Holy shit.

He continues, "Soph was the first person I met when I moved to New York and I thought, this is it. I found my person. We've gone through so much together. Her mom got really sick sophomore year. Then my mom filed for divorce. But through all the awful, we were Levi and Soph. And then with the break, well, I wasn't just going to give up when it got hard, like my dad . . . and I'm rambling but I guess what I'm trying to say is that night I realized maybe the break should've always been a breakup. I'm sorry I didn't tell you. But it felt selfish to admit that my feelings have changed, when you and Dani—"

"Are over too," I confirm to Levi. "We've *been* over since before the kiss. But I'm leaving soon and I didn't want whatever happened on the roof and my feelings to mess up things for you. I thought our plan could still work for at least one of us."

"Well. *Fuck* the plan."

"Fuck it," I agree.

Then I press my lips against his in the darkness.

It's more than a kiss. It's an unspoken, undeniable declaration.

*I love you.*

*I love you.*

*I love you.*

"And to think we're supposed to post about our amicable breakup today," I joke against his lips.

Levi pulls away as the lights flicker. "Is that seriously what you're thinking about right now?"

His furrowed brow wipes the stupid smile off my face. But I don't *want* to post that anymore. Obviously. "Berkowitz—"

"Maybe we should still post it," Levi says.

"What?"

"I mean. You're leaving. So . . ." He shrugs, his voice trailing off. "Maybe it's better to just call it."

"Seriously?"

I hate the panic that is evident in my voice, how terrified I am that Levi doesn't just mean the relationship . . . he means *all* of it. He's running away and leaving me because it's still apparently too hard to be a part of my life if I'm not *right here*. I can't believe him. We're not ten anymore. But already I feel his absence, hear it in his voice even if we're on a stalled subway with nowhere to run.

"You're doing it again."

"What?"

"Leaving me."

"Technically, you're the one leaving—"

"You know what I mean."

Levi looks away and removes his glasses to pinch the bridge of his nose. "It's not because you're leaving. It's because being around you is such a mindfuck."

I flinch. "Ouch."

"I don't know what's real anymore. I . . ." He pauses, considering his words, like he always does. "All that pretending we did? It stopped feeling fake so fast for me. But I could never tell what you were thinking, until that night up on the roof. I thought we were finally on the same page—"

"Were?"

"—so seeing screenshots that said we're 'one thousand percent just friends'? It sucked."

"I promise it did not suck as much as the guilt of kissing someone I thought had a somewhat-maybe-girlfriend."

"I know! Okay? But I didn't know how to tell you when you still seemed so all in on Dani. So it was easier to keep pretending. Until it became actually impossible. But when I stopped, you doubled down and told Soph before I could even say anything. It made me question if I misread all of it."

"That's not fair," I mutter. "You can't expect me to assume or be on your timeline when I didn't have all the information."

Levi shrugs. "It's not. But you haven't been entirely honest either."

Before I can say another word, the engine buzzes below us and we are in slow motion, crawling ahead to the next station. I unclench my palms to find nail marks so deep I'm lucky that I didn't break skin. I spent so much time pushing away my feelings for Levi Berkowitz in the name of preserving our friendship only to feel him slipping away right in front of my face, and I don't even understand why because I think we finally want the same thing? I don't know. We're talking in circles around the truth. Again.

So I say, "You want honest? Bumping into you on this train was the best thing that's happened to me since strawberry-lavender jam. I don't want to lose you again."

I reach for his hand but he pulls back, doesn't let our fingers twine together, and my stomach is on the subway floor. We're inching along at a glacial pace, nowhere near the station, but Levi stands.

It's one thing to know that you always fuck up a good thing, but it's another to feel it in your bones that it's happening and not even understand why.

"I want to call it. I don't want to be a rebound, or your Insta boyfriend. I don't want to always be second-guessing if you're more into our picture-perfect story than you are into *me*."

I—

My heart is now on the floor with my stomach. "What does that mean?"

"Come on, Fitz. We built an entire relationship on childhood nostalgia and real memories and it was so believable that *I* started to forget it was fake . . . until you would pull out your phone and reduce an amazing day we had to a post. With you, everything is reduced to a post."

"Seriously?"

"Part of me gets it. I mean, you're a content creator—"

"Levi—"

"—but I'm not content."

I'm hot, with fists curled at my sides. For the first time, I feel like I'm talking to a stranger and I hate it. I wipe sweat from my upper lip. It's too hot in here. I'm going to be sick.

Where is this coming from?

Levi's expression softens. "Please don't cry."

I wipe my eyes. "That's a messed-up thing to say. That I reduce everything to a post."

"It's how Dani felt too, isn't it?"

My phone slips out of my hand and the screen splinters into further disarray. I reach for it, wordless and just as broken. I confided that to him about our breakup. What Dani said. How it made me feel. The whole reason for my hiatus. Why I got invested in social media in the first place and how complicated that got. He said he understood. For him to throw it back at me cuts so deep and I'm so done. Just as we arrive at the next station. Finally.

Levi scratches the back of his neck. "I just mean. You said . . ."

His voice trails off as the doors open and I exit this hell train without looking back. Levi doesn't follow me and I hate how much I wanted him to. How stupid am I to believe that Levi Berkowitz was the one person who could accept every part of me? I am too much. I am never enough. Always have been. Always will be.

It's a forty-five-minute walk back to Union Square but there's no way I'm setting foot on another subway right now.

So I walk.

And sweat.

And cry.

And feel.

And as awful as this moment and these feelings are, I'm comforted by the city streets and the people who just let me be—who don't ask if I'm okay, or look at me funny, or look at me at all. Everyone here minds their business and lets me unapologetically weep and tearstain these blocks. I hate that I have to leave a place that feels like a custom pair of jeans. A city where I fit just right. Maybe I'm too much for the people in my life. But nothing is too much for New York, where millions of people can be alone together.

## THIRTY-SEVEN

**T**wo days later, I'm an hour deep into a TikTok rabbit hole watching a teen baker re-create book covers out of cupcakes when I'm interrupted by a call from my mom. A photo of us, together, on opening night of *Barefoot in the Park*, replaces the cupcakes on my screen. In it, her arms are around me. My smile is wide. It's a perfect picture. You'd never know she missed the first act of the show because of a work thing. I feel a twinge as my phone vibrates in my hand, because I'm pretty sure I know why she's calling.

I answer on the third ring.

"You're not coming."

I want to be wrong.

"I'm sorry, Ava."

I'm not wrong.

Mom continues, "We lost power from the heat wave, so the city council meeting has been pushed a week. But! You get a few more days in the city out of this. You'll stay with Tessa until we can pick you up next weekend. And she promised to record the fashion show for us."

"Dad isn't even coming?"

"Lana went into labor early, so he's got to cover her shifts. Did you not see the calendar?"

No.

I didn't see the calendar.

Now is when I'm supposed to say that it's fine. I understand. Their jobs are important. But I *don't* understand. "This showcase is really important to me. Can't Doreen cover the city council meeting?"

She sighs. "I wish. But it's a big budget meeting, Ava. I can't miss it."

Doreen is the assistant director of Parks and Recreation. What is the point of even having an assistant director if not to cover in moments of need? But obviously, Mom doesn't consider this to be a moment of need. I don't know why I thought she would. My parents never understood what a big deal this summer was for me. They never even tried to understand.

"Got it," I say.

Not, *It's fine.*

Because it's not fine.

"Even if it has to be on video, we're still so excited to watch you shine."

I pinch the bridge of my nose, then inhale.

Ask, "What if I don't?"

"What?"

"Shine. What if I don't?"

"Oh, Ava. You always are the brightest star in the sky."

It's meant to be comforting, so I let her think she is. I tell her that I love her, that I'll see her so soon, that I miss her too before hanging up and holding my phone against my chest, replaying the conversation. I shouldn't have hoped, not even for a millisecond of a moment, that my parents would choose me over work, that Mom would assure me everything will be okay if I don't shine. Being the brightest star is an impossible expectation. It's also an apt metaphor. Because the thing about stars?

They burn out.

And the brighter they shine, the faster they burn.

I unlock my phone and scroll through my photos—back to before this summer, before *Melted*, before Dani walked into Improv 101, before Massachusetts became home. So many images. So many copies, takes, attempts, at the same photo. Over and over. So much time spent searching for the perfect angle. Photos I'll never post, but also never delete.

I keep scrolling back in time, all the way to moving Tessa into her dorm at UT Dallas. I'm ten and wearing a *Descendants* T-shirt with Dove Cameron's face on it and purple skinny jeans, my hair tied back in a low ponytail. In the photo, my arms are wrapped around Tessa's waist, my smile so wide, so cute, so perfect.

What it doesn't show is the before.

Leaving an hour late and then hitting traffic due to a major accident on the highway.

Dad reminding us that maybe if we *left on time* we wouldn't be in this situation.

Tessa stressing about missing her move-in slot.

All while I did everything in my power to not projectile-vomit all over the back seat of our Subaru.

I failed.

I'd felt nauseous before we even got in the car, but I told myself I was fine. We were already running late. It would pass. But I was not fine. It did not pass. And in a valiant attempt to save the dorm supplies at my feet, I tried to roll down the child-locked window. The vomit ended up on the seat, on my clothes, in my hair.

But not on Tessa, or any of her stuff.

I changed into that *Descendants* shirt in the back seat of the car, but there was no way to wash the vom smell out of my hair. It lingered, even when I doused peach hand sanitizer all over my body. But I was resourceful, committed to not ruining this for Tessa. So I asked Mom for the kitchen scissors to help Tessa unbox her bedding.

Then I went into the bathroom.

Closed the door.

And cut the vom smell out of my hair.

Mom was more pissed about that, me ruining my perfect ringlets. She tied it back for the photos that now give the illusion of a smooth move-in. Then at home, we evened it out into a short bob. I loved it, but I didn't keep it. I grew it back out until the ringlets Mom preferred returned.

I open my camera and use it as a mirror, running my fingers through long waves, from roots to faded pink tips.

Dani chose the pink.

I wanted Dani to like me.

Now, I just want it gone.

I want to move on.

I want that bob again because *I* loved it—and I don't want to keep being a person who isn't honest about what I want just to make my mom happy, just to make Dani like me, just to make Levi not leave me, just to make thousands of people follow me online. Where has that gotten me? I'm more alone than ever. So I'm done caring more about perfect pictures than imperfect truths. Even if the truth is ugly or painful . . . it's real.

I stand, grab the scissors on my desk, and go to the bathroom.

Tie my hair into a ponytail.

And chop off the pink.

I use the same method that I did as a kid with vomit hair. Do not overthink. Cut before I consider Mom's reaction and chicken out. When the pink tendrils surround my feet, I take a step back and assess.

It's blunt in some spots, jagged in others.

I'm a mess.

My phone vibrates on the vanity just as I'm about to spiral, my eyebrows rising when I see the name on the screen.

"Tessa?"

We haven't spoken since the Bennett of it all.

"Hey," she says. "Are you at the dorm?"

"Yeah?"

"Cool. Can you come down and sign me in?"

"You're here?"

"I just said that."

"Right."

"I meant to surprise you but Tate says that is against protocol. Even after I showed him my ID with our last name on it and photos of us—"

"Hi, Fitz," Tate, the weekday security guard, says in the background.

"How's it going, Tate?"

"I'd be better if I wasn't being harassed by your doppelgänger."

I snort. "I'll be right down."

I tie my hair back like I'm ten and make my way to the elevator, processing that Tessa is here. At my dorm. It's the first time this summer that she's ventured downtown, to me. I exhale a shaky breath as I ride down because I'm still so mad at Tessa. My sister. The stranger.

But I'm also so happy she's here.

## THIRTY-EIGHT

*I* rescue Tate from Tessa and the cringe flirty bantering I overheard on the phone against my will. *Keep it in your pants, Tess.* Is Tate hot? Objectively, in a tattooed Abercrombie model way. One time, waiting in line to scan my ID, I overheard a resident ask him if he models on the side. Tate didn't take the bait from an underage teen. Tate is good people.

"I'm all for casting—" Tessa's eyes widen when they shift from Tate's tattoo sleeve to my ponytail. "Um. What did you do?"

I let my hair down. "Can you fix it?"

"No. But I know someone who can."

First, Tessa asks Tate for his Instagram.

"Sent," she says.

"I'll listen on my break."

"Cool."

Tessa . . . blushes?

What is happening?

"Come on, Fitz," Tessa says to me, before pivoting and exiting the building, fingers typing away.

I follow her, retying my hair. "What was that?"

"We listen to one of the same *Survivor* podcasts. I'm just sharing another one that I like."

"Okay? But what about—"

"Me and Bennett? We're done."

I roll my eyes.

Tessa will not fool me twice.

"Bennett has no clue how much I love *Survivor*. He said on our first date that reality television panders to the lowest common denominator and I just nodded like an idiot, enamored by this smart, serious, beautiful boy. But what I actually want is someone to unapologetically love *Survivor* with."

I nod.

Maybe we do the same thing, Tessa and me.

Make ourselves smaller, agreeable, more palatable to the people we love.

She drops her phone in her purse, then pulls out an Insomnia bag and hands it to me.

"You can't just buy me snickerdoodles every time you fuck up."

"I know."

I follow her down Broadway. "Where are you taking me?"

"To Maxine."

This answers nothing but twenty minutes later, I'm entering a studio apartment with countertops covered with crystals, a shower in the kitchen, and a sink full of plants. I bite the inside of my cheek, so pissed that I now have such a visceral reaction to a houseplant. I try to focus on the shower in the kitchen instead. I've seen many a TikTok featuring NYC apartments like this—cramped, outdated, and overpriced—but never with my own eyes.

We're greeted by someone in a low-rise pink satin skirt and a crochet halter top who throws their arms around Tessa before turning their eyes to me.

"Baby Fitzgerald!" they say, wrapping me in a hug too.

"Fitz, meet Maxine Choi," Tessa says.

"Hi," I say, still in their embrace.

"Maxine went to UTD too. She's literally the reason I passed organic chemistry."

"Bitch, we conquered that shit together."

Maxine laughs as she lets go of me, then moves the plants to the counter and I almost ask what their names are but refrain as she pulls a salon chair from against the wall to in front of the sink. I sit as Tessa helps herself to a beer from the fridge and Maxine asks to see the damage. I undo my hair tie and she nods, then mouths *What the fuck?* at Tessa when she thinks I'm not looking. Watching them, I feel that *twinge*. I've always pictured my sister in a lab coat all day and coming home to just Boring Bennett. But of course Tessa has people. Of course she has a life outside of work and relationships. She just doesn't share it with me.

Or maybe I never asked about it.

"What were you going for?" Maxine asks.

"Short."

"I got that."

"I'm thinking, like, Taylor Swift *1989* era?"

Maxine nods. "That's specific."

I show her photos of the style that I'm very much not currently rocking.

Then she gets to work.

Maxine is a chemist and a cosmetologist. A PhD candidate at NYU who started cutting hair "on the side" to pay off student loans but has been steadily growing an audience posting hair-transformation TikToks. She's too cool to be friends with Tessa. I tell her this and Tess flips me off but we laugh, and even though things aren't close to right between us, it still feels okay to laugh with her.

I'm not sure how long we spend in this kitchen salon, but I do know the moment Maxine holds up a hand mirror to show off the final result that I will name my first-born child after her.

It is the textured chin-length bob of my dreams.

"How much?" I ask.

Maxine waves away my question. "I don't charge family."

But I still want to do something to thank her. "Can I pay you in clothes?"

"I mean, I wouldn't say no to a custom crop top."

"Deal."

Maxine's girlfriend is on her way over for a Hayao Miyazaki marathon so we hug goodbye and I follow Tessa to our next stop: ice cream. Without a problem to solve or Maxine as a buffer, we're quiet as we weave through the crowded Lower East Side streets. Tessa asks if I want to share a double and we end up splitting a strawberry chocolate chip and peanut butter cup sundae.

Tessa gestures at my hair. "You look adorable."

I stab the ice cream with my spoon. "Tess."

"What?"

"Are we really not going to talk about it?"

Her eyes meet mine. "We're not good at that."

"Well I'm feeling very *new hair, new me*. So I don't know. Can we try?"

Tessa swallows, then puts her spoon down. "Do you remember the summer before my freshman year of high school when I went to dance camp?"

I shake my head.

Honestly, I have very few memories of Tessa the dancer.

I also have no idea what that has to do with us.

"I *loved* dance," Tessa continues. "But I put so much pressure on myself to be the best. I *was* the best. Then I hit puberty. I gained some weight. I had boobs and hips and I just . . . *hated* that my body was changing. I had internalized so much shame that I pretty much fully stopped eating."

I blink.

"What?"

"It got, um, pretty serious. Clara found me, like, passed out in the bathroom before school one morning. So that summer, I wasn't at dance camp. I was at a treatment center in Dallas."

"Holy shit, Tess."

I close my eyes and try to remember anything at all about that summer, if there were any signs that I missed . . . but my memories are a black hole of nothingness.

"Treatment saved my life. It also taught me that therapy is life-changing."

I swallow. "How do I not remember any of this?"

"You spent a lot of that summer at Levi's house."

"But I should've registered that something was wrong. I should've—"

"You were six."

"Still—"

"*No. Mom and Dad* should've registered that something was wrong. My hospitalization really freaked them out and I thought they changed after that with you, figured out a better work-life balance, made sure you felt supported—" Tessa cuts herself off and presses the heels of her hands to her eyes. "I'm sorry they're not coming to your showcase."

"It's typical."

"I know. But it shouldn't be."

I shrug.

"I'll be there," Tessa says. "If that means anything."

"It does."

It kind of means everything.

"I've been thinking a lot about what you said to me. That we're strangers."

"Tess. I—"

"You're right. We are. Until this summer, the last time we

spent any meaningful amount of time together, you were twelve. A kid. Between then and now you've always seemed so good, Fitz. With school, with friends, with fashion. From so many miles away, you told us you were *fine* and I never pushed because I believed you'd come to us with the hard stuff. If not me, then Maya or Clara. They're much better at being big sisters."

I crumple a napkin in my hand. "I had to be fine."

Tessa's forehead wrinkles. "Had to be?"

"Whenever I wasn't, I was shut out of the conversations."

"That's not true." Tessa's expression softens. "We wanted to shield you from the hard stuff."

"So I got shut out from your hard stuff, but I was supposed to open up about mine?"

"I . . . see the flaw in that logic now. We thought we were being big sisters, but you just saw it as doors slammed in your face."

*We wanted to shield you from the hard stuff.*

I can't help but wonder what else I don't know about my sisters.

"So the FaceTime without me . . . ?"

"It was a mental health check-in that devolved into the tipsy giggling that you walked in on."

*Oh.* Still.

"I'm not six. Or twelve. I can handle the hard stuff now too."

"I get that now and I'm sorry. I love you."

"I love you too."

Cue two sisters sobbing over ice cream in Lower Manhattan.

"Maya and Clara carried me through my adolescence. And I'm such a selfish asshole to never have considered how hard it must have been, to be in that house alone after the move."

"It was lonely," I admit.

"I'm sorry I've been taking you at face value and using your social media presence as an excuse for not checking in more. I'll do better."

"And I'll try to be better at telling you when I'm not good."

Tessa nods. "So. How are you?"

"Shitty."

"Same."

"A mess."

"We can be messes together."

"I would love that."

Through my eyes, my sisters babied and excluded me. Through theirs, they were protecting me. It's amazing how a different perspective reframes everything. It doesn't fix us. But it's much-needed context. I want to ask Tessa so many questions. So I do. She tells me about her experience at the treatment center, about the medication she takes to treat the OCD she was diagnosed with while there, about therapy.

"If therapy is something you're interested in exploring—now, later, *ever*—you can call me, okay?"

She offers but doesn't push it.

Just gently reminds me that an option is there.

"Okay."

"Sharlene, my therapist, hated Bennett too," Tessa says.

"I love Sharlene."

"She said, and I quote, '*Fucking finally*,' when I told her that we're done."

"How did you end it?"

Tessa snorts. "Not the most maturely."

"Tell me everything."

"He read an excerpt of his book to me and used the word 'grandiloquent,' like, not ironically, and . . . I laughed. I guess it was a serious scene? I don't know. It's like a switch flipped and everything that I used to find endearing and attractive about Bennett is now just really fucking annoying."

"Finally."

"As soon as he started reading, I thought, *I don't miss this*. As soon as he finished, I told him that."

I laugh. *"Tessa."*

"Then after he left, I wrote a one-star review on that Goodreads page that Clara made."

"That's real?"

Tessa opening up lets me open up too. I tell her the whole truth about my disaster summer, the ridiculous scheme, the unintended consequences. I tell her about plantscapades and the burgundy shirt and fucking it up because I was afraid of fucking it up. Classic Fitz. I tell her all my impostor syndrome feelings about FIT and the runway show and how much harder the fashion of it all has been than I thought it would be.

"That is so much," Tessa says.

Not, *You'll figure it out.*

*It always comes together in the end.*

*You'll be fine.*

She just listens as I spill my guts.

Then asks, "What do you need?"

"Just this."

So we stay on this bench on the Lower East Side and talk until the sun starts to set—and for the first time in forever, my sister doesn't feel like a total stranger.

## THIRTY-NINE

*I* spend my last weekend in New York before the runway show with Tessa and I'm emotional about leaving to the point where I may or may not have shed a tear when I stepped off the downtown 1 train at 14th Street for the last time. In a much better headspace after our talk, I worked on my project pretty much nonstop from the comfort of Gertie. Tessa made sure I ate real food and took regular breaks. During those breaks, we talked—about school, about life after my parents moved me to Massachusetts, about our mental health.

We felt like *sisters.*

At Tessa's I wrote and rewrote my safe thrift-flip proposal, but I couldn't get my original idea out of my head. So when I get back to my dorm, I'm reunited with my button-up, a bomber jacket, and a decision to make.

I lay both pieces side by side on my bed.

The jacket symbolizes everything that If the Shoe Fitz currently is.

But the button-up is who I could be if I give myself the chance to grow and change . . . and potentially fail.

I don't know what to do.

Do I play it safe?

Or reach?

I know Mal will be disappointed if I don't pivot back, but the jacket is finished and flawlessly executed. The button-up presentation is a half-sewn work in progress. Originally, I wanted to design a unique textile with enough material to create a button-up with matching pants. Obviously, I don't have time to do that. But maybe I have enough time to make matching shorts?

I can try.

I think about how incredible it felt the first time I tried it on.

How clothes have the power to make people feel like the best versions of themselves.

I want to tell *that* story.

Even if the execution isn't perfect.

So I sit with my sewing machine and choose to reach for my stash of textiles. I search my thrift haul for patterns with shades of green and cream to complement the potted-plant print that still speaks to me, and I deconstruct the button-up that feels like me because in order to make a matching set, it needs to grow a few more yards and transform into something new. Headphones on, I blast Harry Styles and get to work cutting fabric into patches and experimenting with the placement until it feels right.

I'm terrified, liberated, every conflicting feeling all at once. Instead of pushing away these feelings, I sit with them. Sit with how many people this summer have straight-up called out these intrusive thoughts.

*You put so much pressure on yourself, Fitzgerald.*

*I didn't want perfect.*

*Perfectionism is a trap.*

I know everyone is right—that the pressure I put on myself is unhealthy. But it's one thing to know it and another thing to address it. To change. It'd be so much easier to end this summer as it began, aiming for perfect pictures.

But maybe I should just . . . not.

Maybe instead it ends with rushing to finish this design, then calling Tessa to ask her more questions about therapy.

"Hey."

Em's unexpected voice pulls me out of my clothes zone. "Hey! I thought you left."

Their creative writing course ended on Friday and I came home this morning to find their side of the room emptied. I didn't think much of it, Em leaving without saying goodbye, considering the combination of us not hitting it off and seeing them holding hands with Dani resulted in a summer spent avoiding them as much as possible that eventually evolved into quietly coexisting.

They open their desk drawer. "Forgot my AirPods."

"Right."

"Bye, Fitz. As far as roommates go, you were adequate."

"I was barely here."

"Exactly."

Home is Pennsylvania for Em, where they'll return for their senior year like me. Also like me, Em hopes to be back in the city next year for college. I follow them on Instagram and despite my still-complicated relationship with social media, I'm glad that it will keep us in touch, even if it's just in a mutuals way.

"Bummer Levi hasn't been around. I wanted to say bye to him, too."

"Oh. We're . . ."

Em nods. "You two are due for a 'Can we survive long-distance?' panic."

I snort. "Bye, Em. See you next year?"

"Probably not."

I nod. "Probably not."

Even if Em and I both end up back in New York? It's a big city.

We're not friends.

And that's okay.

My headphones back on, I settle into a zone that I haven't experienced since I arrived. I forgot that this is supposed to be fun. So much fun, I don't even realize until hours after Em's goodbye that my headphones are on but not playing any music. I can be alone with the clothes and my thoughts without background noise.

I'm on the right track.

I can do this.

Without overthinking it, I snap a few photos of my work in progress to send to Levi—because even after everything, he's the person who I want to share my victories with. Our disaster of a conversation on a stalled subway *hurt*, but I don't want that one awful moment to be how we leave things for another seven years. I want to tell him how much this summer meant to me and that the universe didn't put us on the same downtown 1 train just for us to end like this.

I want to at least say goodbye.

So I send the photo.

And type:

> at least all of the faking it turned into
> something real?
> 2:02 PM

I hope he answers.

I hope he knows I don't just mean the shirt.

His text bubble appears and disappears but I don't want whatever he does or doesn't say to derail my progress. So I power down my phone and focus on the hypnotic rhythm of my sewing machine's straight stitch, losing the entire afternoon to my work.

It's only when I smell pizza that I stop.

I power on my phone.

Levi hasn't answered.

I try not to let the disappointment suck all the air out of my diaphragm.

Dani knocks on my door. "Do you want pizza?"

My stomach screams in response, so I nod and follow her into the common room.

We started this summer with Mamoun's in the park and now we're ending it with 2 Bros. Pizza and the pro-shot of *Legally Blonde: The Musical*. We're the only two remaining in our dorm and it's hilarious because that would've been a dream until it would've been a nightmare and now it just . . . is.

## FORTY

FIT rents out an empty warehouse in Chelsea—the location where Mal happened to first launch Revived by Mal at New York Fashion Week—for the runway show. So my first runway experience is an actual, legitimate Fashion Week location. I've been so focused on finishing my proposal that I haven't had the brain space to fixate on the fact that I have to walk this legendary runway and model my piece for my peers and family and Mal. Cool. No pressure.

It'll be fine.

I model my thrift flips all the time for Instagram.

In the greenroom, where everyone is accessorizing, touching up their makeup, and finalizing looks, I ask Trevor, "Sneakers or heels?"

I hold out the options: a white chunky dad sneaker or a suede olive block heel.

Yes, I'm making a key accessory decision at the eleventh hour.

I'm leaning toward sneakers for a more relaxed aesthetic, but I need a second opinion.

Trevor considers, then confirms my instinct. "Sneakers."

Shoes secured, I assess myself in one of the full-length mirrors that line the walls. I worked on this plant motif patchwork set until the last possible moment. I severely underestimated the time commitment that is patchwork-designing your own textiles from scratch, so I spent too much time perfecting the top and had to leave a rough hem on the shorts. I hope it looks intentional. I style the button-up so it's half tucked, covering some of the hem, but it still bothers me. But just a week ago, I never would've shown an unfinished piece at all.

Is this growth?

I run my hand through my styled curls and adjust the bangs I'm still getting used to, then sweep a mauve crayon over my lips. Earrings are the finishing touch—either large pearls or a chunky gold hoop. I try one in each ear and contemplate as Mal approaches me.

"Ready?"

She stands behind me, so we're both looking at each other in the mirror. She's a leather-pants moment with a checkered blazer and classic black pumps.

"I think so."

"I'm really proud of you," Mal says.

My heart swells ten sizes. "Thank you."

"Seriously, the whole look is great. I love a rough hem."

I can't tell if she calls it out on purpose, but in any case, it squashes my anxiety. "Pearls or hoops?"

"What are you leaning toward?"

"Pearls."

Mal nods. "Pearls."

She moves on to complimenting Lila's couture gown and I suspect if I said hoops, she would've agreed. I know I need to trust my instincts and stop seeking validation for them. Still. It's impossible to not feel a *little* self-conscious in this space because so many of my classmates created high-concept, avant-garde pieces of art while I made a basic two-piece set.

We have five minutes until the runway, so I check my phone one more time.

No new messages.

But I don't have time to dwell on those feelings, because Mal says it's time to head backstage, so it's phone off.

Filter *off*.

We line up for the runway.

First everyone will walk, then we'll present our proposals. Then we wait. Mal says that we'll receive written feedback and any offers from Revived by Mal by the end of the summer. I'm under no illusions that I'm going to get the collaboration deal with Mal, the Fashion Week tickets, the chance to launch. I don't have a line. I have an outfit. But it's the start of an idea that could be a line. And this moment is more about introducing myself and my vision for how I can turn If the Shoe Fitz into a sustainable fashion brand by designing unique upcycled textiles and continuing to do my part to keep clothes out of landfills.

Mal opens with an introduction and I don't retain a word.

My heart beats too loud in my ears.

Cue music.

Bright lights flicker on and my turn comes before I know it.

I step out from behind the curtain and see my sisters in the audience. Sisters. Plural. Tessa. Clara. Maya. *They're all here* and I'm not sure how I make it through the show without breaking down, but I know I walk and at least don't fall on my face. When it's time to present, I start as always with the story about where If the Shoe Fitz came from. Them. But I also know now that my sisters aren't my whole story with fashion, just the beginning of it. I've always seen clothes as storytelling, but I used to focus more on preserving the stories they once held than creating a *new* story. My story. I hit these points. I think? Of course this summer of overcoming creative block and stress and burnout has built up to a moment I don't even remember.

Mal calls an encore walk after all the presentations, so we can show off our work one last time. Before I know it I'm back in line and inching toward the official end of summer. I don't want to forget this moment. I want the sense memories of walking down the runway in this perfectly imperfect outfit that I was too scared to present a mere forty-eight hours ago. An outfit that I can be proud of without comparing it to Lila's dress with a flawless beaded bodice or Trevor's innovative use of tulle that objectively blows my basic button-up out of the water.

I step into the lights one last time.

I am not the best.

But my outfit?

It's *my* best.

My best can be imperfect.

I can be a work in progress.

My sisters' arms are the first to greet me after the runway, wrapping me in a group hug so tight I can't breathe.

"Fitzy!"

"That was *incredible*!"

"You know I'm stealing this 'fit!"

"You're *here*," I say.

"Tessa organized it," Maya says as we untangle from the embrace.

"We wanted it to be a surprise," Clara says.

"How long are you here?" I ask, still in disbelief.

"For the rest of the week," Maya says.

Clara loops her arm through Tessa's. "T is hosting all of us!"

Tessa smirks. "It's going to be so chaotic."

"The *best* chaotic," Clara corrects.

I'm overwhelmed with emotion. "Thank you for being here."

Clara squeezes my shoulder. "Of course! We're *so* proud of you, A."

"We're proud of you and we're here for you," Maya adds. "Always. Okay?"

It means the world to me that they showed up for me. That they don't want me to feel excluded anymore. But my relationship with my sisters is on me just as much as it is on them. And it starts with not filtering my feelings around them, with initiating some honest conversations with Maya and Clara. Maybe I can while they're here. While we're finally *all* here. Together.

I hope so.

"I know this moment is about the clothes, but A! Your hair? It's *inspired*," Clara says.

I run my hand through the short curls. "You think so?"

"I love it," Maya confirms.

"Me too."

Levi's voice spins me around, sending the *flutter* crashing against my rib cage. And it's not just from the sound of his voice. It's also the burgundy shirt that he's wearing, unbuttoned, sleeves rolled up to the elbows. Just like how I styled him at the Brooklyn Flea, the first time I felt it. The flutter.

*Love.*

"Hi," I say.

"Hey."

"You're here."

I'm short-circuiting, just staring at Levi, as if when I blink he'll—*poof*—disappear.

He doesn't.

He's here.

Maya holds out her hand. "Hi! I'm Maya."

"Levi," he says, taking her hand.

Clara's eyes widen in recognition. "Berkowitz? Holy shit."

"It's been longer than a minute," Tessa says.

Maya and Clara look at me like I have so much explaining

to do. I do, but we have the rest of the week for that, and right now? I want to talk to Levi without all the people and noise. His eyes meet mine and even though we're off, I know that we're thinking the same thing. But how do I ask my sisters, who *flew here from Texas to be at my showcase*, to let me leave with Levi?

They don't make me ask.

"Go," Tessa says.

Then my sisters say goodbye for now and wrap me in another super-extra group hug before leaving for SoHo boutique window-shopping. Because when in Manhattan, there's nothing Maya and Clara love more than being basic bitches. Their words. Well. Clara's words.

I promise to meet them for dinner later and then they're gone. I'm shocked they leave me with him without even being embarrassing about it.

"Hey," Levi says again, in the soft tenor voice I love so much.

"Hi."

And then together we walk, wordless, toward the High Line.

## FORTY-ONE

**W**e stop for bubble tea before one last stroll through our park in the sky. I'm not sure what to say. How to begin this goodbye. Neither is he. Levi Berkowitz, who is always so careful with his words until he isn't. So we walk along the tourist-congested path until we find our way to an empty bench surrounded by wildflowers.

We sit.

And let time *tick, tick, tick* closer to goodbye.

Finally, I start. "Thanks for coming today."

He flushes. "I didn't want to miss it. Or apologize via text."

"Oh."

He reaches into his pocket and pulls out a piece of paper folded into eighths and hands it to me.

I gently unfold it.

It's a goodbye letter.

Not to me.

*From* me.

*TO LEVI*, it begins in big blue bubble letters.

*I will miss you when you move to Austin forever—from Fitz (not Ava)*

Underneath is a Crayola crayon rainbow of flowers, the first thing I could draw well enough to show people. It makes my heart swell because I have every handmade card from Levi Berkowitz in a box under my bed and I cannot believe he kept mine, too.

"Levi—"

"I'm sorry," Levi says, so soft I have to lean closer to him. Our knees bump and I don't move. Neither does he. "I was so terrified of my own feelings—that you didn't feel the same way, that you *did* feel the same way, that we've been using each other in a super-unhealthy way. So I chose words that I knew would hurt because I'm an asshole but I—"

I wrap my arms around him, cutting off Levi Berkowitz's quiet apology with a hug, and it is an unspoken promise that we'll be okay.

I pull away. "We are not one thousand percent just friends."

Levi laughs. "Really?"

"But I think we should be. At least right now."

"Oh."

The disappointment in his voice and the adorable furrow in his brow makes me want to say *fuck it*.

But I stay strong.

"You said you don't want to be a rebound—"

"Fitz—"

I cover his hand with mine. "I don't want to be one either. I mean. We both just got out of, um, pretty intense relationships. And I need a beat, to figure some stuff out. My mental health being one of them. If we do this, like, for real, I don't want to mess it up. Because I will not lose you again, Berkowitz."

Levi is quiet, considering like always.

"That makes too much sense."

"I know."

"Whatever we are . . . I don't want to mess it up either."

"Good."

"But you're leaving."

"I am."

"I'm going to miss you so much."

"Me too."

He flips his hand so our palms press together and laces his fingers through mine. We sit like this, hand in hand, looking out at the city that has been home for the past summer, the city where I rediscovered my first favorite person. My *always* favorite person. Just friends is good. Right. A way for Levi to be in my life without becoming the center of it. Because I rediscovered myself here too and I want senior year to be mine to navigate every messy insecurity. To find a therapist. To work on my clothes, my relationship with If the Shoe Fitz, all of it.

"So. Just friends for now?"

Levi nods and repeats, "Just friends for now."

Our eyes meet. Then despite our words, our lips do too. His fingers weave through my hair. My palm presses against his chest and I feel his heart fluttering. There will be time for talking, texting, even video-chatting later when he has to save Lucy the Bamboo from the plant curse that is me. Distance will make "just friends" easier. You can't kiss your best friend when there are over two hundred miles between you. So for now I lean into the kiss and let myself have these final messy moments of summertime.

When I finally pull away, I say, "Just friends. Starting now."

Levi laughs. "Starting now."

But we kiss again.

And again.

"Starting when we say goodbye," Levi amends, his mouth hot on mine.

"See you later," I clarify.

We push it back as long as possible, our *See you later*. Levi walks me to the restaurant where I'm meeting my sisters, who then insist that he stays. He answers every question they ask about where he's been and where he's going. *Staying put*, he says. His eyes meet mine. I'm positive everyone notices. But I don't care.

It would be so easy to lean into these feelings.

To choose Levi.

Instead, I hug him the moment the Lyft that Tessa calls for him arrives.

Whisper, "See you later."

And I choose myself.

*I*t's happening!"

Trevor stands at the door of my bedroom in the apartment that we're sharing, a duffel bag over his shoulder. I've missed his earnest enthusiasm and cannot wait for us to bounce ideas off each other as classmates at FIT. He drops the bag on the floor and I wrap him in a hug.

"Nice sweatshirt," Trevor says when we pull apart.

I laugh. "You too."

We're wearing the same exact sweatshirt with the FIT logo even though it's, like, a million degrees outside, because school pride. Obviously. Trevor and I have become a lot closer in the last year, bonded by the stress and trauma of fashion school applications. Building out an entire portfolio that would determine my future? It was a lot.

But this time around, I let myself lean on people.

Trevor, who gave the best portfolio feedback.

Mal, who wrote a recommendation letter that made me weep.

Natalie, who asked a few underclassmen to assist with

the costumes for *Scorched*, knowing full well I would've never asked for help myself.

Tessa, who helped me find a therapist.

My parents, who listened as soon as I told them I wasn't fine when they picked me up last summer.

Levi, who I can still talk to about anything and everything.

I came out the other side with an acceptance letter to my dream school and a diagnosis. Generalized anxiety disorder. Denise, the therapist who I trauma-dump all my messy feelings to once a week, is the best. I love therapy. It's not that it's easy, or fun. But it helps me make sense of myself. Like, I always believed that being a perfectionist is just part of who I am, but after a lot of unpacking with Denise I've learned that it's not actually a personality trait, but more a symptom of the anxiety that I've always had. And thanks to a combination of therapy and medication, my brain is so much better. Fashion is more fun than not and I'm in a headspace to hit deadlines and handle critique. It's such a relief, to go through something and recognize that hard moments are just that.

A moment.

There's a knock on my doorframe.

"Hey! I'm working on a list of apartment essentials," Elodie says.

Trevor nods. "Sweet."

"Where's your sweatshirt?" I ask her.

I know she has an NYU sweatshirt. I bought it for her for

our move-in photo because sure, not everything needs to be a photo op, but monumental days absolutely do.

"I refuse to be a walking advertisement."

"It's called school spirit!"

Elodie continues to be my favorite killjoy. I can't give her too much shit, though, as she's the reason I have a sweet housing setup. Since the dorm situation at FIT is limited, a lot of students opt to live off-campus. El's parents retired to a small Dutch farm town outside of Amsterdam, leaving her with an empty room in a two-bedroom Chelsea co-op to fill. Trevor and I jumped at the location and cheap rent.

Unlike Trevor, El and I didn't keep in touch this year, but this roommateship of convenience feels like it might slowly evolve into friendship. We're concert buddies at the very least. We have tickets to see Fall Out Boy next week and cannot wait to scream along to the angsty anthems that our siblings raised us on.

My new, intact-for-now phone glows with one (1) new message.

**Levi Berkowitz**
Plantscapade?
1:01PM

My heart flutters.

"How insufferable are they going to be on a scale of one to ten?" El asks.

"Eleven," Trevor teases.

I flip Trevor and El off, then remove my sweatshirt and toss it over the couch on my way out the door. I head toward the Union Square steps in shorts and a ribbed white tank top because I haven't forgotten that August in this city is a humid hellscape. The college sweatshirts were an aesthetic, for a photo op that El can only avoid for so long.

I tie up my hair, which is barely long enough to put in a ponytail, and pick at my chipped blue nail polish as anticipation blooms in my stomach. Levi and I have been texting pretty much daily, but we've only seen each other in person twice since we ended last summer as just friends. Once when I visited Tessa over winter break. Again when Levi showed up to the opening night of our spring musical, *Scorched*, to see me in the role of Featured Tree #2. Both times, the flutter was uncontrollable in the days, hours, minutes before I saw him. No matter how much has changed, that hasn't. And when we connect? It's just easy. We're pretty great as friends. But I think—I *know*—we can be great as more than friends too.

I will live my best fashion life at FIT.

He'll work toward creating his own parks in the sky as an architectural design major at Parsons.

We can support each other.

Together.

Assuming he still feels the same way, assuming he—

"Fitz."

Levi is here. In front of me. Our smiles cannot be contained. I am so happy to see him. I stand and wrap my arms around his neck in a hug that still feels so goddamn safe, and I'm ready for whatever comes next.

"Hey, Berkowitz. Who are we saving today?"

"Polly, a silver pothos that has been struggling in the care of a Wall Street Bro."

I frown. "Wait, aren't pothos supposed to be, like, super hard to kill?"

He pulls up a photo of a yellowing Polly. "Wall Street Bros will find a way."

Ten minutes of sweating while waiting for the L and one transfer later, we are back on a downtown 1.

*The* downtown 1.

FUCK IT stares right at me and I'm not sure what's with this city and the cosmic shit it continues to pull on us, but who am I to deny a literal sign that is right in front of my face?

"It's root rot for sure, so it's just a matter of how much we can salvage—"

"I love you."

I blurt the three words I've kept close for an entire year.

To Levi.

On a crowded 1 train.

Levi blinks. "What?"

"I love the journeys that you will take to save a plant. I love that we can pull all-nighters texting and somehow never run out of things to say. I love that you are just as enthusiastic as I am about the things that bring you joy. I never feel like I'm too extra with you. I even love your cargo shorts. And do I love our story? Sure. It's an adorable story. But that's not, like, the reason. You are the reason."

Silence.

Did I break him? Again?

I clear my throat. "But I mean. If your feelings have changed, I understand. It's been—"

"I love you too."

I smile. "Yeah?"

"Of course I do."

"Tell me more."

Levi laughs.

I love that sound.

I love him so much.

"You take yourself and your dreams seriously in a way that is aspirational. I love that we're always laughing. I love that we talk every day and that whenever I get a new text I hope it's you. I love that we trust each other with real shit. You haven't killed Lucy. I love that! I wanted to tell you last summer how I felt. So many times. I would've jumped too soon. But you didn't people-please me. You prioritized yourself and your mental health and I love you so fucking much for that, Fitz."

My lips crash into his.

In my head, this moment is cinema, despite the truth that making out on the subway is notoriously not cute. I don't care. I just want to bottle the feeling that's finding the one person in this universe who gets you and sees you—the whole unfiltered truth of you—and loves you anyway. But the logistics of bottling a feeling seem too complicated. Kissing is easier. So I'll do that instead.

"I love you," I say again against his mouth.

*I love you.*

*I love you.*

*I love you.*

We just fit, Levi and me.

We always have.

The difference is that now, the timing is right too.

Finally.

# ACKNOWLEDGMENTS

I started writing *Finally Fitz* during a moment in time when my mental health was at the lowest it had ever been. I was used to living with anxiety, but the depression that crept in was new and, quite honestly, scary. So I asked for an extension. And another. And another. And I sought help . . . and slowly but surely, the words came back to me. Fitz came back to me. And I don't think I could've written her story about reckoning with perfectionism and her mental health until I worked on myself and *my* mental health. It's the aspect of this book that I'm the proudest of and I'm so incredibly thankful to have been given the space to work on myself so that I could *finally* find the joy in working on Fitz.

Taylor Haggerty, there aren't enough words to thank you for your unwavering support, especially throughout the journey that was this book. You never stopped believing in me— and for that I'll be forever grateful. Thank you also to Jasmine Brown and the entire Root Literary team.

Alexa Pastor, thank you so much for championing this book and for loving Fitz and Levi as much as I do. I so appreciate being given the time to get this story not just *right*, but to a place that I'm so incredibly proud of. From the beginning, you understood Fitz's story and it was under your guidance that this book bloomed into something beautiful.

To everyone on the BFYR team who had a hand in this

book—Alma Gomez Martinez, Morgan York, Brenna Franzitta, and Sara Berko, thank you for all that you've done and continue to do behind the scenes. Thank you to my publicist, Alex Kelleher-Nagorski, for helping this book find its perfect readers. Thank you to the art and design team—Krista Vossen and Hilary Zarycky—for creating a gorgeous package that perfectly fits, and to Louisa Cannell for capturing Fitz, Levi, and Dani so beautifully.

To the people who (lovingly!) forced me to finish this book—Rachel Lynn Solomon, Kelsey Rodkey, Auriane Desombre, Carlyn Greenwald, Courtney Kae, and Laura Silverman, thank you for the sprints, the group chats, the friendship. I love you all.

To readers, booksellers, and librarians—thank you for all the work you do to connect my books with readers. Thank you to the staff of the Ripped Bodice for welcoming this L.A. transplant with open arms. And a huge thank you to the bookstagrammers who helped out with the cover reveal—Jordan, Sydney, Avery, Tree, Amanda, Kayla, Courtney, Aleah, Elyse, and Melissa.

Jonah, thank you for answering all my questions about, quote, "What it's like to be a real teenager."

Noah, thank you for your genuine enthusiasm, support, and the best avocado toast.

Mom and Dad, thank you for always believing that this dream career of mine would be a reality. You traverse the entire country to attend a book event without even flinching.

Your belief in me and support means more to me than you know. I love you.

Vanessa, I dedicated this whole book to you, so what else can I say? You were this book's first reader, its first champion, and your constant messages demanding new chapters were the motivation to finish it at all. There's a sister love story in these pages that I only could've written because of ours.

Sam, thank you for being my soft place to land, for seeing the whole, unfiltered truth of me and loving me anyway. I love you so much.

# ABOUT THE AUTHOR

© SAM CHEUNG

**Marisa Kanter** is a young adult author, amateur baker, and reality television enthusiast. She is the author of *What I Like About You*, *As If on Cue*, and *Finally Fitz*. Born and raised in the suburbs of Boston, her obsession with books led her to New York City, where she worked in the publishing industry to help books find their perfect readers. She currently lives in Los Angeles, writing love stories by day and crocheting her wardrobe by night. Follow her at MarisaKanter.com.